BETWEEN THE LAYERS

THE DATA COLLECTORS BOOK THREE

DANIELLE PALLI

What this year has taught me more than anything is to cherish your tribe—those friends, family, and colleagues who support you personally and professionally, often unconditionally. Because in a world of uncertainty, it sure is nice to feel supported. Thank you to everyone who has taken the time to read, review, and share my books with others.

I'd also like to thank the people who have been involved in the production of all three books in The Data Collectors trilogy: Cindy Readnower of Skinny Leopard Media, for publishing, editing, and marketing support; Joan Peters for designing all three book covers; Graham Mack for narrating and mastering the audiobook version of the series, and John Palli for his never-ending love, support, and technical insight. Finally, I need to give a nod to the cat who started it all – Ms. Katrina, for being the spark behind the story. I hope there is a special place in the afterlife for kitties who inspire the building of worlds.

I am grateful.

CONTENTS

SECTION ONE

"What I want is revenge. I'd like to see you trapped between the layers where you left me for a hundred years. Do you know what it's like to constantly present myself to the world as a simple domestic cat, lifetime after lifetime, all the while ignorant beings thinking that I was the primitive one, petting me and giving me kibble, calling me stupid names like Tabby, Fluff and Whiskers?"

DRAMATIS PERSONAE

Amy: Erde-born female (Section 1), small-framed, red hair and green eyes.

Roman Aurelius: Human male (Section 0); wavy black hair, green eyes, tall and slender.

The Baby: Born of Sabrina and Fredo (Section 3), now adopted by Hamish.

Bagheera: Male cat (Section 0), black short hair with yellow eyes, very handsome.

Cepheus Baruch: Royal male (Section 1, Section 3), stringy gray hair, yellow eyes; tall and lanky, shapeshifter (lizard/human).

Petrichor Baruch: Erde-born female (Section 1), the late wife of Cepheus, long auburn hair, pale blue eyes.

Tanager Blackletter: Erde-born male (Section 1), curly blonde hair, brown eyes, average height and weight.

Clusaladek: Erde-Born male (Section 1), tall and thin, blonde hair, pale blue-gray eyes.

Constable Melokuhle: Erde-born male (Section 1), bulky with dark skin, curly black hair and brown eyes.

Commander Royce: Erde-born female (Section 1), walnut and gray hair, coal eyes, small and athletic frame with deep wrinkles.

Bryce Cushing: Human male (Section 0), brown hair, blue eyes, medium height and build.

Dallen: Vitruvian male (Section 2), non-shapeshifter, gold hair and blue eyes, tall with strong build.

Far: Macar-born male (Unsectioned by the IPP), blonde hair and green eyes, pale and thin.

Dr. Archibald Ennis: Human male (Section 0), bald, brown eyes, tall and thin.

Fatima Fortunata: Human female (Section 0), purple hair, gray eyes, short and Rubenesque.

Fredo: Lesser Royal male (Section 3), red body and black eyes, large and thick, salamander-like with no noticeable shapeshifting abilities.

Hamish: Royal male (Section 3), brown hair and gold eyes, short and slightly overweight, shapeshifter (lizard/human-like).

Hysechia: Unknown origin, female (Section 1), striped black and white tiger with golden eyes, human-like features.

Ivan (the Tinkerer): Human male (Section 0), red hair and green eyes, medium height and stocky.

Lucene (Lucy) Jones: Earth-born female (Section 0), blonde or brown hair, hazel eyes, average height and weight, toned form.

Kiki: Vitruvian (Section 2), shapeshifter (varied gender, prefers female form), aardvark-like nose and blue coloring.

Mallory: Erde-born male (Section 1), heavyset, dark hair with multi-colored eyes.

Mateo: Unknown origin (Section 1), short and heavy, little hair, has a long tail.

Marzipan: Unknown origin, male (Section 1), firefly and lady-bug-like features, multicolored with wings.

Moksha: Royal (Section 3) assassin, black hair, yellow eyes, petite but athletic build.

Morphinae: Vitruvian (Section 2), shapeshifter (gender, species, coloring), Balance-Keeper, often prefers doll-like and butterfly-like forms.

Neroni: Erde-born female (Section 1), olive complexion, slightly heavyset, red-green hair and brown eyes.

Not Christopher: Unknown origin, male, chestnut wavy hair, brown eyes, youthful.

Odessa: Vitruvian (Section 2), shapeshifter (gender, species, coloring), prefers mermaid-like form the most.

Olly: Between-the-layers troll; male, small with large hands and feet.

Pelimar: Erie-born male (Section 1), pale skin with bright red hair and purposefully goth-like features.

Renenet: Unknown origin, female (Section 5), red/brown fur and fire agate eyes, tall and broad, bulky stature, shapeshifter (lion/human-like).

Sabrina: Royal woman (Section 3), black hair and yellow eyes, tall with average shape, shapeshifter (lizard/human-like form).

Jasper Set: Demon male (Section 4), red eyes, bald, thin legs and barrel-like body, small wings.

Reverend Isabella Simone: Female (Section 0), spiritual advisor, white hair, violet eyes, tall and thin.

Wilah: Erde-born female doctor (Section 1), tiny and thin, translucent glow.

Xeni: Unknown origin (Section 1), pink eyes, heart-shaped face, blue-black hair.

LOCALES / SPECIAL GROUPS

Achel: Main province on Erde.

The Assembly: Intergalactic gathering for the Intergalactic Peace Project (IPP).

Balance-Keepers: Special interest group in Section 2, Vitruvians. Will intervene to ensure all forces remain in balance.

Between the Layers: Alternate realms of reality on this plane of existence.

Data Collectors: Specialized team from Section 1, collecting data on Earth to save species.

The Crosses: Preservation sites and residential homes on Erde comprised of four quadrants.

The Elders: Erde's version of Gods. Wise souls who guide the leaders of Erde and their ancestors.

Erde: Planet in Section 1 known for setting up preserves to rescue and protect humans.

Erdelings: Species from the Erde planet in Section 1.

Global Environmental Agency (GEA): Earth organization for environmental concerns.

Intergalactic Peace Project (IPP): Formed to create and maintain peace among intergalactic species.

International Registry of Alien Residency (IRAR): Created by the United Commonwealth (UC) to record and track aliens living on Earth.

The Null: Crustacean-like species in Section 4 trying to destroy the universe in order to serve the mighty Segue.

Peace-Keepers: Nickname given to all inhabitants of Section 2, in particular, those living on Erde.

Planetary Defense League (PDL): Government entity on Erde for protection.

Royals: Nickname given to all inhabitants of Section 3, no specific planet-base, nomads.

Section 0: Earth and planets from common and neighboring galaxies.

Section 1: Erde and planets from common and neighboring galaxies.

Section 2: Vitruvia and planets from common and neighboring galaxies.

Section 3: Royal landscape and planets from common and neighboring galaxies. Galaxy boundaries change regularly.

Section 4: Home of the Null. Limited communication with neighboring species, located in a section of the universe with multiple black holes.

Section 5: Silva and Trappist solar system as well as planets from common and nearby galaxies.

Singulari: The Null people in Section 4. They bow to their God, Segue and refer to themselves as Singulari (which represents their religion).

Terrestrial Academy of Research and Awareness (TARA): A major university in Achel where the Data Collectors are trained.

United Commonwealth (UC): Earth subdivision of the IPP to keep and maintain peace.

Universal Marketplace: A place where money and goods are exchanged.

Vitruvia: Planet in Section 2 known for its renegade band of Balance-Keepers.

Vitruvians: Species from the Vitruvia planet in Section 2.

PRELUDE: THE CURRENT STATE OF ERDE

The threat from the Royals has worsened after Sovereign Hamish strikes a deal with the demon, Jasper Set, sending the Null to do what they do best—destroy worlds in the name of their god, Segue. To make matters worse, Erdelings have lost the support of the Vitruvians and all Sections within the Intergalactic Peace Project (IPP), including Earth, the very reason they are now in danger.

Meanwhile, after the Data Collectors intervened to help support Tanager and Lucene overcome Jasper Set, the Data Collectors appeared to have lost all of their genetically enhanced powers. Under orders from Commander Royce, Cepheus and Tanager have now been instructed to redistribute the students from the Data Collector training program to other areas of study and create new programming that everyone is less-than-enthusiastic about.

The Terrestrial Academy of Research and Awareness (TARA) and its Makerspace is now being converted to accommodate warcraft, combat training, psychological warfare, espionage, and interrogation and has abandoned its efforts to save Earth from environmental destruction and hostile takeover.

This means that after 100 years of peace, Erde must prepare for war for the first time in over a century. The only problem is, they don't know how. Because they are small in number, they are forced to learn and become experts in things they know nothing about and fast. They don't realize quite how much the odds are stacked against them.

To save Lucene from Jasper Set, Reverend Isabella was forced to open a portal that she thought was to another dimension. Unfortunately, what she actually did was to create a tear in the fabric of reality, whereby beings from other Shamanic realms can come and go in and out of their reality, and not all of them are peaceful.

1

CEPHEUS AND PETRICHOR

THREE WEEKS BEFORE THE END.

"It's unbearable being close enough to touch you, but not being able to." Tears streamed down Cepheus's face as he stood in the living room of his cottage wearing a black pajama set and slippers on his feet—the one's that Moksha bought for him.

"I know, my love," Petrichor answered. Her ghost-like appearance stood before him wearing a gossamer red sundress with strawberries on it, her favorite. There was a yellow daisy in her hair. "Perhaps I shouldn't have come?"

"Of course, you should have," Cepheus moved toward her before remembering that it would do no good. He couldn't hug her fiercely. All he could do was…talk. "You're my wife, and I love you."

Since Reverend Isabella had accidentally ripped a tear between the layers of reality, creatures such as the feline, Hysechia, were released into this plane in their true forms, while others—such as the demon, Jasper Set—were sucked in. Those with unfinished business seemed to be trapped, too. Or, in the case of Petrichor, had chosen to stay and look after those left behind until they were ready to move on. But until the portal was opened, she couldn't seem to break through the barrier in order to get through to Cepheus aside from the occasional dream. She had even had thoughts of using the Data Collectors' intuitive skills to relay messages for her. Still, since Cepheus never specifically asked for this from any of the students, she decided against it—respecting their free will. Without permission, it would be a form of psychic attack and Petrichor was far too kind to do something like that. But when the doorway opened, Cepheus's late wife leaped at the opportunity.

"I don't know how long we'll have the opportunity to keep meeting like this," Petrichor explained, "but I have exciting news." She smiled.

"What is it?" Cepheus brightened a little. "Is it about the children?"

"Two of them, yes." Petrichor reached a hand out. She, too, longed to embrace her husband but could not. "It seems that Tallulah and Cephi have returned."

"You mean—reincarnated?"

"In a manner of speaking, yes," she smiled. "I don't know where they've gone, just that they've moved on."

"And Seth?"

"Not yet," she answered. "But don't worry. Time is different here. And, if I understand the process correctly, he may choose not to return."

"What process? I don't understand." Cepheus was confused.

"I haven't worked it out entirely because—" Petrichor confessed but caught herself. She might have very well worked it out entirely had she not been overseeing Cepheus for the past few decades. "Well, from what I can tell, a soul can return to live again or stay on the higher realms in some other form. Others voluntarily come back as helping spirits."

"Is that what you are, my dear Petrichor?" Cepheus smiled weakly. "You have the kindest heart of anyone I know. That seems like something you would do."

"Not exactly, my love." She smiled lovingly at her husband. "It is true that I have always been here looking out for you. I just haven't exactly…moved on."

"Why not?" Cepheus was concerned. "Are you trapped?"

"No," Petrichor answered. "I don't think so. I just feel as if I'm in a sort of in limbo. I can't move on…until you do."

Cepheus's face contorted in anguish. He couldn't have possibly known how his actions, or lack of them, could have affected his late wife, but that didn't stop the jab of guilt he was now feeling in his heart.

"How am I to ever truly move on from you?" he sobbed softly. "You are the love of my life."

"And you are mine. Yet, I'm asking you to be open to loving again— truly loving again." She eyed him with a knowing gaze. "I'm not asking you to stop loving me, but your heart is so wide, it has room for another."

"If I move forward then, will you be free from limbo?"

"I believe so, my love. But I'm not asking for me."

Cepheus gazed at his wife from head to toe as if memorizing every bit of her features—as he'd done the three other times she'd visited since the tear in the fabric of space—as if it would once again be the last time.

"Cephi," Petrichor called softly. "You are not being unfaithful to my memory. And I am not so selfish as to lay claim to you for all eternity. What I want most for you, my love, is to be happy. That's all I've ever wanted for you." With that, Petrichor's image began to float in and out before disappearing—as she had done so many times before.

He wiped his eyes with the palms of his hands.

"Everything okay out here?" Moksha called softly from the bedroom door, standing there in a long white nightgown that flowed around her ankles. "I thought I heard you talking to someone."

"I'm sorry, Moksha," Cepheus replied. "I had a fitful dream and was working it out by talking to myself again. Give me a moment and I'll come back to bed."

Moksha nodded and retreated into the bedroom, giving him the space she knew he needed. She realized that he felt guilty about their relationship, as if he were somehow being unfaithful to his late wife. Moksha, while sympathetic, had no idea how to help him.

Cepheus looked around the empty living room before returning to the bedroom. He didn't want to lie to Moksha. But what could he tell her? After all, how do you tell your current partner that you were having conversations with your dead wife?

2

THE ROLL OVER
THREE WEEKS BEFORE THE END.

Jasper Set's disappearance unnerved Hamish. He walked the Royal training grounds in Section 3, watching the military regiments with growing disinterest. They always seemed to be training, he mused, but they hadn't actually fought a healthy battle in years. Somehow, just knowing of their existence had been enough of a threat. He took a vague interest in the newly established Poison Patrol, one of Far's more sadistic ideas, and something of which he thought was an odd suggestion…coming from a monk.

"Becoming a great leader," Far reasoned, "means thinking of the survival of your species as a whole. Sometimes, sacrifices have to be made."

Hamish agreed, though he did question why the poisons had to come with cruel side effects (such as gut-wrenching pain or someone's tongue swelling so much that they could no longer breathe). As a Royal who had never been known for mercy, it struck him as odd that his chief advisor had even less compassion than he did.

"I'm only thinking of you, my Sovereign," Far smiled. "And the Great Gods will reward all who have fallen in the afterlife—more so those who have suffered."

Well, I suppose that makes sense, Hamish conceded. But somehow, even he couldn't bring himself to believe this. *There has to be a better way,* he thought, pausing to witness a young soldier watering a small cyrtostachys renda palm that was drying out. He smiled to himself. *Can things be different?* He wondered.

"My Sovereign," Fredo interrupted his thoughts, calling from the palace steps. "I have news. Permission to approach?"

"Granted," Hamish motioned tiredly. While Fredo had turned into an overgrown lapdog, the one thing he never questioned was his loyalty. Granted, Fredo had had an affair with his wife, Sabrina, but that wasn't exactly disloyal as much as it was poor impulse control. And frankly, him sleeping with Sabrina meant that Hamish hardly ever had to. Perhaps that's why he had turned a blind eye to it for all those years, even though a part of him secretly knew.

"It's the Null, my Sovereign," Fredo appeared breathless from the exertion of running.

"What about the Null?" Hamish was concerned.

"It seems that the deal you made with Jasper Set..." he began, loudly, before Hamish shot him a look and motioned for him to keep his voice down. Fredo dropped his tone into a low whisper. "It seems that the demon has kept his word."

"How so? Jasper Set hasn't been seen in months."

"No, my Sovereign. And yet..."

"Yes?"

"The Null people have rolled over nearly all of the Royal hubs across the galaxy. We're the only of our kind left, it would seem."

As they spoke, a hush fell over the training grounds. All training drills came to a halt as they gazed into the distance.

Over the red horizon, a wave of crustacean-like creatures, with their hissing and popping, rolled past them like an ocean during stormy weather. There was nothing that could be done, despite their training, and they knew it. And so, they watched with a combination of awe and terror. Was this the day that all Royals would die?

Instinctively, Fredo bolted toward the palace steps, bounding them two at a time. He was heading for the nursery to check on the baby. Hamish didn't notice. His eyes were transfixed on the Null.

As quickly as they had arrived, the noisy wave rushed past their planet, as if the Null were blind and didn't even know that the planet existed. Sometime later, the noise died down. The Null had vanished.

At that moment, Hamish began to doubt Far's skills as a prophet since he had assured him that targeting Erde was their best plan of attack. Far had planned to manipulate Roman to gain Erde's trust. He would then ensure that the Royals in high command would view the attempt as self-defense. And yet, none of that now appeared to be necessary.

From what he could observe, Jasper Set had kept up his end of the bargain—wherever he was. Was it that Far was mistaken? That Far hadn't anticipated the demon actually having a strange code of ethics? Or, had something changed?

Thanks to Isabella's mistake, strange beings from another realm had been unleashed on Erde, causing an unnatural shift in time and energy that now rippled across the rest of the universe. But Hamish didn't know about that. If he did, perhaps then he would have understood.

3

JASPER'S RETURN (SORT OF)

THREE WEEKS BEFORE THE END.

"There's the princess-s-s sleeping high in her palac-c-c-e." Jasper's voice was right up against Lucene's ear, so close that she could feel the breath, and a bit of spit, in her ear. She jumped up in bed.

"What is it?" Tanager asked groggily. He didn't wait for an answer before he rolled over and quickly fell back to sleep. Lucene admired the fact that Tanager was, what she would call, a 'power sleeper.' There was little that woke him of late, possibly because he was putting in so many hours at work. Unfortunately, in Lucene's case, there was little that *didn't* wake her, and Jasper Set was definitely in the 'things that wake Lucene up' category.

Lucene strained her eyes, waiting impatiently as they adjusted to the darkness. "Where are you, demon?" she whispered.

"Right here," Jasper whispered back. This time, the voice moved from directly behind her to her opposite ear. Lucene quickly climbed out of bed, adjusting her pajamas while turning in circles. He wasn't there. Or, if he was, she couldn't see him.

"No, princes-s-s," he laughed. "You can't see me. I'm right here, between the layers." His voice seemed to bounce off of the surrounding walls.

"Tanager," Lucene tried to call out. Somehow, her voice was caught in her throat. She tried to scream but she couldn't.

"I'm afraid it's just you and me," he grinned, his red eyes, beaked nose, and narrow jaw suddenly appearing like a ghost, flying toward her face. She backed up to avoid him until her shoulder blades banged against the wall. She winced in pain.

"What do you want?" Lucene managed to choke out.

"What do you think I want, princes-s-s?" The demon appeared almost offended. "I want you…to set me free."

"I thought we had," Lucene protested. "Reverend Isabella sent you to another dimension. What happened?"

"You know what happened, damn it!" he growled before composing himself. "Rev…Rev," he couldn't bring himself to say her name. "Isabella's a hack! Instead of sending me to another dimension all she did was trap me between the layers of this one. Even Olly can flit about between parallel worlds and loop his way back and forth in time, but not me!"

"Who's Olly?" Lucene asked. There was something at the core of her being that felt as if she should know, but she didn't.

"Never mind. The point is that he's a nothing of a creature and can do it. Why can't I?"

"Well, how is that Reverend Isabella's fault?" Lucene reasoned. "If this Olly person can, and you can't, maybe it has nothing to do with her. Maybe you don't have that capability."

He flew in like a flame, touching his nose to her nose. "I'm an all-powerful demon! How is this not in my skillset?"

"Don't know, but you also couldn't reach Erde for the longest of times because of our frequency. Maybe you're just not…good enough? I mean, from a kindness standpoint?" Oddly enough, Lucene felt mildly sorry for the demon.

Jasper paused and thought on this a moment. What if he were

good? He wasn't even sure what a good deed looked like. He quickly dismissed the idea as ludicrous.

"And, what exactly are you talking about…*between the layers*?" Lucene was confused. She hadn't spoken to Reverend Isabella in months. In fact, she was beginning to worry that something had happened to her. Lucene wasn't even sure that Isabella was on Erde anymore.

"Arrogant girl!" Jasper chastised. "Just wait until I signal my Null mamas and papas and let them know I'm stuck here. See how your mangy planet will survive then!"

Something jolted Lucene out of the fog…an alarm. Tanager's alarm. The entire scenario had been a lucid dream. She awoke with a start, but not before hearing Jasper's words in her head, "I'm going to get out soon, with or without your help," he promised. "And when I do, I'm coming for you."

4

XENI WANTS A DATE

TWENTY DAYS BEFORE THE END.

Xeni arrived at Lucene's high-home a good fifteen minutes ahead of schedule. She had taken to wearing a trench coat and hat dipped over her eye like Humphrey Bogart in Casablanca. She even had an old canvas courier bag strung across her shoulder. The young woman knocked loudly on the door.

"Hi Xeni," Lucene called from the other side. "Come on inside. Door's open!"

Lucene was spooning batter into small muffin tins. Flour covered her arms, and well, most of the rest of her, too.

Fatima eyed her friend from the other end of the kitchen counter, giggling. "Oh, you poor thing. Remind me to buy you an apron for your next birthday."

"How is it that you are spotless?" Lucene looked Fatima's large frame over, but there was not a speck of flour on her.

Fatima ignored her, instead, systematically relocating soiled bowls and baking utensils to the sink to be washed. "Hi Xeni," she noticed the young woman at the doorway. "Nice get-up."

Xeni beamed proudly. Fatima seemed the only one who "got" Xeni. "Thanks!" She smiled widely, bouncing into Lucene and

Tanager's high-home before remembering and going back to shut the door behind her.

Since TARA shut down the Data Collector training program, all students on the training path were advised to pick a different course of study—or withdraw from TARA. For Xeni's parents this was not an option and so, they encouraged her interest in criminal justice studies—which also happened to be a field where there was a definite need on Erde. Unfortunately, because there only existed a few past video logs of former, now deceased, detectives, TARA had to rely on the research that came out from planets living in Sections 0, 1, 2 and 5. Xeni, however, chose her inspiration from old Earth detective movies and from the few techniques she'd learn in her Data Collection training about 'blending in.'

"We're in the home stretch," Lucene told her young friend. "Let us just pop these in the oven and we can move on to more exciting things."

Xeni nodded, excitedly, silently clapping her hands together and mouthing the word "yay!" Xeni planted herself on a chair at the dining room table by the long window and removed her portable computer from her bag. Meanwhile, Fatima opened the oven and Lucene slid the tray of lemon poppy muffin batter inside.

Fatima was teaching Lucene how to bake, something that somehow, never happened on Earth. But then, ever since Lucene moved into Tanager's high-home, she had been making a conscious effort to learn how to bake and cook—not that Tanager lacked this skill, mind you. It's just that she felt it somehow unfair that he'd had to do all of the cooking himself, particularly when his workload, at least for now, seemed to surpass her own. So, Lucene set out to learn basic cooking skills, and reached out to the only person she knew with such talent —Fatima.

After last evening's disturbing nightmare of Jasper Set, she was relieved to have the company of her friends to take her mind off things. Tanager reassured her that morning that given the trauma surrounding her last encounter with the demon, it made sense that she'd have some post-traumatic nightmares. And, if they continued, they would talk to Cepheus or Dr. Wilah about it.

At that moment, Tanager surfaced from the master bedroom, dressed in casual attire for a Saturday spent working when he would rather be doing something else.

"Oh, hello, ladies," he smiled pleasantly. "I'm just heading to TARA now and will be out of the way." He gathered a few papers from the dining room table, stuffing them haphazardly into his brief-case. Tanager had gotten so used to living alone that having three women in his high-home, even if one of them was his romantic partner, felt odd to him. And yet, he embraced the pleasant uncomfortableness of it all because it meant that Lucene had become a part of his life—something that he had once been afraid to even wish for.

"You're never in the way," Lucene wrinkled her nose and grinned, shaking her head from side-to-side. "And, if all goes well, I'll have dinner waiting for you when you get home."

Tanager's eyed widened in mock terror.

"Very funny, smart ass," Lucene wrapped her arm around Tanager's shoulders and kissed him, playfully. "But don't worry, I have Fatima supervising."

Tanager double-backed for another kiss, smiling at Lucene as if the world belonged to only them…at least, for that moment.

"Thank you, Fatima," Tanager offered, hugging Lucene close and never losing her gaze. "It's nice to have the reassurance that I can return home without our kitchen being on fire with a burnt Mongolian Beef recipe on the stove."

Lucene swatted his arm. "Don't make me smack you in front of my friends," she laughed, pleasantly. "That was one time! And only because the burner settings were different from what they typically are on Earth."

"Yes," Tanager dared, "*that* was clearly the reason."

"Get out," Lucene demanded, grabbing a wooden spoon and

threatening to smack his bottom with it. He went in for another daring peck on the lips, then paused to dust off the flour that had found his way onto his shirt, before making his exit.

"You guys are so adorable," Xeni cooed, letting out a sigh. "That's what I want…real *romance*."

"Xeni, how old are you?" Lucene asked.

"What does that matter?" She seemed almost indignant. If Lucene had to guess, she would have placed her at eighteen or nineteen, and that was being generous. Xeni had all the energy, but none of the angst and drama that Lucene had had more than a decade ago. And while the circumstances were far different, she was hoping that she, Neroni and Fatima might guide Xeni so that she would not make some of the same horrid mistakes that they had, at least when it came to dating.

"Knock, knock," Neroni called out from the door. A sneeze could be heard from the hallway outside. "May you be absolved of illness," Neroni called out to the sneezer.

"Thank you," Tanager answered in the distance. "Damn cat." As it so happened, Tanager discovered not long after Lucene moved in with him that Bagheera was going to be a problem. Before then, he had no idea that he was greatly allergic to cats. And so, Fatima and Ivan became the proud, adopted parents of the black panther-like cat. And while Fatima did her best to de-fur before visiting Tanager and Lucene's high-home, sometimes remnants of Bagheera became apparent.

"Door's open," the other three women called in unison.

"Good morning," Neroni sang pleasantly. "I hope I didn't keep everyone waiting on me."

"Nope," Lucene wiped a bit of flour off her nose with her arm which only succeeded in making it worse. "You're right on time."

Neroni looked Lucene up and down. "Did you lose a fight with a bag of flour?"

"Very funny," Lucene wrinkled her nose at Neroni. "Why don't you three get started while I change into something less…powdery."

Fatima nodded from behind the kitchen counter where she was wiping it with a dish towel.

A few minutes later, Lucene returned wearing denim shorts and a red t-shirt. Neroni and Fatima were standing behind Xeni, the only one who was seated, all peering with interest at the computer screen that sat in front of the young woman. Lucene took a seat next to the Xeni and craned her neck to see.

"What about him?" Xeni stared dreamily at the computer. She was on Achel's version of a dating site. She clicked on the screen and her potential match popped up above the keyboard as a hologram of the head and shoulders version of the real person. His name was Brad. Brad had brown hair that dipped over his left eye and a pointed chin like Xeni. His eyes were an intense brown—so much so that they almost appeared black. "Hi there," Brad flashed a toothy smile with teeth so white they looked painted on. Xeni's pale face turned a beet red as if he could see her (he couldn't). "I'm Brad, and I'm looking for my dream girl. Could you be the one? I like long walks on the beach and candlelight dinners. I love snuggling up by the fire with a cup of warm cocoa. I'm tired of the bar scene and just want to settle down with the right girl. To tell you the truth, I'm starting to think you're not out there. Prove me wrong."

Xeni was about to hit the "approve" button, which would put Brad in the "maybe" category and push him up the tier of potential suitors.

"Hang on," Fatima grabbed Xeni's arm. "You sure about that?" Fatima had always been the open-minded one, giving everyone the benefit of the doubt, and yet even her bullshit-o-meter was triggered.

"What's wrong with Brad?" Xeni pouted.

"Well, for one thing," Fatima began, "he may very well enjoy walks on the beach and candlelight dinners, but he lost me at the cup of cocoa."

"What's wrong with cocoa?" Xeni protested.

"There's nothing wrong with cocoa," Fatima's voice grew louder and more agitated. "I love cocoa! But leading with that seems like bait to me."

"And furthermore," Lucene added, "that whole 'prove me wrong' line? You don't have to prove shit to him." Lucene noticed Xeni's crestfallen face. "Tell you what," she softened, "invariably, it's up to you. But maybe a few more profiles before you decide."

Xeni nodded. She clicked on the next profile. This one's name was Morris. Morris had bright-blue curly hair tied back in a ponytail. He had a rough-around-the-edges sort of face that was intriguing to look at. Xeni smiled. She evidently thought so, too.

"Hey, hey," he sang out. "My name is Morris. I'm fun-loving. I like to bash and have a good time and am looking for a gal who likes adventure. She should be funny, sexy and smart. No drugs. No tragedy. Glitter diggers need not apply."

Xeni was about to hit the "approve" button.

"Xeni!" Fatima and Lucene called out in unison. Neroni remained oddly silent, seemingly fascinated by the exchange.

"What?" Xeni complained. "I'm fun-loving and like adventure. I'm smart and can learn to be funny. And I'm definitely not into drugs or obsessed with money."

"Xeni," Lucene explained. "This isn't a job posting where you have to qualify for the position. Of course, you're all those wonderful things. I just find it oddly suspicious that he has to specify all the traits he doesn't want—particularly for a 'no tragedy' kinda guy. And then he talks at length about what *he* wants. What's *he* bringing to the relationship?"

"Well, he did say fun-loving," Neroni pointed out, literally gesturing at the screen. "Look…right there…fun-loving."

She stopped when Lucene and Fatima shot her a "are-you-kidding-me?" look.

They moved on.

There was Franklin who had a very close relationship with his mother—enough to include that in his profile. There was Tommy who wanted to be friends first and didn't want to be pressured into marriage. And there was Bob who was a movie producer in the middle of casting for his next film and…well, never mind about Bob.

Xeni had taken to pausing her hand over the "approve" button as if she expected the women to smack it. "You guys don't like any of my matches," she whined. "I'm going to be alone *forever!*"

"Well, that's a surprise," Neroni pointed at the screen. They all turned to look. There, on Xeni's matches, was none other than her classmate and friend, Clusaladek. Xeni's eyes grew wide.

"Should I click on his profile?" Xeni asked, nervously.

"You know this boy?" Fatima asked, having never met him.

Xeni nodded. "He was one of the Data Collectors in training, also an assistant instructor at TARA."

"How interesting." Fatima eyed Xeni, encouragingly.

Xeni cautiously clicked on his profile. And there, the Adonis-like Clusaladek appeared with his blonde hair and chiseled chin. While he typically oozed confidence in class, it was clear that this was out of his comfort zone. "Uh, hi. I'm Clusaladek. I'm a senior student at TARA and work part-time as an assistant instructor. My friends tell me I spend too much time in my books and not enough time getting 'out there,' so…uh. This is me getting 'out there.'"

"Aw," Fatima gushed. "He seems sweet."

Neroni remembered a time when he was not so sweet, but they had since made amends. And, there was a possibility that he had been under the influence of Jasper Set at the time. She decided to give him the benefit of the doubt.

"I like hiking in the mountains and star-gazing. I'm not too big on sports, but I enjoy a good tennis match once in a while. I'm honest and loyal and would like to meet a woman with similar interests and values. Uh…yeah…thanks for listening."

"Okay," Fatima declared. "If you don't go out with him, I will!"

"But you're *married*...with a *baby* and kinda...*older-ish*." Xeni was confused.

"I'm joking, my dear," Fatima laughed. "I just mean, he seems nice."

"Err," Lucene noticed Xeni's expression. It was one of surprise and a little...fear. "Xeni?"

"Yes?"

"Do you have a crush on Clusaladek?"

"No!" she protested. "Shut up." She caught herself. "I'm sorry, I didn't mean to tell you to shut up."

Lucene held her hands up. "It's okay," she laughed. Lucene wasn't exactly sure how to advise Xeni at this point. Clusaladek was a little older and more mature than Xeni, and in observing them together, it always appeared as if he treated Xeni more like a little sister. She wasn't sure about this match. "What do you think?" Lucene asked Neroni, who knew the two better than anyone.

"I'm probably the worst one to ask," Neroni offered. "I've never actually dated. My marriage was arranged."

"What?" Fatima was surprised. "People still do that...*here*?"

"Well, it's not mandatory, like in some cultures," Neroni explained. "I wasn't forced to marry my husband. We were just told we were of the same vibration and a matchmaker contacted our families and suggested we meet. We met, decided we liked each other well enough, spent time at family gatherings for a bit, and eventually got married."

"But what about love, and romance?" Xeni seemed disappointed.

"I wouldn't have gotten married if I didn't love my husband," Neroni explained. "At any time, we could have chosen to walk away, but neither of us wanted to." She smiled at the simplicity of it all.

"Huh," was all Fatima could say after a long pause, bewildered.

"Look, one more match," Lucene pointed at the screen.

Xeni forcefully clicked the "approve" button on Clusaladek and clicked on the final profile with some reluctance.

"Hi, I'm Christopher," said the boy with wavy short-brown hair and hazel eyes. He had a pleasant sort of face that seemed gentle. "I'm happy to be here and really looking forward to meeting you… whomever you may turn out to be. I think I have a lot to offer. I'm a nice person, and pretty easy-going. I like to think I'm fairly well-educated and cultured. I try to keep myself healthy and in good shape. I really like music, and while I know it's not a popular thing to say, I actually like going to art museums and plays. My ideal partner is patient and kind. She knows who she is and is comfortable in her own skin. She's happy and looks at the world with the same sense of wonder that I do. I look forward to meeting you." Christopher looked directly into the camera and smiled sheepishly with a lop-sided grin.

"I've changed my mind," Fatima announced. "He's the one."

"You're still married *with a baby*," Lucene joked.

But Xeni hadn't been paying attention. Her mind was still on Clusaladek.

5

"I HATE AMY"

NINETEEN DAYS BEFORE THE END.

There were manuals…lots and lots of manuals and holographic videos from past Erdelings skilled in the areas of combat, psychological warfare, investigation, defense, espionage and interrogation.

Commander Royce checked in with the Elders, a group of ancient spirits that were the closest that Erde had to gods and religion. They were the spirits of ancestors from long ago of which Commander Royce was believed to have descended. Since Erde was a relatively young planet, no one knew exactly how that lineage came to be.

Which is what brought Cepheus, Moksha, Tanager, and Lucene to the Makerspace that Sunday morning when they would have much preferred to be sleeping in. For Tanager, it was his fourteenth straight workday without a break and tomorrow began a fresh week of school.

Commander Royce had given them specific instructions as to what resource materials in the library to study and, so the for now, they worked regularly integrating what they learned and also worked to develop new curricula for the former Data Collectors and other students at TARA. It was also made it abundantly clear that Cepheus and Tanager no longer represented the Intergalactic Peace Project (IPP) as Erde was no longer a member. Instead, their new assignment was to serve the Planetary Defense League (PDL). Therefore, they no longer checked on humans and those claiming sanctuary at the preserves. That duty was now given to Constable Melokuhle and a few of his assistants.

"I never thought I would live to see the day when TARA would go from being the Terrestrial Academy of Research and Awareness to the Terrestrial Academy of Response to Aggression." Tanager rubbed his forehead, tiredly. He sat around a small table in the library with his colleagues in what was now referred to as their private Resource Room. No one else was admitted there, unless one of them were present. The trusted group now included Moksha, who protested to Commander Royce up and down that she was no longer an assassin. However, it was deemed that she had the most knowledge of combat and defense of anyone, and if she wanted to maintain her residence on Erde, she was "encouraged" to use her knowledge to help get the PDL up to speed.

And there was Lucene. No one really knew what she was capable of since all the Data Collectors seemed to short circuit when trying to outmaneuver Jasper Set on the bridge that day, when he threatened to blow them up and half the city of Achel in the process. And yet, somehow, while all of the other Data Collectors went back to "normal," Lucene had these glitchy re-awakenings where like a faulty electrical system, the lights would blink off and on again. For this reason, Commander Royce added her to the list of PDL "agents," citing her ability as "special skills" even though no one knew what they were anymore.

And poor Roman, he was not entirely trusted after he divulged far too much info to his lover, Far (sorry for the pun). Since Far was working on behalf of the Royals and Jasper Set, Roman was no longer privy to PDL knowledge nor was he permitted to teach at

TARA. However, given his skills in anthropology and psychology, the PDL hired him as a consultant on psychological warfare. Therefore, he could enter the Resource Room, but only to provide information to the team. For this, they paid him a small stipend which was enough to keep him in his high-home and well fed (or so they thought). And while Roman still got an invitation to Cepheus, Tanager and Lucene's monthly "reunion" gatherings (since the four of them traveled from Earth to Erde together), he was distinctly out of place—none more aware of it than he.

The one vital person missing from this equation was Ivan. His knowledge of virtual technology, artificial intelligence, machine learning and remote sequencing outweighed some of the most skilled technicians at TARA. His contribution to the new TARA training modalities would have gone a long way to help fill in the gaps of knowledge that the academy now faced. There was just one problem...Ivan was still on maternity leave with Fatima. He didn't officially start back until Monday.

"Perhaps we should take a break," Cepheus suggested, rubbing his yellow eyes which now had tired red circles around them like a sunset before a storm. "We've been at this for three hours now, and I've had about all I can stomach on how to teach our students 'ethical interrogation.' I mean really, 'ethical interrogation?' In the end, it's still violence. We're simply justifying the means."

The four stood and stretched. Moksha nodded. "Now you have some understanding as to why I fled from the Royals." Cepheus took her hand gently, rubbing the back of it affectionately with his thumb. She squeezed his hand in return. Unlike the others, Moksha was wearing a green uniform with pants and a wrap-around top that changed colors and allowed it to blend into its environment as if a hybrid of a green screen and a chameleon. Funny, given that she and Cepheus were of lizard descent.

No one liked the new arrangement but they didn't really have a choice. After all, the Royals were still a threat. So were the Null who were now keenly aware of Erde's existence. There was also the strange phenomena that seemed to be happening lately where odd new species of animals began appearing on the planet, while others disappeared.

Not limited to creatures, the team also noticed random objects from the Makerspace disappearing and resurfacing someplace else. This wouldn't typically be cause for alarm were it not for the fact that the "someplace else" often turned out to be a random location where it shouldn't be, such us under the kitchen sink of someone's residence or mixed with a batch of tomatoes at the grocery store.

Plus, they kept hearing about news reports of supernatural events occurring all around them, of the flying saucer and ghost variety, stories not unlike what one might hear on Earth. The best guess from experts was that it had something to do with the conjunction between Jupiter and Saturn while Saturn was in retrograde. It reportedly sent out a ripple effect across the universe.

What they didn't understand (mainly because Reverend Isabella wasn't around to explain it to them) was that there was a little matter of a semi-open portal between this dimension and others, where Isabella had accidentally unleashed trapped spirits who hadn't moved on to their next life or who had been sentenced there as a form of prison. It was like a sink plug that didn't seal properly. And now, there were beings who were trying desperately to get out and back *to* or *at* the people who put them there. There were also beings who were simply born in the other realm who were kicked out accidentally or reacted like curious cats when a door is suddenly opened, and they felt an instinctive need to dash. Yes, there were a few odd beasts on this plane of existence who dove between the layers just for the experience of it. But all this was lost on the group.

"Here's what I don't understand," Lucene offered as she locked up the Resource Room after them (another new phenomenon, locks!) using a wireless sequence that emitted from her communication watch. "While I get that we need to defend ourselves from outside threats, I thought the whole reason that Erde flew under-the-radar of the Null and other beings was because of its vibration—being peaceful and all."

"Quite," Tanager answered, holding her hand as they made their way back to the Makerspace's main work stations. He had wondered the same thing. What had suddenly changed within Erde's energy field? Was it Jasper Set's presence, the shifting consciousness of Erde's current inhabitants, or something (or someone) else? He really didn't have an answer and that bothered him.

Once at the Transporter, Tanager sent a request for the group to be picked up as the Makerspace was far too large for the team to make the rounds on foot unless they planned on several miles of walking—which they weren't. Or, more specifically, Tanager wasn't. Moments later, Renenet arrived, the usual scowl on her face and her lion-like mane looking particularly aggressive that day.

"Oh, Director Renenet," Tanager greeted her hesitantly. "I didn't expect you to be the one escorting us today. If you would rather I run the Transporter, I can…"

"That won't be necessary, Professor Tanager," she answered. "Given our new protocol, I am most qualified to escort you. And, for security reasons, no one in the work areas can travel from section to section using the transporter unless accompanied by an official PDL director, which I am."

"But I thought we were agents of the PDL, too," Lucene whispered to Tanager.

"An agent is lower than a director," Renenet barked at Lucene, before remembering herself. "You do not have authorization," she smiled sweetly. "Please take a seat."

Take a seat. Take a seat. That's all Renenet ever commands me to do. Take a seat. Lucene thought, annoyed. But there wasn't time to argue. There wasn't time for much of anything anymore, at least not for Tanager, who spent far too many nights working late and long weekends away from home.

Once everyone was aboard, the Transporter made its slow spiral up through the Fibonacci-like tunnels of the Makerspace, making routine stops at sections including the Welding Room which had been renamed the Weapons Room; the Robotics Lab which was now the AI and Military Robotics Lab; and the Transportation Shop which had become the Warcraft Shop. In fact, nearly every area of the Makerspace had been converted to support some military purpose. The only exception to this were the few local businesses who rented out rooms to build products they were unable to produce in their own factories. They had special permits (AKA a lot of money), which was deemed acceptable as they helped support the financial upkeep of the Makerspace and TARA.

There was a bitterness in Lucene's stomach as they made the rounds. It seemed as if overnight the Makerspace went from being a vibrant inventor and artist hub to becoming a military base. This wasn't what she expected when she'd left Earth. Tanager witnessed her crumbled expression, noting a tear forming in her left eye. He brushed it away with his fingers. "Don't lose hope," he reassured her, "this is temporary."

"How can you be sure?"

"Because," Tanager reasoned, as if trying to convince himself, "it *has* to be."

The last stop on the list was the Model Room which had somehow escaped being renamed the Military Model Room. This was their main agenda for the day since it was on their checklist from Commander Royce with the purpose to see how the new architectural defense designs were coming along. This included creating a dome-like defense shield around Erde, as well as additional on-the-ground defense stations and putting protective barriers around their high-risk structures. "High-risk" were the PDL's main offices, Achel as a whole, the SpeedCircuit, entries and exits to and from the crosses, and national landmarks.

Cepheus and Moksha broke off from the group, exiting the Transporter and making their way to the opposite end of an enormously large and bustling room. They were to survey the air defense shield blueprints and models.

Meanwhile, Tanager and Lucene headed toward an expansive model of Achel, the SpeedCircuit and the Crosses which resembled a miniature train set and tiny village that you might buy for your kids on Earth during Christmas. This one was extremely detailed with small plastic figurines distinct enough to identify TARA, Tanager and Lucene's high-home building and even Lucene's former personal cottage in the Eastern Cross. Oddly enough, Lucene could have sworn her old cottage was a little too accurate, making her wonder how it was they were able to see things like a dish sponge, on a sink, by the kitchen window, just from drone footage (if that's, indeed, what they used to collect their images), or the misshapen shingle on the back end of her roof (she didn't even know it was like that).

Renenet waited by the Transporter eyeing Tanager and Lucene with extreme interest.

"Oh, it's you," a small woman with red hair and green eyes popped out from a back-storage room. She looked wide-eyed at Tanager, surprised to see him. It was the same women Lucene had witnessed on her first trip to the Makerspace several months ago, the one Tanager oddly described as "a mistake" with no further explanation. She seemed to like green as she was once again wearing jeans and a green t-shirt that clung rather tightly around her chest.

"Amy," Tanager coughed, "nice to see you again." He dropped Lucene's hand, something that only Lucene was keenly aware of. Lucene's eyes darted between Tanager and Amy, but the two merely gazed at one-another with a mixture of nervous energy and anticipation. "I didn't expect to see you here on a weekend."

"Well, I'm usually off today, but Renenet let me know that

someone called in sick, so…here I am." She waved her hands as if to say *ta-da!* Lucene peered over her shoulder at Renenet, who started at the mention of her name, quickly averting her gaze and then pretending to plug in coordinates on the Transporter as if to fix some inexplicable malfunction.

"And this is—" Amy turned her bright green and obscenely beautiful (in an irritating sort of way) eyes toward Lucene.

"Ah, this is Lucene…" Tanager paused, awkwardly. "She's recently arrived from Earth, is an agent of the PDL, and is…" He lost his words.

"His lover," Lucene smiled, offering her hand. Tanager choked back an uncomfortable cough. "We work and live together."

"Oh," Amy seemed surprised. "I hadn't realized…"

"It's a new arrangement," Tanager offered.

Why is he explaining this to her? Lucene wanted to know. "So, Amy," Lucene assumed control of the conversation before Amy and Tanager tripped over their own tongues. "Can you give us an update on this defense model so we can make our report for the PDL?" Lucene wasn't generally good at being assertive in situations such as this one, so she channeled her inner Drake and Dallen—two men who were terrible people, but great when it came to negotiation and business.

"Of course," Amy answered, dropping her gaze to the ground momentarily, her head slinking downward as she collected herself before retreating behind the model. "So, if you look here," she pointed to a few visible barricades set up at strategic points along the Crosses, "you can see where we have mapped out areas most vulnerable to air and land attack and set up defense systems to support those areas. These would be a combination of energetic barriers and real fortified structures. We've taken into account technologies that outside species might possess that we lack and have planned workarounds to prevent attack."

Tanager was impressed. "Beautifully done, Amy." Amy smiled

proudly at the praise. And there it was again…that look between them, that distinctly did not include Lucene. In fact, she felt as if she were intruding, somehow.

Lucene was forced to endure this odd back-and-forth for a good fifteen minutes before Cepheus and Moksha could be seen returning to the transporter—their cue to return as well. "Well, thank you, Amy," Lucene spoke forcefully. "You've been most helpful."

"Of course," Amy smiled, uncertainly.

Lucene took Tanager by the forearm and all but steered him back to the Transporter.

"Hey," Amy called before they'd left. "I don't suppose the two of you would like to hear a song from my performance next week?"

"What performance?" Tanager asked.

"We're doing a fundraiser for the Dragoste Healing Center. So, I'm playing a classical Earth piece I know." To Lucene, she added, "The Music Hall is just through there, as you know." She pointed to a small door at the other end of the room. "A quick detour…if it wouldn't be a bother?"

"I'm afraid we…" Lucene started to decline.

"We'd love to," Tanager said with a bit too much enthusiasm.

"Great," Amy smiled, hopefully.

"Lucene, would you go invite Moksha and Cepheus? And tell Renenet we will just be a few minutes more."

Wait, what? Have I just been dismissed? Lucene thought to herself. Apparently, she had, as Tanager and Amy resumed a conversation in hushed voices.

Cepheus saw the look on Lucene's face as she approached the Transporter. He didn't have to guess what this was about—Amy. He let out a frustrated sigh as Lucene made the request. He reluctantly agreed, taking Moksha by the hand and escorting her, with some speed, over to where Tanager and Amy stood, presumably laughing at some inside joke that only the two of them knew about.

Lucene paused, filled with a mixture of confusion, jealousy, anger, and bewilderment. Who the hell was this Amy and why was Tanager so taken with her? And more importantly, why had he not told her about this woman before? Lucene leaned against the wall of the Transporter, thinking, before finally conceding to join the rest of the group.

"Nice couple, aren't they?" Renenet seemed to challenge, speaking sweetly over Lucene's shoulder.

"I hadn't noticed," Lucene retorted. "And you seem to be forgetting that Tanager and I are living together now."

"Oh," Renenet feigned surprise. "I hadn't known that. Curious…"

"What's curious?" Lucene demanded.

"Well," Renenet paused. "I really shouldn't say anything."

"Oh, yes you should," Lucene replied curtly. "You think I don't recognize a set up when I see one? Amy was supposed to be off duty today."

"So, she was." Renenet smiled at her cleverness.

"Ahem," Lucene cleared her throat.

Renenet's fire agate eyes turned and bored into Lucene's. "Tanager and Amy were supposed to be married."

"Oh," Lucene felt as if she'd been slapped in the face. "What happened?"

Renenet narrowed her eyes. "*You* happened."

"What? How is that possible? Tanager and I have only known each other for a little over a year. Were they a couple while he and I were traveling back to Erde?"

Renenet paused for an unbearably long time, giving Lucene enough of an opportunity to run all kinds of horrific scenarios through her head, of Tanager's infidelity (of the heart, if not in actuality) as he awkwardly wooed her on Earth, their trip home… *Oh, God.* Lucene thought, *He didn't actually break up with her after I'd gotten here, did he?"*

"No," Renenet finally answered. Lucene let out a sigh so loud that it sounded as if a helium balloon were rapidly deflating. Renenet eyed her curiously and not without a minor hint of annoyance. "They were over long before you arrived." Renenet looked over Lucene, distastefully.

"Then why is your bitch-o-meter set to annihilate?" Lucene challenged. Sometimes, Lucene couldn't put the brakes on her mouth.

Renenet was about to remind Lucene that she was a director and she shouldn't be spoken to in such a manner, but decided against it, instead, choosing the woman-to-woman assault. "Make no mistake," Renenet peered at her, angrily. "They were *supposed* to be married. But Cepheus kept going on and on about the *Earth-born Data Collector, one of Dora and Zan* who was of the same *vibration* as Tanager," Renenet mocked. "Tanager just fell in love with the *idea* of you," she gave Lucene another disgusted once over, "without actually having met you." That last bit dripped off her tongue in a way that suggested, not so subtly, that Lucene in no way lived up to all that was Amy.

I hate Amy, Lucene thought.

"Lucene, are you coming?" Moksha called, waving for Lucene to join them.

"I'll wait here," Renenet announced, smiling to herself.

Lucene joined the rest of the group, Moksha and Cepheus walking hand-in-hand, while Tanager seemed to follow at Amy's heels like a lost puppy. He almost forgot that Lucene was behind him, until she took his arm, just above the elbow, squeezing it a little harder than necessary.

Down the hallway they went, until they'd arrived at the Music Hall which was essentially a large theater with an ornate concert grand piano sitting on the left of the stage. The group climbed the stage steps and gathered around as Amy sat, shaking her hands nervously before beginning to play Chopin's Fantaisie Impromptu, Op. 66. And there, Amy was transported into another dimension as her fingers flew easily over the keys, leaving Tanager mesmerized.

Lucene dropped his arm and retreated into the shadows behind a curtain.

"Isn't she wonderful?" Tanager whispered to Cepheus, who in turn, jabbed Tanager in the ribs with his elbow.

"What was that for?" Tanager whispered in surprise. Cepheus shot him a look and nodded his head over his shoulder.

Lucene, Tanager realized, standing there in the corner of the stage, arms wrapped around herself as if giving herself a hug for comfort. *I'm a complete idiot,* he thought. He walked over to Lucene and wrapped his arms around her. She smiled at him, appreciatively, thinking to herself, *I still hate Amy.*

6

THE ARGUMENT

NINETEEN DAYS BEFORE THE END.

"Lucene, don't you think you're overreacting, just a little?" Tanager asked as Lucene blew past him into their high-home, all but slamming the door in his face.

She began rifling through the cabinet, clanking pots and pans together before settling on a simple sauté pan and dropping it on the stovetop. Tanager cringed, hoping that wouldn't leave a scratch. She then moved on to the leftovers in the refrigerator. Being a mostly unskilled cook, Tanager couldn't help but wonder if this was in some way part of her protest, forcing him to eat something she made by herself without supervision.

"I saw the way you looked at each other," she replied, unwrapping a parsnip and fennel dish that Fatima helped her make the night before and plopping it in the pan.

"Might want to…" he was about to say, "add olive oil to the pan first," but he was too late. She turned the heat up to high. Instead he asked, "How exactly did we look at each other?" He moved around the kitchen counter and lowered the dial on the stove. Lucene ignored him, as she was now on to the utensil drawer where she rummaged for a wooden spoon. "Lucene," he stopped her, taking her by the arm. "Please, talk to me."

"You both had this shared look of…oh, I don't know. I can't read anyone anymore. But it was something that resembled…*affection*."

"And that's a bad thing?"

"Yes, that's a bad thing!" Lucene whined. "You're supposed to be with me now!"

Tanager tilted his head, forcing Lucene to meet his gaze. "I am with you now. And, I love being with you, although, I must admit, this moment isn't one of the best…"

"The point is," Lucene pulled away, crossing her arms. "It was as if you *missed* each other."

"It's not that," Tanager tried in vain to explain. "But Amy and I were almost married. Just because it didn't work out doesn't mean that I suddenly hate her."

"Hmmph," was all Lucene could say, returning to the stew and stirring it violently.

"Lucene, I know we age differently here, but I am still more than two decades older than you…"

"So you keep reminding me."

"You're acting like a child," Tanager's face began to contort in annoyance.

"Again, thanks for pointing out how you are so much older and wiser than I am."

At this point, the stew was clumping to the spoon as if hanging on for dear life. Tanager retrieved if from her, before turning off the stove and moving the pan to an unheated burner. "Can we please just sit down and talk about this?"

Lucene nodded, tearfully, so they went into the living room and sat.

"What I was trying to say, was that because I've been around for a while, it stands to reason that there were relationships pre-*us*. That doesn't diminish how I feel about you now."

"What about the girl at the bistro?"

Tanager was confused. "What girl?"

"When we went to dinner the other night, you smiled at our server."

"You don't want me smiling at people?"

"No," Lucene let out a frustrated sigh. "It wasn't just a smile it was like you were…flirting."

"I don't flirt," Tanager was offended. "Which is not to say that Brie wasn't attractive but—"

"See! That's what I'm talking about!" Lucene pointed at him triumphantly. *I didn't even know her name was Brie.*

Tanager eyed Lucene calmly and tried again. "Lucene, do you think that being in love means you never get a pang in the center of your chest when you remember a pleasant moment from your past that involved another person, or that you never get crushes or never find someone else even remotely attractive?"

"Yes," she answered simply.

"Well, forgive me for saying so, but I think you're being a little naive."

"Again, with the reflection on my age and lack of worldly experience."

"You never think about Dallen, not in a *what if* sort of way, but remembering some of the good times?"

"There weren't many good times with Dallen, and no."

"What about other people?"

In truth, Lucene couldn't really remember *other people* aside from her former crush on Drake Cushing and her brief dating experience with Dallen. And, as far as she knew, she was immune to crushes. "No, Tanager," she answered finally, "I don't think about other people, and you're the only person I want to be with."

Tanager smiled, wrapping his arms around her. "Well, then we agree on something. You're the only person I want to be with as well.

For the record, I don't intend to leave you and I will never be unfaithful."

Lucene hugged him back with all her might, sniffling as a few teardrops landed on Tanager's shirt. *Stupid emotions,* she chastised herself. "I didn't think her playing the piano was all that good," she whimpered.

Tanager's grin grew wider. He took the cue. "I agree, not very good. And, you know what else?" He leaned back, craning his neck as Lucene looked up at him.

"What?"

"I happen to know that's one of only three songs she knows how to play on the piano. She learned them really well to impress people, but really, that's it."

Lucene buried her face in his chest again, slightly relieved. "Tanager?"

"Yes?"

"I think I killed the parsnip and fennel stew."

"I'm pretty sure you did, too. Dinner out?"

"Okay, but not the bistro."

"No." Tanager thought a moment about Brie, the server. "Not the bistro."

NOT CHRISTOPHER

EIGHTEEN DAYS BEFORE THE END.

"Oh, hello. I didn't realize anyone else was here," Lucene shielded her eyes from the sun as she squinted to observe the young man standing over her. She had been lying on a blanket at the water's edge of Tranquil Beach, a small patch of sand and sea located at the farthermost corner of the Eastern Cross. Very few seemed to take the time to visit as it required an intricate connection from the SpeedCircuit to renting a hovercraft and then walking an additional mile and a half from the rental lot.

Most times, Lucene was alone to enjoy the sun, white sand and gentle tepid water as she swam laps, combed the beach, and otherwise did her best thinking about life in general.

Today, however, was not going to be one of those days.

"Lucene, it's nice to finally meet you," the young man said.

Lucene could make out little of his features against the sun's glare, except that he appeared to be of average height and weight, had a thick head of perfectly combed chestnut hair and a clean-shaven light complexion. He was wearing a light blue guayabera shirt and white linen pants. He was tan and his arms were toned.

What was most odd to Lucene was that he gave the immediate impression of being…flawless.

"I'm sorry, do I know you?" Lucene was confused. There was something about him that seemed very familiar, but her memory was sketchy, and she couldn't be sure.

He stepped in front of the sun, casting a shadow over Lucene's face. "Does this help, now that you can see me better?"

Lucene wrinkled her nose at him. "Not really," she confessed.

"Oh well, you'll figure it out." He plopped down beside her, bending his knees and planting his feet in the sand. He leaned forward and wrapped his long arms around his shins for support.

"Oh," Lucene suddenly realized (or at least, she thought she did). "Are you Xeni's Christopher? The one she met online?"

"No, not Christopher," he answered.

"Then, who are you?"

"That's for me to know and you to find out."

"You sound like a twelve-year-old," Lucene retorted. Not Christopher had to have been in his early twenties, at least.

"Exactly," he answered calmly, not in the least bit offended.

"What do you want, Not Christopher?" Lucene asked flatly. After all, she was there to sort out the mess that was in her head about Tanager and their relationship, and his former fiancé Amy who Lucene decided she hated, even though she didn't exactly have a reason to.

"I thought you might want to work through some stuff about Tanager and needed a sounding board."

"How on Earth could you possibly know about that?"

"I know everything you know," he answered simply.

Since the portal had closed incorrectly, somehow leaving a tear and the layers of reality became intermingled, nothing quite made sense. Less so, since Lucene was unaware of this. *Hmm,* Lucene thought. *Another Jupiter-Saturn conjunction?* Somehow, that explanation made less sense each time she relied on it. And yet, here was a neutral stranger willing to listen.

"I think he still has feelings for his ex," she finally told him.

"Is that terrible?"

"Yes, Not Christopher," Lucene whined. "It's awful."

"Why?"

"Because, he's supposed to only have feelings for me."

"Hmm…"

"What, *hmm*?" Lucene demanded.

"Are you sure its current feelings versus a reflection of past feelings?"

"Does it matter?"

"I don't know," Not Christopher answered. "Does it?"

"The point is, we have very different ideas about relationships, and mine don't seem to matter because I'm 'naive'." Lucene put the word "naïve" in air quotes before pausing as the waves of the ocean rolled in and out, a little stronger this time, making it difficult to talk without yelling above the roar.

"Well, if you feel that way—" Not Christopher finally answered when the waves died down, inching back from the water's edge as the foam reached his sandals. They slipped off as the water tugged at them, and the two watched as Not Christopher's sandals floated out to sea.

"That's terrible for the environment," Lucene commented.

"Not to worry," Not Christopher answered. "They'll be back."

"Anyway, you were saying…"

"If you feel he's not taking you seriously enough, or discounting what you say because you are younger and less experienced at life—"

"Hey," Lucene interrupted again. "Whose side are you on, anyway?"

"I'm on your side, Lucene," Not Christopher answered. "I've always been on your side."

"Sorry, continue."

"I was just going to suggest that you should talk about it. Isn't that what couples do? Talk about things they need to work through?"

"I've complained about it often enough."

"That's not the same thing, though, is it?"

"Perhaps not," Lucene admitted. She hated that Not Christopher was probably right.

"Hey" Fatima's voice suddenly called. "Who are you talking to?"

Lucene looked up in surprise to see Fatima making her way toward her. She was waddling a little and huffing a little more. Lucene ran to greet her, at least, as fast as she could run on sand (which wasn't very). She noticed her friend struggling to carry a tote bag and had an umbrella dragging behind her leaving a line in the sand. "Here," Lucene said. "Give me those." She grabbed the tote and threw it over her left shoulder and tucked the umbrella awkwardly under her arm. Lucene offered her left arm which Fatima gratefully accepted.

"Thanks, Chica," Fatima huffed. "I guess I'm still not a hundred percent after giving birth."

"Well, it's still quite a walk from the lot. What are you doing here?"

"What do you think I'm doing here?" Fatima smiled. "I wanted to see my best friend."

"Fatimaaaa?" Lucene questioned in a way that suggested she didn't believe her.

"Okay, well I stopped to drop off a loaf of banana bread I baked for you guys and Tanager said you went to your favorite think spot to sort some stuff out. This was the only spot I could think of."

"Good guess," Lucene praised. "Did he encourage you to come out here?"

"He ever-so-gently hinted that you would probably appreciate a chat."

"Well, I've been getting that," Lucene answered when they finally arrived at the blanket Lucene had laid out. "Fatima, let me introduce you to…" Lucene stopped. There was no one there, not even footprints in the sand or an impression of Not Christopher's weight from where he sat on the beach. Lucene surveyed her surroundings.

"What are you looking for?"

"Did you not see the young man I was talking to just now?"

"No, actually, I thought you were talking to yourself…or rehearsing a play."

"Curious," Lucene answered. Not wanting to stress her friend out any more than necessary given her heart condition and the fact that she had recently given birth, she changed the subject. "And how is baby Talula today?"

"As adorable as ever," Fatima bragged. "Ivan took her to the Makerspace for the first time to introduce her to everyone on his first day back. He's already made her a matching baby-sized hard hat." She motioned on her own head and continued, "Which is really just a soft yellow hat for show."

"Is that a safe space for a baby?" Lucene wasn't so sure.

"He just wanted to show her off to his colleagues. And," Fatima giggled, "he also wanted to give her a tour!"

"But she's a *baby*." Lucene doubted that the baby would retain any of that knowledge. She set the tote down on her blanket.

"I know that, silly. May I remind you that I was there when she arrived," Fatima chided, laughing. "But you know what? Dr. Wilah said that she predicted with 100% accuracy the occupation of all three of her kids based on her sure-fire game."

"What kind of game?" Lucene asked as she fought to dig the long rail of the umbrella into the sand.

Fatima pulled a towel from the tote. "Well, she puts out a series of toys in front of her newborn and see which he or she picks."

"That's it?"

"That's it." Fatima grinned. "And guess what?"

"What?"

"Talula sailed right past the plastic spatula and the yarn and went straight for the adjustable wrench. Ivan was beside himself with joy. 'That's my girl,' he said."

"Good Lord, Fatima," Lucene laughed. "Not one, but *two* tinkerers in the house. Better buy some extra fire extinguishers and flame-retardant baby clothes."

8

FAR'S RETURN

EIGHTEEN DAYS BEFORE THE END.

Roman didn't hear Far enter his high-home early in the morning, but to be fair, Far was waif-like and moved like a silent ninja. And…Roman was one bottle past the point of drunk. It would have taken an army of soldiers to wake him from his current "sprawled-out-on-the-balcony with his bare bottom in plain view to anyone with a decent pair of binoculars and voyeuristic tendencies" state.

The room was disheveled, Far noticed. This was not like Roman at all, who was a perfectionist, minimalist, and mild germaphobe. Yet the living room was cluttered with gin bottles, sushi-style takeout boxes, empty cigarette cartons, and a heap of dirty laundry. In fact, the room smelled of full-strength smoke, nicotine, and unwashed anthropology professor.

Far paused at the wave of feeling that overtook him, allowing it to pass through him before making his way to the balcony. The Royals had done a fair job of de-conditioning emotions out of him but Roman was still his weakness. After all, their love had been real. At least, that's what he believed before the Royals beat it out of him that romantic love and compassion were anything more than false realities. True love came from banding together for the common good of the species, no matter the cost. Emotions had no place. The Royals were much like the Null in this aspect.

Far tip-toed past the mess, careful not to startle his former beloved. Once he'd reached Roman who was lying face-down on the concrete with a tattered robe wrapped haphazardly around him, he leaned over and gently rubbed Roman's back with one hand–just behind the heart.

After what seemed like an eternity, Roman lifted his nose into the air. With eyes still closed he asked, "Far?"

"Yes, my love," Far answered. "I am here."

Roman rolled over as a smile crossed his lips. It was temporary, as if he were waking from a dream and suddenly remembered that in the real world, Far was a large contributor to Roman and his friends almost getting blown up, and that he was now lying on the balcony in the most embarrassing state imaginable.

Roman held his palm to his forehead and groaned. "No," he muttered. "This is not at all how I imagined our reunion to be. I'm afraid I am in an awful state."

"Nonsense," Far smiled, reverting to a version of his old self, removing Roman's hand and staring deeply into his eyes. "Your state is just a testament to how much you've missed me. And while I would never wish this on you, I would be lying if I said that I wasn't a little bit…touched." Far leaned over to help Roman to his feet and nearly fell on top of him, instead. Far was about as strong as a feather.

Eventually, Roman wobbled his way to the couch, flopping into the cushions. The full weight of his body caused the couch to move slightly. Far settled in next to him, crossing his legs and settling his arms on top of them. Roman rubbed his head and winced at the pain. His brain fog had cleared just enough for him to remember a few things from their last encounter. "Why are you here?" he finally asked.

"Isn't it obvious?" Far answered. When Roman's face indicated that it was not—in fact— all that obvious, he continued. "I missed you. And, sensed that you needed me."

"May I remind you that you were going to let Jasper Set blow us to kingdom come."

Far rolled his eyes as if this were insignificant.

Roman leaned forward, his voice becoming more agitated. "Not to mention that on more than one occasion your fist found it necessary to make its way to my face!"

"Oh, you've over-reacted, my love," Far answered. "Look at me. It's not as if I'm a large man. You know I could never truly hurt you."

"Over-reacting?!" Roman shook his head in disbelief. He began ticking off a bulleted list to support his argument, touching one finger of his right hand at a time for emphasis. "Bomb…fist… emotional distress…abandonment." Roman let out a sigh. "I can't believe I've actually been pining over you! Oh, oh…" Roman remembered. "That woman shopkeeper…what was her name? Mallory? Everyone assumed you murdered her!"

Far caught himself before correcting Roman. It was a man that had been killed, not a woman.

"Oh, come now," Far's voice remained calm. "I'm not a killer. Everyone just blamed me because I was the outsider. Be fair. I'm not the only reason for your current state."

"What are you talking about?"

"Here, let me make you a cup of vegetable broth with garlic. It will help you feel better. We can talk after that."

This was Far's method of operation, Roman had learned. When he didn't want to argue, or he wanted to give Roman a chance to calm down, or he simply needed time to reframe his argument, suddenly it was time to make a cup of broth, take a bath, or get some fresh air.

"No, thank you," Roman growled. "I would like you to explain yourself."

Far ignored him. "How's work going at the Terrestrial Academy?" he asked.

Roman grit his teeth. "It seems I am no longer employed at TARA. But somehow, I expect that you already knew that."

Far glanced at the coffee table where several eviction notices sat in plain sight. "And, they're kicking you out, it would seem."

"When one is not working and unable to pay the mortgage, things like that happen."

"Did your new friends not offer to help?"

Roman's face grew red but he wasn't entirely certain if his anger was misplaced or not. After all, TARA had covered the mortgage on his high-home for months after his dismissal. (It was Cepheus and Tanager that pooled their resources to pay his debts, but Roman didn't know that). There was the small stipend that came in from his "consultant" work at TARA, but that wasn't nearly enough to cover both home expenses, and food and drink that matched his typically high culinary standards. Lucene made every attempt to help him find work and stopped to check in on him regularly. But after months of Cepheus, Tanager and Lucene pleading with him to seek out help and offering what support they could, their visits became increasingly sparser. In reality, Erde was low on qualified emotional counselors, and the team had been working overtime as TARA began transitioning its Makerspace and training modules to become more military-focused. Roman was unaware of this and was a bit too self-absorbed in his current state to actually ask how anyone else was doing. He took their distance as abandonment–they had given up on him.

Far waited patiently for Roman to draw his own misguided conclusions and did nothing to convince him otherwise.

Roman flinched as Far put his hand gently on his shoulder. "I never abandoned you," Far explained. "I was merely preparing something better for us."

"Better?" This made no sense to Roman.

"I would never have let Jasper Set harm you. But since he made a deal with the Royals, I had to make it look convincing. And as for your face..." He stroked the side of Roman's face lovingly. "Well, I'm sorry about that. You're much bigger than I, and I lashed out in fear."

"Fear? You were afraid of...me?" Roman whispered, eyes growing wide. It had never occurred to him that Far's angry outbursts may have been a fear response. But it made perfect sense now that he thought about it.

"Let's not talk about all of that unpleasantness." Far waved his hand. "Water under the bridge. What I'd like to talk about is our future."

"What future?" Roman snorted. "What kind of future can I possible provide for us?"

"Come back to the Royal training grounds with me."

"What? Are you insane? The Royals are blood-thirsty monsters. I can't believe you still support them."

"They are not what they seem, my love." Far balled a fist and took a deep breath. He quickly released his clenched hand and ran it through his fair hair before Roman had a chance to notice. "Most of their decision-making is self-preservation."

"So, you support destroying species living on other planets if it means the survival of your own species."

"If it's self-defense, I most certainly do."

"Self-defense and self-preservation are a bit different," Roman argued. "What are you getting at?"

"Why do you think the Intergalactic Peace Project really kicked the Vitruvians and Erdelings out?"

Roman thought back to the past two IPP Assemblies. "First, because the Vitruvians were allegedly working with the Royals to take over Earth, Erde was wrongly accused of kidnapping Earthlings for the purposes of experimentation and having their own designs of inhabiting the Earth. And, at the second Assembly, Jasper Set clouded everyone's minds into believing that Vitruvians and Erdelings were only interested in war."

"But what if none of that were true?" Far questioned.

"Not true?" Roman was incredulous. "I think you've been brainwashed."

Far took a deep breath. "Don't take my word for it," Far suggested. "Why don't you clean yourself up and go see what's happening at TARA? After that, make some of the rounds at the Preserves and see what they've got in place. When you're done, come and find me."

"And why would I do that?" Roman challenged.

"Because you need me," Far answered. And, after witnessing Roman's unconvinced expression, he added, "And, you will soon learn that I am right."

"How shall I find you?" Roman asked.

"Take the only SpeedCircuit that stops at the Northern Cross and try to be inconspicuous. I'll be waiting for you there."

"That barren wasteland? Is that where you've been all this time?"

"To you, it's a barren wasteland. But for the adventurous, it is ripe for exploring. Crispy dessert gliders cooked on an open fire are rather tasty."

Roman wrinkled his nose.

"But no, my love." Fare finally answered. "I have not been in the Northern Cross for the entire time. "Rather, I have been preparing a place for us at the helm of a kingdom."

"There you go again. What are you talking about, you beautiful, crazy man?" Roman was certain Far was delusional. But then, he himself once thought he was an alien Data Collector sent to Earth instead of a washed-up anthology professor and was put on probation for psychotic episodes once Far received his Cancer diagnosis and had fled to another planet seeking help. There was plenty of evidence to make him question his own sense of reality.

"I am now second in command to Sovereign Hamish, having

been named the official Prophet of the Court. I have a very comfortable living arrangement planned for us, my love…if you still want to be with me." Far pouted a little, letting his eyes fall sheepishly to the floor.

Roman pulled Far over to him on the couch, wrapped his arms around the monk and prophet and hugged him tightly. He buried his head in Far's neck. Far sniffed to avoid a sneeze at Roman's rather unsavory aroma. Roman thought his beloved was crying and merely hugged him more tightly. "Of course, I still want to be with you," Roman sobbed. "You're all I've ever wanted." After a long pause, he added, "Let me make the rounds, as you've suggested, and see for myself."

With his head burrowed into Far's neck, he couldn't see Far's sideways grin. Roman was like putty in Far's hands and Far knew it. In a single conversation, Far had managed to manipulate every concrete truth that Roman held dear.

9

___

KIKI "THE NOSE"

SEVENTEEN DAYS BEFORE THE END.

Lucene once again found herself on Tranquil Beach for the second day in a row, walking along the water's edge as the sea foam rolled in and out, tickling her toes. She thought about what Fatima said to her the day before, on that very beach, a sentiment that she later learned was also shared by Neroni–that it all came down to trust. Of course, she trusted Tanager, he was the most honest and noble man she'd ever met. What she wasn't so sure about, was whether even *he* could trust his emotions. What if he discovered one day that it was Amy that he really wanted all along, and that Lucene *did* get in the way of destiny? And what Lucene also didn't trust, was herself. She didn't trust that she'd remain stable of mind. She didn't trust that her social anxiety and insecurities wouldn't flare up, and she certainly didn't trust that she was …well…good enough.

And then there was Amy, who she would come to learn, spoke three languages, was a skilled artist, played classical music (at least three songs), and was an expert chef.

I hate Amy, Lucene thought to herself.

Just then, she caught sight of something flitting in the water. Not Christopher? *No, the thing was distinctly fish-like.* A dolphin? *No, too big for a dolphin. Wait, it has a blue and green torso resembling the Northern Lights. Was it…?*

"Odessa?" Lucene was surprised.

Odessa stopped swimming for a moment, treading water as she tried to make out the image of the woman in front of her on the beach. Finally, she nodded and swam over.

"Lucene," she acknowledged simply. "What are you doing here?"

"I *live* here," Lucene was surprised. "The larger question is, what are *you* doing here?" Even more surprising to Lucene, was that the Vitruvian shapeshifter, while still adopting her mermaid-like tail for swimming also seemed to be wearing…a bra?

"Something the matter?" Odessa made a face at Lucene's glance, transforming her lower half into legs. She wore a wrap skirt around her waist. Somehow, she felt more awkward covering up than she did being uncovered, and was feeling very…conspicuous.

"No, just surprised to see you."

"Well," Odessa explained. "After the last Assembly, we were ordered home; but somehow it got out that I was helping Erde against the wishes of my superiors, and now I am somewhat of a fugitive."

Odessa had become an unlikely ally. Originally an informant for the Vitruvians, she claimed to have no allegiances whatsoever, and was simply doing her job. Yet, she had helped Lucene on more than one occasion: once when Tanager was trying to rescue her from the Royals, once when the Peace-Keepers were fleeing Earth, and again when The Vitruvians and Erdelings attempted to form an alliance and return to the Intergalactic Peace Project (IPP). When the Assembly denied their re-admittance into the IPP, Vitruvians demanded that Odessa return to Section 2—her mission was over and she was being re-assigned. However, instead of returning, she hid out on Earth as long as she could, and then escaped to Erde.

Morphinae, a Vitruvian and a member of an elite group of

Balance-Keepers went against his better judgment, and supported her escape. But he didn't go with her.

Lucene and Odessa began walking the length of the beach, Odessa dripping from sea water, Lucene in the same simple yellow sun dress that she'd worn far too often for the better part of a year. It was now faded and had noticeable holes in several places. Her feet were covered in white sand that would get washed away every time the water reached the shoreline and then replaced moments later with a fresh batch as they walked.

"Does anyone know you're here?"

"Yes," Odessa answered. "Commander Royce granted me sanctuary since I'm helpful to Erde and supportive of its mission to help Earth."

"Where do you live?"

"Up there," Odessa pointed to a tiny shack, strung together with what appeared to be palm fronds.

"You live on the beach?" While it sounded lovely in theory, it didn't seem terribly practical.

"I love the water," Odessa sighed. "Aside from being close to it, I don't need much and I was able to build my home quickly."

"But, what do you do for income?"

"You sure ask a lot of questions," Odessa commented. "I'll tell you…but only because I'm bored and I haven't talked to a single person in days. I don't mind, but I'm told that socialization is 'important.'" Odessa put air quotes around the 'important.'

Lucene waited.

Odessa seemed to lose her train of thought. "Oh, right, so I'm sort of a part-time undercover investigator reporting back on any activity that may be construed as subversive to the Erde government."

"Like…a spy?" Lucene was curious. "If that's true, should you be telling me that?"

"Good point," Odessa answered. "Forget I said anything."

"Well, now that you've dropped that bomb, you have to tell me more!" Lucene reasoned. Lucene doubted Odessa's undercover skills, given her propensity for wanting attention, but was dying of curiosity.

"Okay, fine," Odessa relented. "Back on Earth, I was sent on behalf of Vitruvia to collect information on Earthlings and the Royals, and…well…*you*. Kinda like the Data Collectors, only using shapeshifting talents and good old-fashioned detective work. Something, which I might add, that Erde severely lacks. Hence why Commander Royce thought my services would be invaluable."

"Agreed, but…" Lucene pointed to the rickety shack. "Surely they pay you better than this."

"Don't be rude," Odessa whined. "Look at this view!" Odessa pointed. "No one is allowed to build here, but I got special permission, so long as I avoid the sand dunes and cover my windows at night so the light doesn't affect the sea turtles when they're nesting. This is million-dollar property back on Earth!" It was clear that Odessa was very proud of her misshapen hovel.

A shadow passed over Odessa's form as a cloud floated by, only to reveal the bright sun moments later making her Northern-lights-skin flicker.

Lucene was suddenly struck by a thought.

"What?" Odessa stopped. "What is that look for?"

"I was just thinking about something…something that has been bugging me for a long time. Recent happenings have brought it to the top of my mind again." Lucene was momentarily lost in thought.

"Please," Odessa waived her hand in mild annoyance. "Sometime in this lifetime?"

"You just gave me an idea," Lucene was cautiously optimistic.

"About what?"

"There was a girl at the Embassy Club. She had a long aardvark-like nose. Told me I smelled sweet."

"You do," Odessa nodded, as if this were common knowledge.

Lucene paused for a moment, not sure what to make of that

assessment, but then continued. "Anyway, the one time I was there last year, she mentioned that my backpack smelled briny."

"What does that mean?"

"I don't know. I didn't think about it at the time, but my watch was missing when I got my bag back. I later found it in my cottage, but I was sure I had brought it with me. And…Xeni said that she was certain someone had been in my cottage. Xeni is–" Lucene started to explain.

"I know who Xeni is." Odessa crossed her arms, gesturing to herself with her hands, "Spy, remember?"

"So, the same thing has started happening again, with things vanishing and resurfacing later. I thought it was some weird energetic reaction to the whole Jupiter-Venus thing."

"Saturn," Odessa corrected.

"Whatever. The point is, what if it's not? What if…" Lucene cringed, her mind going to Jasper Set, to Dallen, to Drake, to Sabrina and the Royals. They all began flashing in front of her as if on a movie screen.

Odessa clapped her hands in front of Lucene's face. "Stop that!" she commanded. "Right now!"

"Right," Lucene blinked, awkwardly. "What if someone was following me then? What if someone is following me now?"

Odessa wrapped one arm around her waist, resting her elbow on it and tapping her fingers under her chin, thoughtfully.

"What? You think I'm paranoid, don't you?"

After what felt like an eternity, Odessa finally answered, "No. I honestly don't."

Lucene wasn't entirely sure why she needed Odessa's reassurance, but it felt good, nonetheless.

"So, who do you think was following me?"

"Well, clearly, I wasn't here at the time but, if I had to guess, a Vitruvian."

"One of your people?"

"*Not* my people…anymore. Their claims of non-interference have always been somewhat murky."

"Does Morphinae know this? Where is he, anyway?"

Odessa's face contorted and Lucene realized she must have said something wrong. "He left the Balance-Keepers, but wouldn't say why. And, from what I've heard, he is no longer in communication with our former superiors. I haven't seen him in over a month, but I suspect he became disenchanted when he realized that the Vitruvians weren't much better than the Royals. They wouldn't out-and-out kill Earthlings, mind you, but they certainly wouldn't mind helping things along."

"But I thought they were on Earth's side…eventually."

Odessa let out an uncomfortable cough. "I'm probably saying more than I should, but their interest in aligning with Erde and Earth was simply self-preservation against the Royals and the Null. Not entirely sure how long-lasting that friendship would have been even if the IPP did agree to let Sections 1 and 2 back into the IPP."

"What about now?" Lucene asked. "Now that they have abandoned Erde and their help was rejected by Earth, what will they do now?"

Odessa thought a moment, shuffling through information in her head as if passing it through a filtering system. "Lucene," she answered finally. "I suggest you go about your life and don't worry about things that are out of your control."

Lucene hadn't been listening. She was lost in her own thoughts. "Well, there's one thing I know for certain," she exclaimed suddenly, not really taking in much of what Odessa had just told her. She was fixated on finding out who had been spying on her and why. She suspected that the girl at the Embassy Club may be able to shed light on the subject.

"What's that?"

"Come on," Lucene said while, not-so-gently, grabbing Odessa's arm. "We need your morphing skills and we need her nose!"

That evening…

Xeni met Lucene and Odessa around the corner from the Embassy Club, wearing her usual trench coat and hat, despite Lucene advising her to wear something more…neutral. Odessa had shape-shifted into the coat-check woman at the club, at least, according to Lucene's sketchy description. After all, Lucene wasn't always the most observant of people; she was tired that night and her memory was not the best. But for some reason, the woman leaning over and telling her, "smells a little briny, don't you think?" in reference to her backpack, left her with questions—particularly after her watch went missing. Therefore, her recollection of the woman turned out to be reasonably clear. She had a blue, aardvark-like nose and patches of dark hair protruding from around her ears. She was thin and tall, her nose excessively large by comparison to the rest of her. And yet, she carried herself with a sense of grace. After a few transitions, Odessa morphed into what Lucene deemed as passable.

"Perfect." Lucene surveyed Odessa's transformation. She turned her attention to Xeni and let out a long sigh. "Xeni, I thought we talked about this," Lucene protested, gesturing to her coat and hat.

"What?" Xeni appeared hurt. "You said to dress neutral. These colors are super neutral!"

Lucene rubbed her forehead with her thumb and forefinger. "That's not what I meant."

"Heh," Xeni let out a chortle. "You looked just like Professor Tanager just then. He does the same thing."

Odessa noticed Lucene's cheeks turn a visible shade of pink and bit her lip to stifle back a laugh. She was well aware of Lucene's burgeoning relationship with Tanager. However, it was one thing to have people be aware of it, quite another to have it pointed out.

To Odessa, Xeni turned and said, "Nice to meet you. I'm Xeni," she held out her hand like a bona fide human.

"I know who you are," Odessa bragged, taking her hand in an overly gentle manner. "I'm Odessa, nice to officially meet you."

Xeni wasn't surprised by this, but mainly because she couldn't help but keep looking at Odessa's very large aardvark-like nose. It bobbed up and down as Odessa shook her hand and Xeni was mesmerized by it.

"I'm usually much more beautiful than this," Odessa commented, which confused Xeni. "Shapeshifter, right?" Odessa explained, making a large, sweeping gesture over her body.

"Oh, yeah," Xeni nodded, putting the pieces together. She'd met a few shapeshifters in her young life, but they were always just one… well, shape. Come to think of it, she hadn't recalled witnessing them ever shift into something else before now.

"Xeni was in the animal lab the other day and smelled something that she described as 'briny,' a weird saltwater smell that she'd never noticed before. And, she had also felt the energy of something in my old cottage. So, unless you have any ideas as to who or what we're dealing with—"

"I don't," Odessa answered curtly. "Frankly, I think you're grasping at straws…on a wild goose chase…making a mountain out of a molehill…"

Xeni's eyes grew wide with fascination at Odessa's use of Earth lingo. She grabbed a notepad from her pocket and began jotting them all down, feverishly.

But there was something in the pit of Lucene's stomach that told her that something big was about to happen. "We need to investigate," she proclaimed, defiantly.

"Yes," Xeni made a fist and drew her elbow toward her in victory.

"Except you, Xeni."

"What?" Xeni pouted.

"Don't get me wrong, you have a beautiful heart-shaped face and pink eyes, but between your striking features and your trench coat, you're a bit…"

"Obvious," Odessa finished.

Xeni sulked.

"But," Lucene offered, "you gave me a great idea, and we will need your super-sleuthing skills when we're back."

"Back from where?" Xeni wanted to know.

Lucene pointed to the Embassy Club and explained their plan. Lucene was not a Vitruvian and wouldn't be allowed in unless accompanied by a dignitary, or, she reasoned, someone who worked at the club. She was hoping the coat-check woman would be working that evening since it was a Friday and about the same time she'd worked when Lucene had had her first date with Dallen, in what now seemed like ages ago. If Odessa could make the guard out front think Odessa was an employee, then they might have a way in.

"Ready?" Lucene asked.

"I was born ready," Odessa winked.

To Xeni, she said, "Wait here." Xeni sulked a little, but nodded agreeably.

At the door, the guard eyed Odessa curiously. "Kiki," he stammered. "I almost didn't recognize you. You look…ahem…taller," he finished. Something was wrong with Kiki, but he couldn't exactly point at what. "You're here a bit early for your shift."

Odessa dropped her voice to sound sugary and snakelike, as Lucene had instructed. "This Earth woman accidentally forgot her purse the other night. I thought I would retrieve it for her before guests arrive for their refection. I just need her to confirm which one is hers. There are several in our lost-and-found."

The guard looked Lucene over, distastefully.

"Well," he was uncomfortable. "It's highly uncustomary for a non-Vitruvian to be allowed inside unaccompanied by a dignitary. Most uncustomary." He shook his head. "I will need approval from my superiors."

"This is no ordinary human," Odessa smiled at him, seductively. Unfortunately, this maneuver did little to entice the guard as she still looked like an aardvark. "This," she leaned in and whispered, "is a special friend of Representative Dallen." Lucene cringed at the name. And, what did she mean by "special friend?"

"Oh, I see," the guard gave this some thought. "Didn't know he was on Erde…haven't seen him in quite some time. But I have been working odd hours lately, so maybe I missed him." He paused. "Alright, Kiki, but be quick about it, else both of us will be looking for new jobs soon." He held the door open and motioned for them to go inside.

Odessa and Lucene quickly made their way to the coatroom. "Okay," Odessa stated and then asked, "now what?"

"We lay low and wait for the real Kiki to arrive."

"How is she going to get inside without the guard being suspicious?" Odessa whispered from the back of the coatroom. "And, what if she isn't even on duty today?"

"Hmm, I hadn't thought of that," Lucene pondered. Maybe she should have asked for Xeni's detecting expertise after all.

Their questions were answered moments later, as the real Kiki arrived at the door, seemingly perplexed at the guard's asking her what happened to the *distasteful mistress of Representative Dallen? And, you'd think someone of his stature could have done better."* Suddenly, Kiki sniffed the air suspiciously, turned her head toward the window and smiled.

Can she smell us from out there? Lucene wondered.

Kiki appeared to have made some joke and the guard finally laughed, letting her inside. She made her way behind the counter and to the coatroom, pulling the cloth drapes that separated the coats and purses from the main counter closed. "Okay," she said quietly. "I know there are at least two of you here. Show yourselves."

Lucene appeared from behind a furry coat that tickled her nose. She had been fighting back a sneeze. Odessa, on the other hand, who had turned herself into a tiny moth, transformed back into her standard female form. "Oh, a fellow shapeshifter," Kiki acknowledged. "I like your shape," she complimented. This was not a sexual reference. It seemed almost standard behavior among Vitruvians, not unlike, "I like your dress," or "I like your new hairdo."

"Thank you, and…" Odessa was trying to think of something nice to say, but was coming up short.

"I know," Kiki sighed. "Shapeshifting mishap."

"Whatever do you mean?" Odessa was curious.

"Well, you know how on Earth," she eyed Lucene, "they tell kids not to make ugly faces at people or else they might freeze that way?"

"Yes," Odessa answered.

Lucene nodded in agreement.

"Well, mine did." Her face fell to the floor. "I shifted one day and couldn't manage to shift back."

"Oh, you poor thing," Odessa was not typically known for her empathy, but she found herself putting her arm around Kiki, encouragingly.

"It's not so bad," she answered. "On the plus side, I've got this killer nose. I knew, even from outside, that there were two different species in my closet and I was right!" After pausing for a moment she asked. "And, what are you doing in my closet?"

"We need your nose," Lucene answered, catching herself when Kiki gave her a quizzical look. "I mean, we need your help in identifying scents. It's…" Lucene tried to think of something that might warrant her buy-in, and continued with, "a matter of national security!" This made no sense, but she lifted her chin and puffed out her chest and as they would say on Earth, "owned it."

"Oh, how intriguing," Kiki's eyes lit up.

"I don't suppose you remember the night I came here with Representative Dallen about six months ago?"

"No," Kiki shook her head. "But I've only been working here for a month."

"Oh, but..." Lucene paused. "Is there another girl who works here who..." she pointed to the nose. "Looks like you?"

"Fortunately, no," Kiki answered.

"How odd. Well, okay, but whomever it was had told me that I smelled sweet and she knew I was a human."

"You do." Odessa and Kiki chimed in, in unison. Lucene looked from one to the other, wrinkling her forehead, perplexed. "Well, when you, or whomever it was, told me my bag smelled briny...I was wondering if someone had somehow gotten into my bag while I was at dinner an... left a scent?"

"I honestly don't remember this," Kiki confessed, "if it was even me working that night. But a briny smell could be any one of three: a lower class shapeshifting Vitruvian—"

"I resent that," Odessa interrupted. "I don't smell briny."

"No," Kiki smiled. "You are much saltier...mid-west?"

"Hmmph," Odessa crossed her arms. Kiki knew she was right.

"You were saying?" Lucene coaxed Kiki into continuing.

"Or a rare type of fish found in the ponds in the Western Crosses, which doesn't make sense because they're not edible and they're found in brackish water that most people wouldn't want to swim in. So, the other option could be—" Kiki thought a moment.

"What?" Lucene asked.

"Well, I'm not sure you believe in such things, but there are species from other realms that tend to leave odd scents behind... flowers, oaky smells, and bitter food smells—such as olive brine."

"I vote for Vitruvian," Odessa was convinced.

At that moment, Kiki sniffed the air. She furrowed her eyebrows in a very confused manner. "You two need to stay here. I'll sneak you out in a moment."

With that, she lifted her chin, pulled her shoulders back and emerged to the front counter in time to see an alternate Lucene, dressed in a form-fitting red dress appear behind an impatient Representative Dallen. Her eyes grew wide, but ever the professional, she quickly covered it up. "May I take your purse, Earth woman?"

Lucene peered through a crack in the curtain. She almost let out a yelp until Odessa put her hand over Lucene's mouth. She was witnessing her arrival and her first date with Dallen, months ago. But how was this possible? Her heart seemed to take a up a place in her throat as she forced a gulp of air. When Odessa was confident that Lucene had her emotions under control, she removed her hand. The two retreated behind rows of coats, capes and purses, hiding until receiving new information from Kiki.

Minutes later (which felt like an eternity to Lucene), Kiki made her way to the back with Lucene's backpack. "Is this yours?" she asked.

"Yes," Lucene whispered. "Can I see it?" Kiki handed it over. There, buried beneath her day clothes, lay her communication watch. She passed it back to Kiki. "Kiki, I need you to tell me what happens this evening. Please. How can we reach you after tonight?"

Kiki thought a moment. "Here," she handed her a business card that showed a glam shot of Kiki with a microphone. "I'm sort of a singer on the side. Either call me on this number," she pointed to the card, "or, if you ladies are free tonight, I've got a singing gig at The Beacon."

"Thanks," Lucene accepted the card. "I know Odessa will have no trouble morphing her way out of here, but how can I leave?"

"Easy," Kiki answered. "Dignitaries are always smuggling mistresses in and out of this place." Lucene took offense. It made her wonder exactly how many "special friends" Dallen actually had. Kiki pulled aside a throw rug, revealing a handle that was folded down on a hinge, fitting neatly into a trap door. She lifted it and gave a tug. "This will drop you on the street, the backend of the club."

"Thanks, Kiki, you're a champ."

"No problem, Earth woman." After Lucene climbed in, Odessa followed suit, choosing the moth form again for simplicity. Kiki closed the door behind them and covered it with the carpet...and waited.

That night, Kiki was called from her station exactly one time—a guest needed to be lent proper attire that evening, and so it was requested that Kiki hand-deliver the garment to a private club room. She hadn't been gone more than a few minutes. But when she returned, she checked Lucene's bag, curiously. Sure enough, the watch was missing.

Then, she smelled it...sweetness. It was the alternate Lucene passing her counter. Lucene was about to leave *with* Representative Dallen but *without* her backpack. When she remembered, Kiki leaned in, knowingly, warning her new Earth friend, "Smells sort of briny, don't you think?"

"So, what happened?" Xeni asked eagerly when Odessa (now back to her most human-like form) and Lucene met her a block from the Embassy Club.

"I'm not sure," Lucene filled her in on the weird time warp.

Xeni's eyes grew wide. "Oh my gosh! But I thought that two of you couldn't occupy the same space at the same time. How could you have been there at the same time that last year's "you" was there?"

"Who told you that?" Odessa challenged.

"Just every science fiction movie ever," Xeni explained.

"Well, that explains it," Odessa remained unconvinced. "If it's a rule from a science fiction movie, it has to be true."

"You don't have to be rude," Xeni pouted. "Hey," she had a thought, "were there any other duplicates, I mean, aside from you?"

"No, come to think of it." Lucene thought a moment. "At least, not that I could tell."

"So, what do we do now?" Xeni wanted to know.

Lucene flipped Kiki's card over and over in her hand. "Xeni, since you're new to the dating scene, maybe it's time for a gal's night out."

Xenia's eyes grew wide. "Yessss," the young woman did that annoying thing where she made a fist and pulled her elbow in with excitement. "We should invite Neroni and Fatima, too." Xeni paused for a moment. "How about you, Des? Will you come with us, too?"

It took Odessa a moment to realize that Xeni had just given her a nickname, and was about to protest, until it occurred to her that no one had ever done that before. And, she rather liked it. After all, that was a term of affection and friendliness, wasn't it? She hadn't really done a great job of maintaining friendships, the closest being Morphinae, but he seemed to be avoiding her.

"Oh, I'm sure you'll see me there," Odessa winked. "If I remember correctly, Kiki's got a regular spot at 10 o'clock."

Lucene tried to remember the last time she'd been out anywhere where things were just getting started at ten in the evening. In fact, she was usually asleep by then.

"Okay," Xeni decided. "Meet you out front of The Beacon by 9:30. If you call Fatima, I'll call Neroni, deal?"

Lucene nodded. *Right after I take a nap,* she thought.

"Catch you later, alligator." Xeni waited for a response that Lucene absolutely refused to give her.

"In a while, crocodile," Odessa offered. It was the least she could do now that she had been given a nickname. Xeni smiled before darting toward the bridge connecting Achel with the SpeedCircuit. Odessa morphed into a little bluebird and flew away, leaving Lucene to walk home alone and wonder how she was going to explain all of this to Tanager.

10

THE BEACON

SEVENTEEN DAYS BEFORE THE END.

Lucene could hear The Beacon before the nightclub actually came into view. Multicolored strobe lights marked the entryway in a light stream that scanned High Street from the top of The Beacon's outdoor signage. The Beacon had a glass, pentagonal prism roof, making the light waves brighter and more wave-like. The club was a stone's throw from Big Ben (one of Achel's many Earth-like replicas) which, sadly, began to chime at that very moment.

Xeni stood next to Lucene wearing a bright red sequined party dress with an unfortunate tulle fabric at one side of her neck that fanned out in front of the right side of her face, making her pink eyes seem almost fluorescent. (*Maybe that was on purpose?*) On her feet, were high-heeled, cuffed sandals as white as snow. For the briefest of moments, Lucene missed the trench coat that the girl usually wore when she was "detecting."

The chimes, the music, and the sounds of people crowding around the club grew louder. Lucene clasped her hands over her ears but it was too late. There were flashes of light in all directions, the street appeared to be wobbling up and down around her, and more and more sounds manifested in her mind as if her brain were cycling through a radio dial. She began to lose her balance.

Xeni grabbed her arm. "Are you okay?" she all but yelled, concerned.

Suddenly, someone grabbed her other arm for support. "Don't worry, we got you," Fatima smiled. The two women stood flanked at Lucene's side until the spinning slowed to a stop. A moment later, Big Ben had finished chiming and the rest of the world seemed to return to a normal level. It was still too loud for Lucene's taste but at least it was…bearable. Lucene opened her eyes.

"Sorry," Lucene apologized.

"No need to apologize," Fatima shook her head. "I know crowds aren't exactly your thing, but it's for the greater good."

In this case, the *greater good* was Fatima getting a reprieve from mommy-duty for the evening and, possibly, helping Xeni get a date. Or at least, making sure she didn't do anything stupid her first night out on the scene. Lucene had a different agenda in mind. She wanted to seek out Kiki to find out what happened after she and Odessa fled the Embassy Club.

It was then that Lucene noticed Fatima's outfit. She was wearing a dark brown steampunk corset dress with a hem that poofed at the bottom, and knee-high boots that laced all the way to the top. With her hair newly died a deep frosted purple, she was quite a sight to behold. It was then that Lucene realized that maybe she was the one who was out of place, wearing the simplest of black cocktail dresses with no lace, sequins or anything remotely interesting about it other than it made her look as if she actually had cleavage. She looked down at her dress. *(Cleavage! Who knew?)* On her feet were black ballet flats. To her, these seemed the most practical for dancing.

"Where's Neroni?" Fatima asked.

"She bailed," Xeni explained as the three made their way to the front door of The Beacon, where they gathered in line for admission.

"She said it was family game night at her house. But I think it was more that this really isn't her scene."

Not my scene either, Lucene thought. *And yet, here I am.*

The guard at the door stopped them with a smile. "Hi Xeni, how many in your party?" he asked.

"Uh, three," Xeni answered, counting again as if she were somehow unsure. Lucene was surprised that the guard actually knew Xeni enough to call her by name. Lucene shot Fatima a questioning look, who merely shrugged her shoulders.

"300 Units," he called out.

"I got it," Fatima electronically transferred the money from her watch.

"Thanks," Lucene responded.

"Likewise. That's really good of you," Xeni offered.

"Enjoy your evening, ladies," the guard admitted them.

It took a moment to adjust to the dark lighting as the women found their way inside and headed to the bar nearest the entrance. "How come they didn't ID Xeni?" Lucene wanted to know.

"That's an Earth thing," Xeni waved her hand as if she were someone now an Earth expert. She took a seat on a pub stool and pounded the bar top with her fist to get the bartender's attention. A seven-foot-tall thin man wearing a paisley shirt and lime green tie walked over to them from behind the counter. It was almost as if his top half hadn't figured out how to balance on top of his bottom half, so his torso swayed awkwardly as he approached.

"Refection?" he asked.

"Yeah," Xeni answered. "I'll have a chilled Corsica Slam with a splash of vermouth and a sprig of thyme; don't forget the thyme," she cautioned.

The bartended laughed. "Don't worry, Xeni, I won't."

"Wait!" Lucene pointed her finger between the two of them. "He knows your name. How does he know your name, and how did the guard know your name, if you've never been here before?"

"It was a ruse," Xeni flashed an open palm across her face as if to dazzle. "You need to get out more, and I knew the only way to do it was to make it seem like I needed protecting. Besides, we've got some detecting to do!"

"No," Lucene corrected. "*I've* got some detecting to do. *You* are going to dance and have fun and…whatever it is that people do in places like this."

The bartender cleared his throat. "So, what'll you guys have?"

Lucene thought a moment. "Red wine?" she said it more like a question. The bartender nodded. Apparently, they only had one kind, and that was what she was getting. He looked at Fatima.

"I'll just have an unsweetened iced tea," Fatima answered. "I'm the designated pedestrian," she joked. No one was driving. They were walking. Also, no one but Fatima got the joke. She didn't care, she began laughing, giggling up and down as she did.

The bartender nodded and wobbled away.

"So, what was all that about needing help on the dating site then?" Fatima asked Xeni, as the three huddled in one corner of the counter awaiting their drinks.

"Oh, that part is true." Xeni sighed. "Just because I go clubbing and do the whole 'bar scene' doesn't mean I'm any good tracking down a boyfriend…at least, not a good one."

"Maybe it's your approach?" Fatima offered. "*Tracking?*"

Just then, a haunting voice filled the room. A woman was singing. While the Erde tongue was songlike and beautiful all on its own, that wasn't the language. It wasn't one that Fatima or Lucene had ever heard before. The notes were off-pitch by many musical standards, and yet they somehow worked in this context. The crowd became entranced as they gazed toward the singer on the main stage.

It was Kiki. She was accompanied by an electric violin, a harpsichord and some other wind instrument that Lucene could not identify. The stage, itself, was simple enough, a black backdrop with those awful multicolored strobe lights floating across them.

Kiki was wearing a long yellow evening gown that hugged her slim waist and billowed out all around her on the floor. The yellow offset her blue skin. She was still a sight to behold with her over-grown aardvark nose. But in that moment, she didn't care. And neither did anyone else.

It was then that Lucene noticed something. She peered around the room. There were exceptionally tall and thin people, small and wide people, dancers on the floor with wolf-like faces similar to those living in Section 5, a few baboon-shaped beings, and even several shapeshifting Vitruvians who seemed to change form every time the rhythm of a song changed. But they all stopped dancing when Kiki began singing. Lucene realized that while most of the time she was surrounded by many people who looked largely like herself, a human, in this place, she was as much a rarity as they were…if not more. It seemed as if The Beacon was one of those unusual places where everyone could be exactly who they were, and no one else seemed to care.

After the song, which went on for an unprecedented fifteen minutes or more, Kiki belted out a final high note, holding it for what seemed like an eternity while the room stood frozen. It was followed by a moment of silence as Kiki took a majestic bow. The room erupted in applause, along with some weird clicking noise that people seemed to produce from the depths of their throats. Xeni exaggerated the sound and motioned for Fatima and Lucene to follow her lead, which they did with some difficulty. Clapping was, by far, easier.

"You finally made it, Earth woman" Kiki squealed, all but leaping from the stage. She climbed down and untangled her dress, heading straight toward Lucene. She embraced her in an unexpected bear hug, as if they were old friends. Without waiting for a response, Kiki did the same to Xeni and Fatima. While Lucene was flum-moxed, Xeni and Fatima automatically hugged her back with all the zeal of people who'd known each other for years. This was not at all the reserved version of Kiki Lucene observed at the Embassy Club. This one, was noticeably more animated.

"Oh, sorry," Kiki remembered herself. "I'm Kiki," she introduced herself to Fatima. "I've been told I'm not great at boundaries but after being bound and gagged and on my best behavior at the Embassy Club all day, I tend to go a little overboard."

Xeni looked wide-eyed with glee at Kiki's use of Earth lingo. Fatima resonated with Kiki's warmth; it reminded her of the family she'd left behind when moving too Erde. There was this strange moment of familial love between them that, sadly, was lost on Lucene who watched the scene with a minor amount of confusion.

After all, she had been imbued with empathic powers that had been stripped away when they short-circuited trying to banish the demon Jasper Set before he could destroy her and her closest allies. But they seemed to be returning at oddly inappropriate and uncontrolled times, a fact that she'd been hiding from Tanager until…actually, she couldn't even articulate to herself what exactly she was waiting for. He knew about some of it, of course, but not the severity at which it was starting to flood back into her being. All Lucene knew was at this particular moment, she wasn't feeling the love…or much of anything, for that matter.

"I see you've found your watch," Kiki motioned to Lucene's communication watch on her wrist. "Or, at least that someone returned it to you."

"Yes, the day after it disappeared. That's why I'm here. I wanted to ask what happened today after we left."

"Today?" Kiki was confused. "Honey, have you hit your head? That happened more than six months ago. I was wondering why you never came in to ask about what happened."

"Kiki," Lucene answered, confused "In our timeline, it happened earlier today."

Xeni nodded in agreement.

"Hmm," Kiki considered this. "Maybe I'm the one who's hit her head." She felt her skull as if this could be a possibility.

"Given that there were two of me at the Club, I'm going to guess it was something else…some weird time warp," Lucene offered.

Another fact that she'd kept from Tanager when she mentioned going out with the ladies that evening. She knew he'd want to come along and act as chaperone to protect her. Or, he might talk her out of going altogether. And while she appreciated the fact that he cared enough to worry about her, she didn't feel as if she needed protecting.

Fatima stared in wide-eyed fascination as Kiki and Xeni swapped stories about what transpired at the Embassy Club following Lucene and Odessa's visit. Kiki's memory had become a bit faultier as more time had passed. For example, she remembered that the watch had disappeared, but had no recollection of how, when, or who had taken it. So, the hunt led to a dead end. The only memory blazing in her mind from that night was another Vitruvian who had taken on her form. *It's unnerving to run into another you*, Kiki decided.

Lucene wandered from the group. She didn't know where she was going, exactly, but with the loud house music, flashing lights, and dancing, which resumed immediately after Kiki's number, she moved in a hazy, dreamlike fashion. People moved past her, appearing in odd shapes and colors. She stopped after almost walking directly into what appeared to be a human-sized metal birdcage. Except, inside, there wasn't a bird; there was a woman dancing. There were several rings hanging from the top and a bar at its center which she expertly maneuvered in both a seductive and yet artistic manor. Frankly, Lucene hadn't ever seen a person able to contort that way. The woman looked up with one leg somehow flipped over her shoulder.

"Lucene." Odessa dropped from the bar at the center of the cage and fell expertly to the floor, landing like a cat ready to pounce. "Somehow, I didn't think you'd actually show up here."

"Kiki invited us, remember?" Lucene reminded her. "Why would you think I wouldn't show up?"

Odessa thought a moment. "No reason." She held her hands on her hips as if trying to blend in with the scenery. It wasn't working. "You did figure out the time glitch though, right?"

"Just caught on," Lucene acknowledged. Odessa merely nodded.

"Yeah, I remember when I first met her months back, she seemed to know me and was surprised that I didn't remember her. Seemed almost hurt, actually." For a moment Odessa was lost in thought over the incident.

"Um," Lucene finally commented, pulling Odessa back from her daydream. "What are you doing in a cage?" At that moment, a surly looking man with brown fur that framed his entire face and head walked by.

"I gotta get back to work." Odessa nodded to the man. "This is sort of my expressive…outlet."

"Oh, I see." (Lucene really didn't.)

"Listen, if you happen to see him, don't tell Morphinae you saw me here, okay?"

"Morphinae?" Lucene was confused. "I thought you hadn't seen him in months, the last place being back on Earth. Has he contacted you?"

Odessa's face actually turned slightly pink. "No," she confessed. "But he and I have spent so much time together in the past that I, sort of, well, *feel* his energy in the distance. And, I don't know how he'd feel about my dancing. So, just between us?"

"Sure," Lucene furrowed her lips in confusion. Why would Morphinae care about her dancing? More to the point, why would Odessa care what anyone thought of anything she did? She never had before. It was then that Lucene made the connection. *Boy, am I oblivious sometimes,* Lucene thought to herself.

"There you are!" Fatima yelled above the music, waving as she,

Xeni, and Kiki made their way over to the cage where Odessa was resetting for the next dance number. Kiki sniffed the air.

"Oh, I didn't realize you were working tonight," Kiki said to Odessa. "I smelled something salty and figured it must have been you."

"I do not smell salty," Odessa protested. "And I work here most nights. I just shift forms regularly. The boss said it makes it more interesting for people."

"Ah," Kiki nodded. "You're the kind that changes scent with each form. I guess I hadn't smelled you enough to realize that."

"You really need to stop saying weird stuff like that," Odessa advised.

"Sorry," Kiki smiled. (She really wasn't sorry.) Modesty was not a particularly strong trait among shapeshifters.

"Now, shoo," Odessa shooed them away. "I am an artiste, and I have to get back to work."

"Me, too," Kiki nodded. To Lucene, Fatima and Xeni she said, "Thanks so much for coming out tonight to hear me sing. It means a lot to me. Please come back again soon." With that, she went back to the hugging thing. When she hugged Lucene, she rubbed her arms and her back a little, awkwardly. No, boundaries did not appear to be a thing among Vitruvian shapeshifters, either. This was quite a bit different from the dignitaries and high-ranking officials from Vitru-via, Lucene noted.

"Time for my next set," Kiki announced. As she returned to the stage, Fatima's eyes turned to Xeni. The young girl seemed to be staring absentmindedly into space. Fatima waved her hand in front of Xeni's face. "What's wrong with you? Are you okay?"

There, in the distance, working his way through the crowd, was none other than Clusaladek. It only took Lucene a few seconds to realize the real reason Xeni frequented The Beacon…it was Clusaladek's favorite hangout.

Today, he had replaced the toga-like garb he frequently wore in class with black spandex pants and a burnt orange tunic. "Lucene, Xeni, so nice to see you here," he smiled as if they were visiting him at his home. "I'm sorry, we've not met," he said as he turned to Fatima.

"Oh, but I know you," Fatima giggled. Clusaladek seemed confused. "I'm Fatima," she offered her hand.

He shook it, hesitantly. "You must originally be from Earth," he surmised.

"What gave me away?" Fatima asked. Between her heavy Brooklyn-inspired accent and handshake, it really wasn't all that hard to guess.

"Just a hunch," he answered, with that same sheepish, lopsided grin that he had shown in his dating profile. Fatima actually blushed a little.

"Hi, Clusaladek," Xeni greeted, her eyes even wider than normal with a stupid grin plastered across her face. The gauze around her neck somehow seemed to poof up so that it covered the entire side of her face. Clusaladek reached over and attempted to push it down for her in an effort to be helpful, but it just sprang back into place. Xeni couldn't take her eyes off of him.

At that moment, Kiki launched into her next number—a slow ballad.

"Why don't you kids dance?" Fatima suggested, pushing Xeni toward her classmate.

"Of course," Clusaladek flashed an Adonis smile. "Xeni, would you honor me with a dance?"

Xeni nodded, letting out this strange gurgle from the back of her throat as she accompanied him to the dance floor.

As they were walking away, Lucene could hear him whisper to Xeni, "Why are you acting so weird?"

"Young love," Fatima sighed. "Isn't it romantic?"

"What they have isn't romantic," Lucene shook her head. "What they have is a friendship. He sees her like a little sister. And once Xeni figures that out, it's not going to be pretty."

"Oh," Fatima's face dropped. "You're probably right. Poor thing. I guess I shouldn't have pushed the two of them together."

"It's a dance," Lucene reasoned. "There's no harm in that."

Lucene had barely gotten the words out when a loud crash erupted. The glass ceiling shattered as a large, cat-like frame landed on the floor and on top of the two unfortunate shapeshifters who were dancing at that moment. Had Lucene been in contact with Isabella, she would have recognized the creature as Hysechia, the cat formerly known as Tabby, the house cat from the animal lab, now in full lion form.

Much like candy glass, the ceiling's properties changed when shattered. While bits of the glass would have normally cut into the flesh of those in its wake, it was simply a minor annoyance to those covered in it, not unlike people covered in glitter or confetti.

But for Lucene, it brought back memories. Suddenly, she was a little girl in the back of a green SUV as her father fought to stay on the road during a storm. The glass had shattered around her, embedding into her arms as the car toppled over and over repeatedly, with her hanging helplessly upside-down from her seatbelt, and then falling unconscious until days later when she awoke in the hospital. That was where she met her lifetime friend, Fatima, and learned of her parent's death. Lucene crawled under one of the nightclub's tables and wrapped her arms around her head, fearfully.

"Snap out of it, Lucene," Fatima commanded with uncustomary harshness, leaning under the table and slapping her friend's face lightly with the back of her fingers. "We need you."

Lucene's eyes fluttered open as she fought to adjust to the incoming stream of lights. For once, she wasn't fighting the sights and sounds in her head. They were actually coming from the world around her.

There, in the center of room, Hysechia had downed a Vitruvian shapeshifter who had unfortunately chosen the shape of a lamb. Hysechia was now feasting on its flesh while the lamb's dance partner had shifted into a flying black dragon, belching a hot flame onto Hysechia's back. The feline's eyes grew wide in pain and fear. At that moment, she resembled Henri Rousseau's "Tiger in a Storm" painting. The flame-ridden cat began rolling on the floor. Someone thought to open The Beacon's main doors and Hysechia sprang through it, setting a few tables and chairs ablaze along the way— not to mention a few bystanders who dropped to the ground as several bar servers pointed flame suppressors at them, dampening the fires in a coat of white snow.

Now, the dragon shifted back into its preferred form—a woman, as she held her lamb-shaped partner in her arms, bloodied and nearly dead.

"Don't just hide like a mouse. Use your powers and do something!" Odessa commanded of Lucene, leaning over to peer under the table where Lucene was crouched. Lucene let out a relieved sigh. While she had just been talking to her friend, she had had a momentary mental glitch, *was that Vitruvian Odessa? Was the other Morphinae?* Odessa all but dragged the woman out from under the table as Fatima helped steady her friend. The two flanked Lucene and guided her clumsily to the dance floor.

"But I don't know how," Lucene protested.

"Of course, you do," Odessa barked. "The only other person I've witnessed with your level of empathic healing power is Morphinae." Her face crumbled. "And he's not here right now." She pushed Lucene toward the fallen man.

Lucene reluctantly knelt at his side, blood pooling around him with bits of his neck hanging out. Lucene fought back the queasiness in her stomach and focused on the task. Holding her hands over the man, she attempted to imbue her hands with loving energy, sending it his direction. She looked down at the branch-like patterns of her arms, but they were dark…nothing.

The crowd grew restless. The Vitruvian woman stood over her love, hopefully. She may not have had the powers that some other Balance-Keepers on her planet had, but she recognized the ability in others.

Xeni pushed her way through the spectators. "Excuse me!" she called loudly. Behind her, she clasped Clusaladek's hand and dragged his tall frame after her.

"What are you doing?" Clusaladek was embarrassed. "We lost our powers, remember?"

Xeni's body shook as if she were bubbling up energy from the soles of her feet. "I don't believe that," she tucked her head, determined. "Let's go. Lucene needs us."

Clusaladek caught sight of the body and gagged.

"Focus," Xeni, punched him in the arm.

"Ouch!" He recoiled slightly, annoyed. She motioned for him to kneel on the other side of Lucene. He had never seen Xeni quite so determined and obeyed. Odessa and Fatima stood behind Lucene for moral support.

"Medical help is on the way," Fatima told her friend, just as the strobe lights and music stopped. The room fell silent and dark.

Lucene held her hand over the man's neck, being careful not to actually touch him. This time, Xeni and Cluseladek did the same, just as she, Cepheus and Morphinae had done back when Fredo, Sovereign Hamish's guard, had almost killed Tanager on Earth when he was attempting to rescue Lucene from the Royals.

Lucene remembered, of all things, the words that Neroni's young child had told her recently when trying to use telekinetic powers to make a coin slide off the table and onto the floor, *just think why the coin would want to fall on the floor.*

Why would healing energy want to flow through my arms? Lucene asked herself. It was then that she realized that this had nothing to do with her, her ability, or lack of it. The Universe didn't really care who she was as a person and whether her life was purposeful or not, whether she was a good person or a bad person. Once she took herself out of the equation it was easy…it was simply convincing the energy that life and love were the most important things in the universe and then…

The patterns on her arms began to turn a deep brown and then a red. This time, however, the red seemed to give off smoke and the heat hurt her arms. She bit her lip and fought back the pain as light began streaming directly from her arms and flowing into the fallen Vitruvian.

Seconds later, he coughed up a little blood and then turned his head slowly and smiled groggily at his partner. The medics arrived and hoisted him onto a hover unit that transported him to the Dragoste Healing Center with his partner at his heels. She turned to shoot Lucene a grateful look before disappearing through the front doors.

"We did it!" Xenia's eyes grew wide. "We really did it!"

Xeni stood between Clusaladek and Lucene as the other two stumbled to their feet. Xeni wrapped one arm around Clusaladek, the other around Lucene, pulling them in for a group hug. "We're not broken, after all," she smiled proudly.

Fatima knew she wasn't exactly a part of this healing trio but was still overcome with emotion. She wrapped her big arms around the three of them, "Of course you're not," she whispered, blinking back tears.

Odessa stood behind them and crossed her arms, curiously. "Hmmm…" was all she said.

11

THE RESEARCH CONTINUES

SIXTEEN DAYS BEFORE THE END.

At Commander Royce's insistence, following a long night of questioning by Constable Melokule and his men about what transpired at The Beacon, Xeni, Clusaladek, Lucene, Tanager, Cepheus and Moksha were "requested" at the Planetary Defense League (PDL) for further interrogation.

"This is not an interrogation," Commander Royce assured them upon arrival. (But it really was.)

Xeni clutched Clusaladeks's arm with both hands, nervously, her pink eyes wide. She shivered like a nervous chihuahua and was beginning to think whether she was cut out to be a detective after all. Here she was, crumbling at the first sign of potential trouble. Clusaladek put a hand over hers. "It'll be okay," he told her. She sucked in a deep breath and held it. "Breathe," he whispered to her. Remembering, she exhaled like a tire losing its air pressure all at once.

"Sit," Royce commanded, and then, as if remembering she added, "please."

They sat.

She nodded for an attendant to go around the room offering water to those she had summoned. Lucene, Tanager, Moksha and Cepheus were used to Commander Royce at this point, but Tanager's students were not. Xeni accepted the water, her hands still shaking nervously. So much so that she was worried she might accidentally dump the contents of the glass all over herself. Clusaladek retrieved it for her and set it on the table.

"Quite the evening the three of you seemed to have had," Royce singled out Lucene, Clusaladek, and Xeni.

To be clear, Lucene was operating on about three hours of sleep, and it showed. After a long silence, she answered, "We didn't expect a large tiger to come crashing through the ceiling of a night club and trying to feast on one of the attendees, that's for sure."

"No," Royce answered, "I expect you didn't. I'm growing tired of these weird anomalies from Erde's reaction to the conjunction between the Jupiter-Saturn shift. Frankly, I never believed in such things before now. But I have it on good authority that the shift will end in another two weeks or so. Until then, my men have been scrambling to manage unusual emergencies, such as this one."

"May I ask," Tanager interjected, "why you called us here?"

Lucene shrank into her seat. She was so tired when she finally arrived at their high-home that she gave him the briefest of explanations about the evening, none of which included that she and two of his former students used powers they were no longer supposed to have, to save a shapeshifter's life.

Commander Royce was surprised, until she caught a glance at Lucene's expression. "Oh, she hasn't told you?" Both Tanager and Cepheus looked at Lucene, questioningly. The hairs on the back of Moksha's neck bristled. She suspected she already knew where this conversation was going, and it wasn't good.

All eyes were on Lucene for an explanation. Finally, she relented. "The tiger mauled someone on the dance floor," she began.

"Yes," Tanager answered impatiently, "you told me that last night."

"But what I didn't get around to telling you was…that the three of us," she pointed to Xeni and Clusaladek, "combined our energy to keep him alive long enough for the medics to arrive."

Tanager bit the back of his fist, fighting back anger.

"Lucene," Cepheus interjected calmly. "Why didn't you tell us?"

"I didn't get a chance to," she defended. "This just happened last night, and here we are at the butt-crack of dawn at the PDL after only a few hours of sleep!" (It should be noted here that Lucene didn't function well when sleep-deprived.)

"But," Xeni gathered the courage to speak up. "How did you know about it?" she asked Commander Royce.

"There were hundreds of witnesses at the club," Royce explained as if the girl were daft, "all saying that there was a woman with 'lightening flowing from her arms' with two 'regulars' at The Beacon helping her. It didn't take much effort to determine who those 'regulars' might be."

"Are we in trouble?" Xeni asked weakly.

"No," Royce softened, just a little. "But what I want to know is… have your other powers returned? We assumed you lost them permanently." No one answered her. She resorted to a grade-school inquiry. "Show of hands," she demanded. "Who has noticed signs that your Data Collection powers are returning? Not just the glitches that Lucene has experienced…I mean, full-on power?"

Xeni, Clusaladek, and Lucene all nervously raised their hands.

"Why didn't we hear of this sooner?" She glared at Tanager and Cepheus as if they had been hiding something from them all.

"To be honest," Clusaladek spoke. "My memory was shot for about a month after the incident on the bridge. But then it began to sharpen again." He smiled, proudly. "I just thought it was because I'm very smart."

Royce resisted the urge to slap the grin off his stupid face. Commander Royce used to be a patient woman, but now that she was working past when she was originally set to retire at the behest of The Elders, she had grown irritable.

"What about you?" Royce pointed to Xeni.

"I…" Xeni paused, peering down at the table. "I didn't want to say anything until I was sure, and…" Her eyes teared up a little.

"It's okay, Xeni," Tanager offered gently. He may have been angry at Lucene's omission but Xeni, he reasoned, was an innocent bystander with far less life experience than Lucene.

"I don't like what TARA has become," she finally blurted out. "It used to be fun, and creative, and a place where we could learn and develop our skills in a supportive environment. Now, it's just a military school and I didn't want my powers to be exploited as…a weapon."

Tanager's heart sank. He understood. He and Cepheus had been feeling the exact same way. In their case, it was their livelihood and much harder to walk away from the financial security TARA provided. It wasn't until that moment that he fully appreciated what his former students must have been going through—suddenly shuffled into different courses of study with minimal psychological support to address the emotional affects they must be feeling from having initially lost their powers. Tanager and Cepheus adapted to the change easily, but for their students, who had never gone through this type of trauma before, it must have felt as if they'd suddenly lost a limb. The emptiness of not having one's powers must have been devastating for them. At that moment, there was no one that Tanager disliked more than himself.

"I'm sorry you feel that way," Commander Royce answered, matter-of-factly. "I hope one day you can learn to appreciate how your services have become vital assets to the government of Erde."

"What are you talking about?" Lucene demanded. Moksha's face felt flushed. She already knew what was coming.

"I am requesting the re-assembly of all the Data Collectors. Training will resume immediately with you, Professors Tanager and Cepheus at the helm."

"But many students dropped out of school when this happened," Tanager protested. "And others, including Xeni and Clusaladek, have already chosen other fields of study."

"I am requesting that they switch back," Commander Royce made it abundantly clear that this was not a request. "These classes will resume Monday morning and I'm putting in a medical request that all three of you have a full battery of bloodwork and tests to see if there's any other reason why you should have lost your powers to begin with."

Tanager left Dr. Ennis' name out of it and addressed only Erde's most respected physician, Dr. Wilah. "Dr. Wilah confirmed that they, in essence, short-circuited from an explosion of energy. Perhaps they just needed time to recharge and heal," Tanager reasoned.

"Let's reconfirm that, shall we?" Commander Royce eyed him coldly. She stood, her hair much grayer then even a month ago—possibly from stress—and her gate a little more unstable.

"And those who have dropped out of school altogether?" Tanager asked.

"I suggest you convince them to return," Royce answered simply.

Tanager started to belt out an angry reply but Cepheus stopped him.

"We will do our best," Cepheus answered calmly.

Xeni shot Lucene a furtive glance. *Should we tell them?* she thought. Surprised, Lucene heard her. *No*, Lucene answered. *Not yet. I don't trust her.* Xeni nodded. She was, of course, referring to the fact that she and Lucene were the only ones in the room who knew about the strange time shift at the Embassy Club.

The group stood to leave.

"Be happy, Professor Tanager," Royce finished. "TARA will receive full funding and I will see to it that you and Professor

Cepheus are well compensated for your efforts. As for your students," she smiled, "they have long, bright careers ahead of them."

Somehow, at this moment, the future didn't seem very bright at all.

12

HYSECHIA CONFRONTS ISABELLA

FIFTEEN DAYS BEFORE THE END.

Mateo (or "Mati" as he preferred to be called) was in a state. He searched every corner of the animal habitats at TARA, sweeping his own office and scouring the hallways with the diligence of a curious ferret. But his friend, Marzipan, was nowhere to be found. Marzipan, his longtime tiny friend with the face of a young boy, body of a ladybug and legs like a firefly, was missing from the small cage that served as his habitat. He knew the little bug couldn't last long outside of a carefully balanced atmosphere, and Mati became so desperate, he called his wife and eight children to help him search.

This was the second animal he'd lost from the lab within the past few months—the last being Tabby, an ordinary house cat that caretakers recently brought from a neighboring ally planet in Section 1. They left her at TARA for the planet's required quarantine period. He apologized profusely to her heart-broken adoptive parents. But what else could he do? She'd vanished.

Mati had no way of knowing that when Isabella accidentally sent Jasper Set between the layers of ordinary and non-ordinary realities, that she had managed to unlock Tabby's true form—a very large tiger that went by the name of Hysechia. Hysechia was not nearly as docile as her house cat form. What Mati feared was that maybe little Tabby hadn't gone that far after all. Perhaps she lived as a feral on the streets of Achel, and somehow found her way to his office, where Marzipan lived and ate Mati's friend as a snack. Mati wiped back a tear as his wife patted him gently on the back, trying to console him. His long, rat-like tail swished mournfully.

He was on the right track, as it turned out. Had Reverend Isabella not interfered, Hysechia would have eaten Marzipan straight away, which would have provided about as must sustenance to a tiger as a human eating a rice cake. Really, it was hardly worth the effort.

But when Hysechia wasn't busy losing her temper, and actually took time to think things through, she was then able to devise a cunning plan. It was a plan that took her several months to figure out, but then, it wasn't every day that one had to research how to close the gap between realities, now was it? And to think, she almost ate the little bug that was the key to Isabella's undoing.

"It's about time, bruja," Hysechia greeted Isabella at a remote location in the Northern Cross, a barren land with unpredictable weather and few inhabitants. Strapped to her back was a little self-contained travel cage where the air circulated enough to keep one little Marzipan safe…for now. Today, the weather at the Northern Cross was pleasant and the winds were calm.

"I'd like to say that it's nice to see you, Hysechia," Isabella offered, "but we both know that's not true." Isabella had created a large circle of pebbles around herself, wide enough for her to lay down and stretch her arms and legs out like angel's wings if she wanted to. Inside, sat her hand drum, a small medicine bag of copal, a feather, an iron bowl, a mortar and pestle, a canteen of water, and an assortment of dried herbs in a tied linen bag.

"On the contrary," Hysechia's voice had a sexy, slithery quality that few felines could match (not that many tried). Several tiny orange hairs that Hysechia had on her otherwise black and white body stood up excitedly. "I, for one, am thrilled to see you. And, as you can see," she motioned her eyes up toward Marzipan, "I have something of value to you."

Isabella knelt in the center of the circle and added herbs to the mortar bowl as if adding a pinch of salt, a sprig of thyme, and a dash of pepper to a recipe. She then used the pestle to furiously grind them together. "What use could I have for a firefly?" Isabella glanced at Marzipan out of the corner of her eye.

"You and I both know that you can't seal the tear between the realms without him," Hysechia began pacing back and forth, tracing the outer circle of the pebbles, pawing at them lightly but not crossing them.

"Do we know that?" Isabella's mind worked quickly. Her calm exterior didn't match the jumble of anxiety she felt. She thought she merely sent the demon Jasper Set to another dimension. Instead, she trapped him between the layers of this reality, and in doing so, somehow let Hysechia out. Once free, the feline had immediately transformed into her true form, still feline, but decidedly larger and more aggressive.

Isabella heard other news reports of animals being snatched from a local sanctuary, only to have their carcasses turn up later, having been eaten by what could only be assumed were of canine or feline origin. She suspected this was Hysechia's doing, but the number of dead animals found seemed out of sync with Hysechia's slender form. Did she really eat that much?

There was also a new breed of insect fluttering around. They resembled flying ticks. They didn't carry disease from what scientists could tell so far, but they liked to burrow under the skin and leave an itchy rash, leaving its host little option but to submerge their body under water until the nasty insect gave up and floated away. It was no use to only submerge an arm or a leg because the tick simply moved to another part of the host. So, it became a battle between host and bug to see who could hold their breath the longest.

This is only what she knew about. She shuddered at what else she may have trapped or let out.

"What is it that you want, Hysechia?" Isabella finally asked.

Hysechia now made full circles around Isabella, as if searching for a way in and sizing up her opponent. Her tail twitched irritably. "What I want is revenge," Hysechia answered, honestly. "I'd like to see you trapped between the layers where you left me for a hundred years. Do you know what it's like to constantly present myself to the world as a simple domestic cat, lifetime after lifetime, all the while ignorant beings thinking that I was the primitive one, petting me and giving me kibble, calling me stupid names like Tabby, Fluff and Whiskers?"

"Would you have rather I killed you?" Isabella asked, curiously, looking up from her work, where she was now adding a few pieces of copal to the iron bowl. "I thought what I did was more merciful."

"Merciful!" Hysechia choked. "That's like forcing a rich man to live as a pauper, a god to be trapped as a powerless human, a piranha that only knows how to jump in the air like a directionless mullet, a—"

"I get it," Isabella interrupted the verbal diatribe before it became personal. "So…no?"

"No," Hysechia growled under her breath. "As I was saying before I was rudely interrupted, I would love to see you thrown into an open portal where you'll be stuck between the layers forever, but that's an impractical goal." Hysechia was rather proud of her turn of phrase. She thought she was setting up a suspenseful tale, only to look over her shoulder and find that Isabella was all but ignoring her. "Fine, I'll just eat the firefly now and be done with it."

Hysechia, while mostly feline, seemed to move the digits on her paws with the same agility as a human. She unlatched the leather-like strap that held Marzipan's travel cage in place. Then, she sat on her haunches while the cage fell to the ground with poor Marzipan tumbling around and narrowly missing hitting his head on a rock in his habitat. Somehow, the cage landed right-side-up.

Instinctively, Isabella leapt over her circle of protection to go to the little bug's aid. She immediately realized her mistake, but it was too late.

Hysechia pounced, and the two rolled on the ground, Isabella no match for the tigress. Hysechia pinned Isabella's shoulders, pausing for a moment of self-satisfaction and victory before moving toward the vein in Isabella's neck.

Isabella reached an arm across her makeshift circle of pebbles and grabbed the first thing she could—the hand drum—sandwiching its smooth white, round surface between she and Hysechia's mouth. The feline was surprised for a moment as one saber tooth pierced the drum. Hysechia backed away, annoyed, flicking her head violently back and forth as she tried to free the drum from where her tooth clung to it before realizing she had paws for that. She tossed the damaged drum aside and leapt.

Isabella had just enough time to roll over the pebbles, replacing a few that scattered in the shuffle. Hysechia flew through the air, but then, as if an invisible force-field blocked her path, smacked into something that sparked a few blue bolts of light as she fell backward, letting out a howl in pain. Hysechia rolled over and sat up, her fur slightly singed.

Both Hysechia and Isabella were out of breath. Marzipan sat up, helplessly.

"Excuse me," he finally asked. "Do I get a say in any of this? I mean, whether I get eaten or not or help stitch tears in the fabric of reality and such? Seems awfully unfair of you."

"What do you propose, little one?" Isabella asked.

"Well, let me clarify a few things first." Marzipan stood and began pacing around his little grotto, which didn't last long as the cage wasn't very big. He finally settled one foot on the roots of a tiny tree, his other foot firmly on the ground. "A portal gets opened and stuff gets in and stuff gets out, right?"

"Correct," Isabella indulged his questions.

Hysechia huffed. *What a waste of time*, she thought.

"And sometimes, it's like a seam on a pair of pants that fit too tightly. It doesn't close exactly right, and when the owner of the pants bends over, it splits, revealing his undies, right?"

"That's the general idea," Isabella answered.

"So, when you seal it, does stuff that's out stay out and stuff that's in stay in? Or is there some…flexibility?"

Isabella thought about this simple question. Her eyes suddenly lit up. *Marzipan, you brilliant little bug*, she thought.

"What?" Hysechia saw the exchange between Marzipan, outside the protective circle, and Isabella, still within the circle. "What am I missing?"

"It means, my dear Hysechia, that things *born* between the layers will eventually return there, all on their own once this realm is sealed. Whereas, things that have been *placed* there, such as a tiger wanting revenge or an evil demon trying to wreak havoc on the universe, would have to be *re-placed* since they were born in *this* realm. So you see, you are not automatically going to return to the other realm when I seal the doorway between worlds. You are free!"

Hysechia let that information sink in. This still didn't solve her problem of wanting Isabella dead.

"So, if I hand the bug over to you and let you close the portal with me on the outside, how do I know you won't open up another one someplace else in the future?"

"Hysechia, we don't even know that Lucene's powers are strong enough to open a portal a second time. So, once it's sealed, it's sealed. Secondly, I would have to find the Crossroads, which I have yet to locate."

"The Crossroads?" This was news to the feline.

"Surely you stumbled upon this in your research when you discovered that little Marzipan is a necessary ingredient for sealing the leak between worlds."

"Apparently not," Hysechia spat.

"Think of the entryway as a moving target. I have to find it again to seal the damage. I am told that this is at what is known as the 'Crossroads,' a strange intersection where time and space behave differently."

"Why not return to where you were when you opened it in the first place and track it?" Hysechia sniffed the ground to demonstrate.

"I'm not certain that a portal to another realm has a scent," Isabella grumbled at Hysechia's suggestion. Though, to be fair, it was as reasonable a hypothesis as any.

"In that case, how do you plan on finding it again?" Hysechia was curious, although her motives were primarily self-serving.

"As I mentioned, I need to find an anomaly of time and space. Everything at Lucene's old cottage where it was first opened, appears normal. The timeline makes sense. I need to find the place where it *doesn't* make sense. That's why I'm here attempting to meditate and get answers from the Great Spirits, before you interrupted me with your vendetta."

"If you had left me alone a century ago—"

"Hysechia, you single-handedly wiped out an entire village! *My* village. It was the first time in history I had a home with people I actually cared about, who cared about me, too!" Isabella fought back the emotion.

Hysechia thought a moment. "I was hungry," she answered simply.

Isabella was too enraged to speak.

"Why didn't you just go back in time and warn them about me. I would have gone about my business and you'd still have your precious village. Aren't you a time traveler?"

Isabella let out a sigh, followed by a pause that lasted for an eternity. "I can only go forward in leaps and bounds," she finally confessed. It was a confession that she'd never shared with anyone, and yet somehow, the words rolled off her tongue easily. Suddenly, her heart felt as if a weight had lifted. She'd never worked out how to go backward and actually save people from dying, thinking that maybe it was punishment from the Great Spirit for having betrayed her people all those centuries ago. So, while she could spring herself through time like hitting the fast forward button on a video, she had no way to get back once she did.

Hysechia let out a laugh so hard she spat a little.

"What's so funny?" Isabella demanded.

"Your family is a joke," she said between bouts of laughter. "Your descendent, Far, can't tell how to get from point A to point B. You can't work out traveling backward and forward in time—you can't even locate the Crossroads. Your cousin Nettle couldn't transport herself more than ten feet in any direction, and as for the gift of prophesy, your own father couldn't predict more than five minutes into the future!"

Isabella's anger bubbled over. She would have transported herself away from this conversation were it not for the fact that she had to ensure that Marzipan was safe first. It would have been irresponsible of her to abandon him.

"Excuse me," Marzipan chimed in, "I don't mean to complain, but all the water splashed everywhere when I fell from Hysechia's back. It's really hot out here and I'm ever so thirsty."

"A dead bug won't be of use to either of us," Isabella commented. She placed her canteen of water which she had intended for her own use, outside the circle. Hysechia relented, dragging the canteen over to the cage, flipping the lid and pouring a spot of it into a watering hole.

"Thank you," Marzipan acknowledged, diving face-first into it and drinking thirstily. "Now, about your dilemma," he offered, wiping his mouth.

"Yes?" Isabella answered.

"What if we pinky swear that once we find the Crossroads and seal the tear, that no one attempts to open a portal or seek revenge on Hysechia again? After all, as a priestess, Reverend Isabella, you do have a code to keep your word. Everything that's supposed to go back, goes back, and everyone's happy." Marzipan rubbed his furry front legs together as if dusting them off.

"Or," Hysechia reasoned, "we leave it open on the off-chance you are lying to me. I kill the bug, and everyone's happy…except him, of course. Sorry," she nodded to Marzipan. She didn't seem sorry.

"But then Jasper Set might eventually free himself. I have no idea how a demon might adapt. He could already be out for all I know. Plus, we still have things that don't belong here wreaking havoc on this world. How is this a solution?" Isabella demanded.

Hysechia had been waiting for this, not very long, as she'd only just thought of it. Her intention was simply to kill her nemesis for sealing her up for so many years—deservedly or not. But maybe she could have her wish after all?

"I have a new proposal," Hysechia offered.

"Yes," Isabella asked.

"You deliberately open the portal again assuming your precious pupil Lucene can manage it. But *you* go through it. I use firefly boy over there to seal you in—poetic justice."

"There's a bit more to it than that," Isabella answered flatly. "Do you actually know anything about the ceremony involved in making sure the worlds are separated?"

Hysechia flashed a smile. "Of course, I know. I knew what you did before you even did…except for the Crossroads. That was new. And…" she paused dramatically, "I'm pretty sure I won't make the same mistakes you did in sealing it." Hysechia paused for Isabella to digest the situation. "Bruja, this is the only way you can be held accountable for what you did to me and for what you unleashed on this world in the first place. Not to mention all of those pesky regrets you've had about your abuse of power in the past. Consider this —redemption."

Hysechia was right, Isabella thought to herself. This could be what she deserved. But she'd have to find a way to warn Lucene and the others what Hysechia's being on the loose would mean for Erde. She needed more time to muddle through this, but time was something she didn't have in this very moment.

"I agree to your terms," Isabella said, finally. "Now hand over Marzipan."

"Not so fast," Hysechia answered. "Why don't I just hold onto him for safekeeping and you let me know when you've found the Crossroads."

Isabella looked at Marzipan who merely held his chin up bravely and nodded. With that, Hysechia strapped Marzipan to her back once more; this time being a little more careful with him, because now she had a reason to keep him safe. Her day was turning out much better than she had anticipated.

13

EMBASSY VISIT

FIFTEEN DAYS BEFORE THE END.

"I don't understand why you didn't tell me sooner," Tanager stated as they approached the front of the Embassy Club.

"It just happened two days ago," Lucene protested.

"But an overlap of time and space where you literally saw yourself walking into the club with Dallen? This is rather a big deal, wouldn't you say?"

Lucene had lots to say, actually, but she wasn't sure where to begin anymore. She knew Not Christopher was right. She needed to communicate better, but she wasn't entirely sure how to do that. Honestly, it was easier at the beginning when they were empathically connected. Now, it was only Lucene that seemed to be regaining her skills, another factor that she felt bothered Tanager, but he would never admit it. She felt it every time he was disappointed in her, when he thought she was acting immature, and when he disapproved of her decisions, like now.

Unfortunately, he couldn't feel anything that she was feeling. And she wasn't great at explaining it to him.

"Could we just focus on the task at hand, please?" Lucene

changed the subject, the one thing she *was* becoming increasingly good at.

Tanager let out a sigh.

"Excuse me," a guard dressed in a regal red uniform blocked the two from entering the club. He held a hand up for emphasis.

"Yes?" Tanager eyed the guard quizzically. "Is there a problem?"

"Unfortunately, we only allow members of the club admittance. And you are clearly *not* members of the Embassy Club." Lucene remembered this guard from two days ago when the fake Kiki helped her get inside to retrieve her purse. Apparently, he remembered her as well. "You sure are popular, aren't you?" He eyed her distastefully.

Lucene was indignant. *Who*, or more specifically, *what* did he think she was anyway?

Tanager ignored the statement. "This is highly irregular. I know of no culinary establishment on Achel, or anywhere in Section 1 for that matter, where exclusive membership is enforced."

The guard puffed up his shoulders. "Well, then you are apparently unaware of Vitruvian customs."

"Perhaps I am mistaken," Tanager grit his teeth. "But we're not on Vitruvia, now, are we?"

The guard was about to respond when Constable Melokuhle passed by. "May I be of assistance?" he asked quietly. It was always odd to the outside observer just how timid the constable was given his height and girth. It was as if he were trying to overcompensate for his profound presence by speaking as gently as possible.

"Constable Melokuhle, so nice to see you again. I believe we haven't spoken since our last meeting with Commander Royce." Tanager eyed the guard for a reaction but received none. "We were just about to have dinner at the Club. Care to join us?"

"No, thank you," Constable Melokuhle answered. "Gotta get back home myself. The missus has dinner on the table and little Charlemar needs help with his schooling tonight." He thought a moment. Constable Melokuhle wasn't the quickest of studies, but given a moment of reflection, he was eventually able to put two and two together. After a momentary glance at the guard, he told Tanager and Lucene, "Enjoy your dinner. I'm certain that agents of the PDL will be treated extra special at the Embassy Club. They are well known for their…hospitality."

The constable tipped his hat and moved along. The guard wrinkled his nose but conceded to open the door. "Enjoy your dinner," he murmured in a way that clearly indicated that he didn't mean it. They had barely made their way inside when the guard could be heard contacting the inside host, speaking into his communication watch in hushed tones.

"May I take your purse or jacket, Earth woman and Erde man?" Kiki asked politely.

"Hi Kiki," Lucene answered pleasantly. "Can I just say, you were awesome the other night?"

Kiki blinked for a moment. "I'm sorry," she answered politely, barely above a whisper. "You seem to know me, but I'm not sure I know you."

The back of Lucene's neck tingled as the hairs on it stood up. She really didn't remember. "Oh, I'm sorry," Lucene spoke in a hushed voice. "I heard you sing at The Beacon. You have no reason to know me. I'm just a fan."

The corners of Kiki's eyes turned upward and a few tears formed, but she fought them back. This wasn't the place for emotions. At that moment, the host arrived. Kiki resumed her duties, looking expectantly at the couple.

Tanager jumped in, taking off his cardigan even though he thought it was rather chilly. He offered it to Kiki. "Thank you," he answered. "I believe my companion would prefer to keep her purse with her."

Lucene didn't have a purse. She had a little black backpack slung across her shoulders. But she didn't argue; it was true. After the last time, she wasn't willing to let it out of her sight.

"Very well," Kiki smiled, accepting the cardigan. "Enjoy your refection."

The host was just as Lucene remembered, wearing the same dull uniform as before, using as few words as possible. "Welcome," he coughed. "I have a table that I believe will be most agreeable for you this evening." He paused. An awkward silence ensued.

Lucene leaned over to Tanager and whispered. "I think you have to flick your first two fingers at him."

"Really?" Tanager whispered back. "Like this?" He motioned slightly, not really sure that that was right at all, but the host nodded his head and quickly directed the two to a small table in the further-most corner of the club—in the shadows and largely away from everyone. Lucene was slightly disappointed that she didn't get to ride up the old-fashioned elevator again.

Lucene had time to forget parts of her last visit, either willfully because of the company, or because of her sleep deprivation at the time. Yet, it was slowly coming back to her as three female atten-dants seated Tanager first and seemed almost appalled that he paused to pull the chair out to enable Lucene to take a seat at the table before he did. He then raised his arms, uncomfortably, as one attendant placed a cloth table napkin in his lap before eventually doing the same for Lucene. This time, she didn't protest, having learned the drill.

They offered Tanager a beverage to start and handed him a menu. "Just water for me," he fumbled over his words. "And you?" he turned his attention to Lucene. "What would you like, my darling?" If the servers could turn a shade whiter, they would have. This was highly uncustomary. She tried to remember the bubbly beverage she had the only time she'd been there with Dallen, but she couldn't. "What have you got that's fizzy?" she finally asked. The server closest to her seemed confused, but finally offered, "A peach effer-vescence?"

"That sounds perfect," Lucene smiled, resting an elbow on the table, knowing full well that they, and probably Fatima, would take issue with this. But she didn't care and she was certain that Tanager didn't either.

"Excuse me," Tanager asked. "But do you have a second menu for my companion?" He did the finger and wrist flick thing again, stumping the servers for the second time in only a few minutes.

One server leaned in helpfully. "It is usually customary for the male to order for the female in this establishment," she whispered.

Tanager nodded, before whispering back, "But I have no idea what my lovely date would care for this evening. And without seeing the menu, I'm sure she doesn't know yet, either." He smiled politely. Therefore, for the first time in the history of the Embassy Club's existence, a woman received a menu.

Unfortunately, the descriptions were written in a foreign language. Therefore, when the servers returned to take their orders, Lucene asked candidly, "Any specials this evening?"

"Specials?" the server was confused. To be fair, the three looked identical, so Lucene was never quite sure which one they were addressing when.

She tried again, "What is the most popular dish on the menu?"

The server thought a moment. "Many guests find the mutton and vegetable stew delightful."

"Okay, I'd like that please."

The server eyed Tanager as if seeking his approval. After a long pause, he finally answered, "I shall have the same, thank you."

The attendants took the menus and returned a moment later with beverages, always serving Tanager first and then Lucene. And when dinner arrived, they gasped in horror as Lucene immediately took a bite of her food without waiting for Tanager to sample his meal first (she was *very* hungry). They peered anxiously at Tanager for a reaction that didn't come. He merely smiled pleasantly and asked, "How is it?"

"Delightful," Lucene smiled at he and the attendants with an overabundance of enthusiasm. At that moment, Lucene noticed something that caused her face to drop in concern.

"What is it?" Tanager asked, touching her wrist from across the table. She couldn't find the words, so she just motioned.

There, across the restaurant on the balcony level, she witnessed herself on her first date with Dallen. He had just received the vegetable dish with assorted chutneys and sauces. He flicked his wrist at her indicating that she was permitted to eat.

At that moment, the console at the center of the room shifted and the band emerged from the floor as the host stood to announce them —just as it had been when she was there with Dallen.

"It's happening again," Lucene choked. "Yesterday, I watched as I walked past the coatroom. Now, this. It's the same event from a different angle."

Tanager resisted the urge to pay too much attention to the *other* Lucene and her date with a man he had been somewhat jealous of at the time. Instead, he answered, "I don't know of any planetary alignments that would cause a shift of this magnitude."

"Then, what do you think it is?"

"I don't know. All I can tell you for certain is that these inconsistencies in reality, and the odd occurrences all began after Isabella used you to send Jasper Set into another dimension."

"And now, Isabella is missing," Lucene was concerned. "Do you think she is in danger or trapped somewhere? Or do you think she returned to Earth?"

"I don't know," Tanager confessed. "But I would wager that she is the only one who can shed light on this subject."

The two became quiet as the band started to play. Afterward, exactly two people started clapping, Tanager, and old Lucene from the balcony. Lucene grabbed Tanager's wrist. "I don't think clapping is done here," she smiled.

"Is it stuffy in here or is it just me?" he asked.

"Definitely stuffy," she confessed. "But I'm not leaving until I've finished my stew. Eat up, because you know damn well, you're not going to get this at home from me."

"Good point," he nodded, digging into his plate.

They eyed Dallen and the other Lucene curiously. Today's Lucene had to put it out of her mind that she was watching herself, trying to observe the situation objectively. She found that as she watched her other self, she had a strange empathy coupled with the realization that after only a short period of time, she wasn't that woman anymore.

Just then, something bumped into her leg as it shot past them.

"What the—" Tanager started.

Lucene squinted her eyes in order to see what just flew by. Actually, she smelled him first, a little elf that gave off the scent of a dry martini.

How odd is that? Lucene wondered to herself.

"Look, they're leaving," Tanager noticed.

Lucene was distracted from the elf. "Oh, then we should lay low," Lucene offered. "They're going to come down the elevator behind us at any moment."

"I don't think we can lay any lower," Tanager retorted. "They've got us in a shadowy corner closest to the kitchen."

Nonetheless, Lucene found herself ducking her head, shielding her face by resting her palm across it, as the old version of herself and Dallen walked by, not three feet from their table.

After they had gone, Tanager let out a loud and long sigh. The two smiled at one another, relieved. Moments of connection seemed harder to come by lately and they both appreciated when they did.

Finally, the check arrived. One of the servers slipped a notice on the table closest to Tanager's arm.

"Oh, I've got it," Lucene snatched the check before Tanager could respond. Once again, the three attendants turned a whiter shade of pale. Lucene was even worried that one might actually pass out. "It's okay," she explained. "It's not as if we're on Vitruvia now, is it?"

One of the server's eyes twitched, ever-so-slightly, as if she wanted to smile but knew that wasn't permitted.

"There," Lucene smiled pleasantly, "all set." The attendants didn't move. "Oh, please don't make me flick my fingers at you. That's just so condescending."

Still nothing.

"We're all finished here," Tanager finally chimed in. They nodded and retreated, but not before one of them recited, "Thank you for your visit to the Embassy Club, an exclusive club on Erde that caters only to the highest ranking of Vitruvian dignitaries. We would be delighted to serve you again soon." With that, they bowed and made their exit.

Tanager pulled out Lucene's chair as she stood, offering his arm as a few diners at neighboring tables eyed the exchange with a mix of discomfort and curiosity.

Tanager had forgotten all about his cardigan until Kiki whispered loudly, "Don't forget your sweater, Erde man." She held it out for him.

"Thank you," he paused. "I don't know your way of doing things here," he confessed. "Tell me, is tipping customary?"

"Yes," Kiki whispered back, "and I have one for you." This time, she peered deeply into Tanager's eyes. "There are times when fear is good," she said. "It must keep its watchful place at the heart's controls."

Tanager looked at her quizzically, having no idea why she was spouting Earthen Greek literature at him. Still, he smiled, finally noticing a collection bowl filled with traditional Erde coins. He dropped a few in. Kiki bowed her head politely and retreated dramatically into the coatroom.

Outside, the air was crisp and had the scent of fallen rain.

"I don't remember hearing the rain from inside, do you?" Tanager asked.

"No, but it wasn't raining the night I accompanied Dallen to the club. It may have been raining here, today. But I don't think we were having dinner in the 'now,' if that makes any sense at all."

"Not really," Tanager admitted, putting his arm around her as they walked home. Had he given it a moment's thought, it *would* have made sense. It's just that his mind was elsewhere. "But there's one thing that I am sure of."

"Yeah? What's that?" She wrapped her arm around his waist.

"I'm sure of how much I love you," he looked down at her, with an odd mix of hope and expectation.

Something in Lucene's chest tightened a little. "I know," she smiled up at him. It wasn't as if she didn't feel the same. It was just that those words didn't come to her easily.

Tanager kissed the top of her head. "Let's go home," he said.

14

VIRUS

FOURTEEN DAYS BEFORE THE END.

Lucene was busy smudging their high-home with sage the next morning when the computer sitting on their living room table lit up. There was an incoming message from Dr. Archibald Ennis from Earth. It was not typically safe for him to phone these days, and so she summoned Tanager hastily from the bedroom where he'd just emerged from the shower, clean-shaven and struggling to pull his trousers over still-damp legs.

Lucene accepted the call on the last ring, sitting at the table with Tanager hanging over her shoulder, towel-drying his hair.

Dr. Ennis, who was normally much more cordial, didn't wait to exchange pleasantries.

"You should be getting a call from Dr. Wilah shortly about your test results, Lucene." he explained quickly, occasionally glancing over his shoulder.

Tanager was surprised. Those tests were conducted only two days prior at the Dragoste Healing Center on Erde. How did Dr. Ennis know about them? More specifically, how did he know about them before they did?

"I only have a moment," Dr. Ennis explained hastily. "But here's what you need to know." He leaned in toward the screen, causing his holographic image to emerge directly in front of Lucene's nose. "It was a virus."

"What?" Tanager asked.

"You may recall that over a year ago several students became ill but quickly recovered?"

Tanager did remember. He and Cepheus had been discussing that very topic when traveling back to Earth with Roman and Lucene.

"We didn't know if it had to do with the genetic splicing or an odd bacterial infection. But know we now. It was a virus, likely carried back from Earth at some point in our early Data Collection stages when we brought Earthlings to the preserves."

"But there have been no unusual illnesses on the preserves over the past few years," Tanager reasoned.

"Just because they have built an immunity to it, doesn't mean *we* have. Given the general constitution of our Data Collectors, we might hypothesize that they would recover more quickly than the average Erdeling. On the other hand, no one outside of the Data Collectors appears to have been affected by it. We don't know whether it's simply that the virus infected the general Erdeling population but caused no noticeable side effects, or if the genetic splicing made the Data Collectors more sensitive. However, more tests on the entire Data Collection class will likely be required until we know for sure. They will also likely want to test all students at TARA to check for the presence of a virus in their systems."

"Will Dr. Wilah force us to quarantine?" Tanager asked the next logical question.

"I don't know. Not likely at this time since months have passed since any reported incidents. However—"

"Yes," Tanager persisted.

"I suspect that Commander Royce will use it as an excuse to ban any travels to and from Erde and Earth."

"I don't understand," Lucene interjected. "Why would she need an excuse?"

"I've already said more than I should." Dr. Ennis cleared his throat. "I should be going."

He didn't wait for them to say goodbye before cancelling his call. The computer screen went dark.

"Now what?" Lucene asked, staring at the blank screen.

"Now," Tanager rubbed her shoulders, "we wait for Dr. Wilah's call and pretend nothing has happened." Tanager appeared calm, but on the inside, his mind was racing. *Were the odd outbursts and mental health issues they'd witnessed that day in class because of the demon Jasper Set's influence, genetic splicing, or some odd virus? Or worse, was it that he had simply done a terrible job at helping students mentally and emotionally adjust to their new abilities?*

Lucene put her hand on his shoulder, sympathetically. *You are a great teacher,* she thought. *Clearly, it's not that.* But Tanager couldn't hear her.

The phone rang a second time, pulling him out of his thoughts. The first notification hadn't even finished before Lucene accepted it. It was Dr. Wilah.

They acted appropriately surprised at her news. But Dr. Wilah filled in some gaps that Dr. Ennis missed. It seems that Xeni, Clusaladek, Cepheus, Tanager, and Neroni had a larger viral load than Lucene, which might explain why her powers never went away completely and she seemed to be getting them back at a faster rate. Otherwise, how could Reverend Isabella have opened the portal to send Jasper Set into another dimension?

"Is it the odd smudging that Lucene insists on doing each week?" Tanager asked, wrinkling his nose at the realization that Lucene had set the burning sage stick and abalone shell on the table, and it was now smoking up the entire room. Lucene quickly went to extinguish it, opening the sliding glass doors to air the place out. "We live together now, but Lucene spent the better part of last year living alone."

Dr. Wilah smiled politely. "I am a medical doctor, not a witch doctor, Professor Tanager. While there is some evidence to suggest that smudging kills airborne bacteria and viruses, I'm afraid I couldn't tell you for certain if that is what has made a difference."

"Fair enough," Tanager offered, one of the newest Earth expressions he had come to start using. "But how does this explain the short circuit, all at the same time, on the bridge earlier this year? Did Jasper Set have something to do with it?"

"Again, I'm not a witch doctor, and I know nothing about the supernatural. I don't know what influence a demon may have on the situation, or if a combination of factors might be at play. But what I can tell you is that stress puts significant pressure on one's immune system. I can definitely see where the threat of a bomb explosion and death could trigger such an extreme stress response in our Data Collectors, particularly if they are more empathic."

When Lucene returned, Dr. Wilah explained the next steps of the protocol. Since the test results all came back post-virus, and no one was currently sick, the school testing was more to collect data of her own—to see if anyone was currently sick and who had antibodies in their system. The same protocol was to be put in place for all Earthlings living at the preserves. Since the only noticeable symptoms were a lack of extra sensory skills, there appeared to be no logical way to test the general public unless they collected a random sample, which they weren't prepared to do…yet.

"What if they refuse?" Tanager asked.

"We lost more than a third of our population a century ago due to an uncontrolled pandemic," Dr. Wilah answered calmly. "While I don't anticipate anything of that magnitude here, I'm afraid that Commander Royce will insist upon compulsory testing."

Tanager was of mixed mind as he reflected on how the villagers burned Moksha's house to the ground and threatened to kill her. Was it fear? Frustration? Or, as Dr. Wilah may be suggesting, exposure to a virus that affected their otherwise sound judgement? Clearly, they were lacking empathy, the main trait noticeably missing with those infected. His thoughts also went to Clusaladek and the classroom all those months ago, where students became borderline angry and violent—completely out of character with their normal personalities.

Dr. Wilah interrupted Tanager's mind chatter by politely ending the call, leaving Tanager and Lucene left with more questions than answers.

"Why did Dr. Ennis bother to phone us at all?" Lucene wanted to know. "He told us essentially the same thing except for—"

Tanager nodded. "Exactly," he finished her thought, "except for the fact that Commander Royce will be closing the borders between Earth and Erde travel. He wasn't just imparting information; he was trying to warn us."

As expected, Commander Royce declared the borders closed until further notice, leaving those on the preserves, including Fatima, who was already concerned about when she might get to see her family again, to wonder if that would ever happen.

Fatima rubbed Talula's back gently as she bounced her little girl up and down in the baby carrier that was wrapped around her waist.

"It will be okay," Lucene tried to comfort her friend after having told her the news. Ivan was at the lab—his home away from home—and Fatima was about to head to Cepheus's home to help Moksha with an old grape-treading ritual. It seems that stomping on grapes, barefoot, was not limited to wine growers on Earth.

"How do you know?" Fatima whined, sniffing back tears. Usually infused with unbridled optimism, Fatima was being uncharacteristically morose. "It's easy for you to say it will be okay. You didn't leave family behind. Everyone you love is here."

Lucene thought a moment. *Not everyone.*

Fatima read Lucene's facial expression. She had the luxury of growing up with both parents. Lucene lost both of hers at a young age.

"I'm so sorry," Fatima touched her friend's arm. "That was rude."

"It's okay." Lucene leaned over to roll the hems of her linen pants up and use a threaded strap to secure them in place. "Before you and my makeshift family here on Erde, I've never had anyone like you did with aunt Keti, Tai and your family. It couldn't have been easy not having them around at Talula's birth and being isolated on an alien planet."

"Eh, forget about me. It's no big deal. I'm just being melodramatic." Fatima started down the path to Cepheus's house where Moksha was waiting for them. While she was taking off weight since giving birth, her movements were still a little stiff.

"No," Lucene stopped her. "You're not. How you feel is how you feel. And, that *is* a big deal." She wrapped her arm around her friend, reaching out a hand to pat a very bouncy little Talula on the head. The baby gurgled bubbles and then giggled as if they were the funniest thing ever. She and Lucene exchanged bright smiles.

Just then, something in the distance caught their eyes. They could barely make out the shape of a dog-like creature bounding toward them from across the desert planes, kicking dust up everywhere in its wake. Logically, an animal couldn't possible move that fast and yet, in a matter of moments, it descended on them. And, it was much larger than they realized.

Before them, stood a snarling black dire wolf with flame-tipped ears, red eyes and foam and saliva dripping from its mouth.

Fatima let out a scream.

Instinctively, Lucene jumped in front of her friend and baby, her arms outright as if to shield them. They had just reached the front door of Moksha and Cepheus's cottage.

"Get inside," she ordered Fatima.

15

DESERT GLIDERS AND DIRE WOLVES

THIRTEEN DAYS BEFORE THE END.

Before Fatima had time to react, the dire wolf leapt at them with Lucene in its most immediate path. Its jaws went right for her throat. Lucene leaned as far back as she could but kept her stance. She had to until she was certain that Fatima and Talula were out of harm's way. Lucene crossed her arms in front of her, helplessly as the wolf descended.

Suddenly, she heard a loud thunk. The wolf still landed on her, but it was so stunned it did little more than topple Lucene onto her back, drooling on her arms as its weight landed on her. It regained its wits quickly and stood, its front paws pinning Lucene's shoulders to the ground, its back paws balancing on her thighs. It was about to attack again when a second whack came. This time, Lucene could see where it had come from. The wolf's eyes widened in surprise as it toppled sideways.

Over them stood Moksha, bloodied staff in hand from the aggressive strikes to the wolf.

Fortunately, Fatima sidestepped before Lucene and the wolf could land on them. Ordinarily, Fatima wouldn't have run, were it not for the fact that her baby was strapped to her chest and needed to be out of harm's way. She darted away from the altercation, heading up the lined path to the cottage, fumbling with the doorknob as a confused Talula, now pressed lightly against the door, began to cry. "Shhhh, it's okay, baby," Fatima whispered, her hands shaking as she was finally able to open it. She slammed it behind her instinctively, and quickly began unwrapping Talula from her chest, looking around for a safe space she might be able to deposit the infant until she returned. She finally settled on the only container she could think of that Talula, who had not yet learned to crawl or roll over, would be safe…the deep-basin that was the kitchen sink. She grabbed the first cushion she could find, Cepheus's black cape that was hanging by the front door, pillowing it onto the bottom of the sink. She rotated the faucet out of the way and gently laid Talula down, who immediately began staring at the faucet, curiously. Something about it amused her and she began giggling. Ordinarily, Fatima would have cherished this moment, but she had other things on her mind.

She searched for a weapon, but the closest thing she could find was an iron skillet. "That'll have to do," she exclaimed out loud and bounded back outside.

Moksha did a good job at keeping the beast at bay, but it was relentless. It ducked back and forth, as if looking for an opening between Moksha's staff and her flesh. It snarled; its red eyes almost reading Moksha's movements. It was beginning to predict her next moves, darting out of the way before she could strike and then lunging immediately after.

Lucene had no weapon and did the only thing she could think of. As the beast's teeth connected with Moksha's calf, Moksha let out a painful wail. Lucene leapt onto the wolf's back, reaching around to pry its jaws from Moksha's legs, cutting her hands in the process. Then she rolled onto her back, using all of her might to keep the jaws from closing.

From beyond the hills a team of desert gliders on high alert scattered, their wings fanning out to make themselves appear larger and more aggressive, and to warn their clan of danger. Behind them, two more dire wolves appeared, an amber-colored one with longer and thicker fur, and a gray one with mangled patches of white around his back and head.

Lucene heard the noise but couldn't see the turmoil. Instead, she thought a moment. *It worked on humans sometimes,* she reasoned, *maybe...* She tried to command the wolf to stop the attack and to retreat. Nothing happened. Her powers hadn't fully returned yet, and who knows how well her methods affected animals?

So, when that didn't work, she tried to tuck her legs to propel him away from her, adding in the intention that he should sail backward. But he followed her movements as if he knew exactly what she was going to do next. Her arms were getting tired and the jaws were beginning to bite into the backs of her fingers which were now sandwiched together in the beast's mouth. Finally, she attempted to give the illusion that she was much bigger and scare him away...all of this happening in less than a minute. At that moment, she could have sworn she heard the wolf in her head saying, *you're pitiful.*

It bared its teeth as if to smile at her. From her look of surprise, he knew that she had heard him.

What the beast didn't see coming, was Fatima, wildly swinging an iron skillet. It connected with the top of the wolf's head. He fell to one side, long enough for Lucene to roll over and rush to her feet. It was then she witnessed an injured Moksha trying to fight off the other two wolves with her staff.

Had their lives not been in danger, it would have been comical to witness Fatima now coming to Moksha's aid, skillet clenched in both hands as she swung it like a tennis racket at the amber wolf. It caught the edge of it in its mouth and somehow managed to bite into the pan and rip a piece off of the front of it as if it were nothing more than a thin piece of cloth. Fatima's face went pale. *What the hell kind of wolves were these?*

In a last-ditch effort, Lucene did the only remaining thing she could think of. She focused all of her intention on the desert gliders. *What will inspire them to fight instead of retreat? Ah,* she thought, *hunger.* She sent the message of immense hunger, allowing herself to feel that starvation deep within her. As she did, she also imagined that the women in her group were very thin, while the wolves were very large and meaty…but feeble.

Suddenly, the gliders began arriving en masse, rolling across the desert like a dust bowl. They began biting at the red and gray wolves' legs and then climbing up their backs.

"Head for the house!" Lucene ordered Moksha and Fatima, trying not to lose focus.

"Are you sure?" Moksha backed away. She wobbled slightly from the effects of the blood loss in her leg. Fatima caught her arm and steadied her.

"I'm very sure," Lucene was determined. The scene that followed was grotesque. As Moksha and Fatima headed for safety, Lucene kept her stance as the gliders devoured the wolves, leaving disgusting bits of bone and fur on the ground. Two gliders climbed up her back, one even making eye contact with her. She visualized herself as nothing but a raw, upright skeleton. The glider sniffed her ear and then signaled his friend. They leapt from her body, gliding through the air, as their name implied. Unfortunately, since they had just eaten, their landing was not delicate. They both plopped on the ground with a loud thud.

There were now at least two dozen overstuffed gliders waddling off into the sunset like penguins. When they were finally gone, she peered down at the wolves' remains, stepping away from them, queasy. It was then that exhaustion overtook her and she fell to the ground and quickly lost consciousness.

Lucene woke to find herself laying on a long couch in the Baruch house, a pillow beneath her head and a blanket covering her. She had a splitting headache.

"How are you feeling?" Tanager asked gently, touching her shins. He was sitting upright at the end of the couch, Lucene's legs strewn across his lap.

Once she'd opened her eyes, the bright lights blinded her, and the searing pain returned. She quickly shut them. The only problem was, it was now night, and there was nothing but low lights, not much brighter than candles illuminating the room.

"Fine," she answered in a way that suggested that she was not fine. "As long as I don't open my eyes, move, or breathe too hard."

Tanager smiled, sympathetically, trying to think what might help. *Magnesium tablets? A cold pack for her head?*

"Here," Fatima brought over a ceramic cup. "I've mixed you a tincture of magnesium, feverfew, butterbur and vinegar. It'll help." She guided her friend's head forward to take a sip.

"Bleh," Lucene coughed. "It tastes awful." She scrunched her face at the bitterness.

"Don't be such a baby. Drink," Fatima commanded.

Lucene drank it, before falling back onto the pillow. It seemed to help almost immediately. Within a few minutes, she could open her eyes and keep them open. She surveyed the room.

Moksha sat on a recliner in the corner of the room, her injured leg propped up, having been wrapped tightly in gauze. Cepheus had just returned from the healing center with an antibiotic—highly uncustomary for them to provide one without actually seeing the patient. But it seemed they were overwhelmed with calls of strange wild animals randomly attacking pedestrians throughout the Western Cross. Oddly enough, as night fell, the incidents stopped altogether. From the glass door overlooking the room, the waxing half-moon shone brightly with a small and full pink moon floating just behind it.

Ivan was busy entertaining Talula, who seemed to like being in the sink so much that he stood over her rotating the copper faucet back and forth while she gleefully clapped her hands. Just to mix it up, he occasionally rattled a set of metal measuring spoons and threatened to steal her nose with an oven mitt. Oblivious to what happened hours earlier, Talula seemed to be having the best evening of all.

"Constable Melokuhle should be here shortly to make a report and photograph the scene before the remains can be removed," Tanager explained, putting his hand over his mouth and fighting back a gag reflex. He refocused on Lucene and put the wolf carcasses out of his mind. "Are you up to speaking with him?"

"I guess so," Lucene sighed. All she wanted to do was go home, climb under the covers, and sleep for the next 48 hours. *Why am I so exhausted?*

Tanager jolted in surprise. For the first time since the short circuit on the bridge, he *heard* her. As training at TARA resumed and the effects of the virus wore off, it seemed that his own skills were finally returning. At least, he hoped that was the case and it wasn't a fluke. He kept this to himself because he was also becoming increasingly aware of the searing pain in Lucene's head. He had to mentally block it out to avoid becoming overcome with pain and exhaustion himself. "Moksha and Fatima said the gliders suddenly attacked the wolves," Tanager commented. "Do you remember?"

"Yeah," Fatima chimed in, looking at Lucene. "We were gonna try and nab you but then we saw your arms were glowing. Figured we had to let you finish doing your thing."

"We rushed to pull you inside after the desert gliders retreated. Well," Moksha pointed out, "Fatima did most of the pulling." She looked down at her leg.

"Don't let her fool you," Fatima commented. "Now I get why Moksha has the reputation of being a badass. By the way, your arms shocked me, *literally*! It was a hundred times worse than the shock of static electricity when you drag your feet across a carpet."

"Sorry," Lucene moaned.

Moksha considered herself the gentle sort, former Royal assassin or not. She wasn't sure she really wanted to be known as a 'badass.' But the thought gave her an idea.

"You know what?" she exclaimed. "This world isn't safe anymore. I need to train you how to fight—all of you."

"How often do you plan on having to defend yourselves against wolves?" Tanager wanted to know.

"Sadly, a stun gun is still the best option for that. Don't know that we can procure something like that around here though."

"Weapons are typically frowned upon on Erde," Tanager said while dropping his lips in a down-turned expression, not for emphasis, just to express his disapproval as he considered all manner of weaponry that was likely already in production at TARA these days. "Though," he looked sadly at Lucene's current state and continued, "we've never had to deal with wild and formerly extinct wolves before."

"Well, never mind that," Moksha continued. "There's a lot we can't seem to defend well against—chaos-loving demons, wolves, neighbors who burn your house down…" She paused for a moment, thinking about her old cottage with a minor level of nostalgia. The original plan was to grow new vines on Cepheus's land while hers recovered, but since the relationship blossomed, Moksha moved in with Cepheus and gave up her cottage to someone else who might need it. "And, as much as I hate violence, Erde hasn't been able to shut other worlds out. I just think that on this point, Commander Royce may be right. Self-defense should be taught in school, but not limited to students. I'm offering this to you, my friends." Moksha almost teared up a little as she said it. It took her a long time to establish any place that she'd call *home* and she'd become rather protective of it. "It may not be the best against wild animals, but it can certainly help in hand-to-hand combat. And really, what else have you got?"

"Moksha," Cepheus protested calmly, "while I appreciate the sentiment, that's not something I would choose for myself."

Tanager nodded. "And I am working insane hours as it is. When would I have the time?"

"I'll train with you," Fatima piped up. "Lucene will, too."

"Wait, why are you volunteering me?" Lucene protested, rubbing her head.

"Aww, c'mon," Fatima smiled. "Remember all the new stuff we tried on Earth? Bocce ball? Yoga? Sailing? It'll be fun."

Moksha hadn't intended on making it *fun*, but if it got her buy-ins, she was all for it.

"What about you, Ivan?" Fatima called into the kitchen. "You wanna train with Moksha and learn how to defend yourself?" She bit back a smile as if the only one in on a joke.

Ivan's face became flushed. Baby Talula wondered why he stopped clapping the plastic oven mitt together and reached up to touch his face, curious. There were a few things from his younger years that he hadn't gotten around to telling Fatima.

"Nah," he answered. "I'm good. But ye go ahead. I think the training will be good fer ye. Wouldn't want another incident like this to ever happen again."

SECTION TWO

"There you go, questioning again. The Netherworld is the opposite of the Hitherworld, which is where we are now. In the Netherworld, a finely-dressed bloke by the name of Jasper Ssset—lots of esses in his last name, it would seem. He let on that you might be able to use someone of my skillset."

16

ISABELLA'S CONFESSION

ELEVEN DAYS BEFORE THE END.

Classes weren't due to start for another hour, but there were still a handful of students wandering the campus at TARA. The newly appointed "agents" of the PDL were surprised to find Reverend Isabella waiting on a picnic bench outside of the Makerspace Monday morning, none more so than Lucene.

"Isabella," Lucene called, running up to her mentor and friend. "Are you okay? Where have you been?" While Isabella was a kind soul, one thing she wasn't was a hugger—something Lucene had become aware of in the short time living on Erde. She lifted up her arms, noticed Isabella's expression, and then dropped them at her side.

"I am fine, my dear," Isabella answered with her usual calmness. While she often wore colorful, flowing jumpsuits and scarves that caused many to mistake her for a supermodel, today her outfit was surprisingly subdued. She wore an amber-colored wrap-around tunic and matching headpiece. On her feet were what appeared to be recycled plastic brown flats. Make no mistake that Isabella still stood out. It was impossible for her not to. "What I want to know is, how are *you*?" She eyed Lucene's hands and arms, covered with several small bandages where she had fought off the dire wolves not a day earlier.

"I'm okay," Lucene glanced at her arms, self-consciously. The branch-like tree patterns on her arms kept routinely glowing on and off all evening. They would become uncomfortably warm for a few minutes and then stop, which did little to help her sleep, but seemed to do wonders for her injuries. One would have assumed that her attack had been several weeks ago as most of the marks on her hands were starting to scar.

"Fighting off dire wolves with your bare hands," Isabella commented. "That was pretty brave of you."

"How did you know that?"

"I know many things," Isabella answered calmly as Tanager, Cepheus and Moksha gathered at Lucene's side. "Perhaps we could talk…somewhere private?"

"Of course," Tanager responded. "The Resource Room would be most appropriate."

The guard at the new security station didn't think so. "I'm afraid this woman does not have authority to be on school property," he answered gruffly.

Cepheus began protest when Isabella spoke up. "*This woman*?" she was incredulous, mocking the guard. "Is that any way to speak to the spiritual advisor who delivered two of your babies last year in a large tub of water while you cowered in the bathroom because you couldn't take the site of blood?" The guard paused for a moment. "How are Verny and Zachery by the way?"

The guard awkwardly cleared his throat, reaching to adjust his belt uncomfortably as if he'd just finished eating a large meal. "Growing up fast," he laughed. "They've even started talking a little, just a few simple words here and there."

Isabella nodded and smiled encouragingly. She had been a temporary resident of Erde since she opened the portal to save Lucene and banish Jasper Set last year, though that didn't seem to stop her from flitting from one planet to the other when it suited her.

"Surely," Cepheus seized the opportunity, "there could be no issue with Reverend Isabella, our spiritual advisor, meeting with us on official business. You can clear it with Commander Royce if you care to phone her this early in the morning."

"Er," the guard rocked back and forth on his heels. Behind them, several faculty and students began to line up, impatiently. "I suppose it would be all right." He finally agreed to let them pass.

"Ridiculous," Tanager mumbled under his breath. "We've never had to go through such measures before just to walk into a damn building."

Lucene rubbed his back with one hand, supportively. "It will get better," she said. She wasn't sure she believed that, exactly, though she did hope that it was true.

Once they'd reached the library, Cepheus opened the door to the Resource Room which, to an onlooker, was camouflaged to look like a wall mural.

"The Knights Templar," Isabella remarked as she walked inside, eyeing the room in front of her.

"Please," Tanager offered her a chair.

"Thank you," she replied, winking at Lucene as if to commend her on her choice in partners. Lucene sat to her left, Moksha to her right, with Tanager sitting at Lucene's other side and Cepheus taking his place at the still unoccupied seat beside Moksha around the table.

"Reverend Isabella," Cepheus began, cautiously. "We have been searching for you for quite some time. We need to ask you some questions, but are curious as to what brought you to us today?" Cepheus drummed his fingers nervously on the table, while Tanager cleared his throat several times before Lucene eyed him oddly. Moksha sat calmly with her hands resting in her lap, a neutral expression on her face.

Isabella let out a sigh. "I confess," she declared suddenly, her face dropping shamefully, her eyes downcast. This was an uncharacteristic display of emotion from the woman. *There is no point prolonging the inevitable,* she thought.

"What?" Tanager sat upright, confused. "Confess to what, exactly?"

"To opening the portal, of course!" Isabella thought this was obvious. "The strange happenings all over town—a tiger-like feline terrorizing the zoo, dire wolves back from extinction, dead men walking, subtle and inexplicable distortions of reality—surely you had noticed these things?"

"We did," Tanager answered, cautiously, "But we assumed these were strange anomalies because of the conjunction between Jupiter and Saturn sending out ripples to neighboring planets. We just thought these oddities were…celestial."

"Celestial?!" Isabella couldn't believe what she was hearing. Though, to be fair, when Lucene had questioned her about the portal that seemed to evaporate when closed (becoming nothing more than the burning embers on her arms), Isabella explained it away as simply a metaphysical side effect of being an Erdeling born on Earth, imbued with special empathic powers. When Lucene had been struck by lightning, it triggered an anomaly in time and space. So, sending Jasper Set into an alternate plane of existence was simply an expression of that anomaly. That last part was a lie, though she hadn't realized that she had been lying at the time. Now, she had to come clean.

"I was wrong," Isabella blurted out. "As a time bender and a descendent of a prophet, I should have known better, but I made a mistake. Seems to be a family trait," she grumbled, thinking of Far's bumbling about the universe, making one miscalculation after another.

"What, exactly, do you think you were wrong about?" Tanager wanted to know.

What, exactly, is a time bender, Lucene wanted to know. That seemed to her the more interesting question.

"I didn't send Jasper Set into a parallel world," she sighed. "I sent him between the layers."

"What does that mean?" Moksha asked.

"In Shamanic culture, they talk about our reality and the non-ordinary realms," Isabella explained. "It would seem that he is still here, just between the layers."

"Oh," was all Tanager could think to say.

Isabella eyed him, questioningly.

Cepheus spoke up, "We were actually going to ask about something completely different," he said hesitantly. "We wanted to know if you were aware of any special arrangement between the Vitruvians and Commander Royce?"

Isabella was confused. "I don't know what you're talking about. I may be a prophet, but I'm not omnipotent and I certainly can't see and know everything. I only get bits and pieces of insight through prayers and meditation." People always seemed to believe she had special knowledge regarding just about everything. Being a prophet was hard.

"But you were supporting Representative Dallen, Odessa, and Morphinae at the last IPP assembly."

Isabella eyed him cautiously. "That was at the behest of Odessa who thought it the only way to help preserve Earth and Erde." She paused. "What is all this about?"

What this was about were some odd internal anomalies at TARA, particularly in the animal lab and the aerospace lab. Items went missing, only to return later in the exact space in which they vanished… random items like reamers and parts of a winglet kit, skin scrapings from the exotics room, and in one case, a missing litter box. (It should be noted that the litter box was one of the few items that never actually returned.) This was an improvement from two weeks prior, where items resurfaced in remote locations. It was as if whatever (or whoever) took them figured out how to recalculate and return them to their original location.

When they shared this information with Commander Royce, letting her know that they suspected someone was pilfering bits of information from TARA, she dismissed it. She even went as far as to suggest that one of the local businesses who rented the Makerspace for production were simply trying to get a leg up on the competition. "I'll have Constable Melokuhle look into it," she promised. But this answer made no sense, given the lockdown of the Makerspace. You needed to ask permission to use the bathroom these days.

"While we have no proof," Cepheus explained. "I have reason to believe that Commander Royce has been selling secrets to an outside source, perhaps the Vitruvians. Technology that could, essentially, be used to destroy us."

Suddenly a light bulb went off in Isabella's brain. She smiled, knowingly.

"So, you did know?" Tanager asked.

"No," she shook her head at her own ignorance. "I did not know. But it makes sense. How else could all of this," she motioned to the library around her, "be here."

The reality sank in their collective chests like the end of a movie where the dog dies and everyone is grieving. But in this case, it was as if they were, in part, responsible for the animal's passing.

"So," Moksha finally interjected, "if it turns out that TARA has been funded by the Vitruvians this whole time on the pretense of helping Earth, you mean to say that not one of you were even remotely suspicious of this before now?"

"No!" Tanager fought back anger. "Certainly not!" He shot Moksha a look of betrayal. Whose side was she on, anyway?

"Sorry," Moksha's voice softened. "Didn't mean that to sound quite so confrontational." Sometimes, her automatic defenses went up when she didn't intend for them to.

"Don't worry about it," Tanager grumbled.

Cepheus smirked, in spite of the current situation. Tanager was sounding more and more Earth-like the longer he was around Lucene which, these days, was all the time.

Isabella thought a moment. "I am not sure what to do with the information I have just been given, but about the portal I mentioned, the other realms?" This, to Isabella, was a far more immediate danger.

"What is it, Reverend Isabella?" Lucene asked, concerned.

"We have to seal it," she declared. "Unnatural spirits are getting in and out because it didn't fully close properly. Or, perhaps that *I* didn't close it properly."

Cepheus cringed. He didn't think of his visitations of Petrichor as *an unnatural spirit* at all.

"Jasper Set will get out," she continued. "And when he does, I have no idea how he will retaliate. Plus, we can suspect, but can't be entirely certain, that those vanishing items are being snatched by something else, or simply floating in and out between the realms all on their own," Isabella reasoned.

"Why haven't you told anyone of this sooner?" Tanager challenged.

"I did," Isabella answered, deflated. "I just told the wrong person."

"Commander Royce?" Moksha put the pieces together.

"Commander Royce," Isabella confirmed. "She asked me to keep this information to myself for now, but after the dire wolves—" For the first time ever, Isabella's eyes began to well up.

Lucene touched her arm gently. "It's okay," Lucene told her friend. "We're okay."

"What do we do now?" Moksha asked.

"I've been searching all my resources and everything I know about portals. From what I have found, we need to close it, but to do that, I will likely need to re-open it altogether to reset it. But to do *that,* we need to find a glitch in time and space."

"A glitch?" Tanager asked. "What does that mean?"

"It means that in the everyday realm, we have a timeline—a past, present and future. Whereas, in other Shamanic worlds, such as the upper and lower realms, time does not exist in the way it does here. We can, theoretically, float between time and space. In the non-ordinary middle world, however, there is a timeline. But..."

The group leaned in, eagerly.

"There is a vortex at the Crossroads of the non-ordinary realm where time and space can be manipulated. It doesn't follow an ordinary timeline. That's what we need to find...the Crossroads. Only then can we re-seal it."

"How in the world are we to figure out where that is?" Moksha asked.

"That, my dear," Isabella answered, "is the million-dollar question."

"Well, prepare to open your checkbooks," Lucene joked as she and Tanager exchanged knowing glances. "Tanager and I know *exactly* where it is."

Unfortunately, knowing the exact location of the Crossroads wasn't the only impediment. According to Isabella, they had to wait until sometime between a full moon and the *waning gibbous* (her words). It also had to coincide with the end of the Saturn and Jupiter conjunction or at least the energy it was kicking off. No one particularly understood what this meant aside from Isabella. But no one else had a better solution. She made the mess. She had to fix it.

And so, they waited.

17

———

TRAINING

TEN DAYS BEFORE THE END.

"How's this?" Fatima jabbed the air clumsily a few times and followed up with a full-on punch with an energy that sprang from her back heel to her hips and out through her right fist. Her face had the seriousness of someone who just passed a kidney stone.

"Wonderful," Moksha answered flatly, limping slightly over to Fatima, who smiled proudly, "if you want to break your wrist."

Fatima's facial expression sank.

"Here," Moksha reached out and adjusted her fist so that it aligned with her wrist and forearm. "Think of it as a kink in a garden hose. You have to keep it straight for water flow. The same is true of energy. "

The women began training at Moksha and Cepheus's house, oddly enough, on a small patch of grass surrounded by rows of grapes. They still had grape smashing on the agenda, a plan that got discarded the other day because of the wolves. Moksha was leaving that for last because it was the most fun and the messiest.

It would also give her a chance to demonstrate on the grapes how to smash someone's instep, break a knee, or scrape someone's shin with one's heel. The repeated movement would build muscle

145

memory, and she'd end up with crushed grapes for a first season of wine—greatly enhanced by science, of course. Thanks to Cepheus's idea of using the same technology on grapes as they do lab-grown clean meats, production was fast.

They replicated grape vines from a sample of Petrichor's bottled wine, grew parts in a lab and transplanted them to the vineyard. They also discovered that as Lucene's skills were returning, she seemed to be able to influence the vines. As she moved throughout the vineyard, the vines actually bowed toward her as she passed. And, Lucene couldn't help but speak to them lovingly as one might speak to their children. This was another reason why Moksha insisted on training in the vineyard. She believed Lucene's energy helped them grow faster and heartier.

That wasn't all. Lucene's own wounds healed at such a rapid rate that she began hovering her palms over Moksha's injured leg, and in two days, Moksha was able to walk on it again and the wound had sealed as if the injury were several weeks old. Like most things, it was a power that became stronger with practice.

After a few more rounds of straight and reverse punches, upward jabs, and backhand *hammers* and elbow strikes, they moved on to wrist and shoulder locks.

"Is this it?" Lucene asked, standing in front of Fatima and attempting to peel her friend's hand off, which was grasped firmly around her own wrist, and then lock her 'opponent' in a new, reversed wrist lock.

Moksha let out a sigh. Somehow, Royals seemed to understand combat instinctively. This did not appear to be the case with humans. And they hadn't even gotten to defending against species with more than four limbs yet.

To Fatima, Moksha asked, "How do you feel, Fatima?"

"Fine, thanks," Fatima smiled, not really understanding where Moksha was going with this.

"Here, Lucene. Try it on me," Moksha instructed as Fatima

released her grasp and took a step back. Moksha grabbed Lucene's wrist enough to make her wince.

Lucene reached her left hand across her body and tried to peel Moksha's hand free. Moksha let out a fake yawn. "My turn," she said. "Grab my wrist."

Lucene obliged, and within a split second found herself kneeling on the ground crying *uncle*. Moksha had taken Lucene down with a simple but effective lock that forced her to contort her body just to avoid the pain. There were many counters to this maneuver, of course, but Lucene didn't know any of them yet.

Moksha was curious how a combination of Lucene's powers with training would serve her in the long run, but that was a discussion for another day. The only stipulation in her training was that she didn't attempt to use any telekinetic or mind-altering skills during basic training, at least not until they could be sure that she wouldn't accidentally hurt anyone, including herself. Lucene made a mental note to talk to Tanager about this. The Data Collectors might do well with these skills, but only when they could be trusted. And after the incident at the school last year, when the students became violent, this type to study may have been a long way off.

"Sorry." Moksha released her grasp and helped Lucene to her feet. "I know you want to be careful not to hurt Fatima, but you need to develop better speed, pressure and accuracy, unless you simply plan on holding hands with the enemy."

"Very funny," Lucene rubbed her sore wrist.

"All right, shake it out, ladies." Moksha rapidly shook her hands and wrists in the air as if trying to shake something off that had gotten stuck on them. This was followed by a few cool-down shoulder, hip, knee and ankle rolls and some light stretches. "I think it's time we take a break before the last part of today's training."

Fatima groaned. "I'm not sure my sore body can handle any more of this."

"Oh, don't worry," Moksha assured her. "We're moving to the

lower body, which tends to be easier since we typically have more power in our legs."

"Still—"

"Humor me for fifteen more minutes." She led Fatima and Lucene to a large outdoor basin. "It begins with smashing and it ends with wine."

"That fast?" Fatima wrinkled her nose, curiously.

"No," Moksha smiled. "I cheated and bought a bottle from the market for us. It was the least I could do after torturing you both all day."

"So, how long does this training last, exactly?" Lucene wanted to know.

Moksha wanted to answer that the training never stops but given the deflated look they both had on their faces, she decided to side-step the issue altogether.

"Let's mash some grapes, shall we? We can discuss it later."

18

WAR

TEN DAYS BEFORE THE END.

"Cepheus, old boy," Ivan knocked on the closed door of his friend's office at TARA.

Cepheus, who was presently napping on the bench that had been his bed for a number of years, groggily lifted his head. He'd been having trouble sleeping ever since Petrichor's ghostly nighttime visits. Mainly because he eagerly awaited for her to return and was afraid he might miss her. And then after, there was that dreaded mix of sorrow, grief and guilt.

Plus, after years of sleeping on a hard bench with little back support, he'd actually gotten used to it. Therefore, when at home with Moksha who insisted on purchasing one of those cushy, form-adapting mattresses, he slept on something unnaturally comfortable. Whether this was some type of suppressed self-flagellation, he didn't know. All he knew was, these days he needed a nap to fill in the gaps of restless nights if he was going to continue to function well at his job. Cepheus finally made his way to the office door, accidentally hitting his forehead on the door's edge after not backing away quickly enough after opening it.

"Ye okay?" Ivan questioned. "Ye seem a little…stressed."

Cepheus rubbed his forehead, surprised. After all, Ivan was typically so hung up on the thoughts in his head that he often paid little attention to people's emotions unless someone else pointed them out. He did, however, miss the part where Cepheus smacked his head on the door.

"I am a little stressed, yes," Cepheus confessed.

"What's stressing ye, if you don't mind my asking?" Ivan suspected it might be the very thing that had been stressing him out, too.

"I question everything that's happening at TARA and the Makerspace of late. And, after a lifetime here, I am also starting to question my role…if I should even be here."

"I hear ye," Ivan nodded. "Been asking meself the same questions lately." The two were silent for a moment while Ivan carefully formed his words. He rubbed his earlobe with his thumb and forefinger nervously. "Er," he finally continued, "not to add to yer stress, but—"

"What is it, my friend? You can speak freely."

"Well, when I first arrived, it was all about building out technology for efficiencies, like transportation, growing food, clean energy. Now, I'm just back a week and suddenly it's…"

"What?" Cepheus knew the answer but somehow needed the perspective of someone outside of he and Tanager, both of whom had been tied to the school for decades and possibly lacked objectivity.

"Well, pardon me fer saying so, but now it seems to be for war." Cepheus's face dropped. "I don't mean to upset ye," Ivan continued. He wished Fatima were here right now. She was the better communicator.

At that moment, a member of Renenet's security team passed the office. He was wearing a crisp, tan uniform with brown boots and a distinctive, government-issued hat. The officer's manner suggested a clearly defined purpose of surveying the halls for anything that shouldn't be. He didn't walk, exactly. He marched.

"Perhaps we should take this conversation in my office," Cepheus stepped back to leave room for Ivan's bulky frame to slide past him before shutting the door.

It was only after the sound of the officer's footsteps had passed that they resumed communication. "I get that they want to be proactive about defending Erde from the neighboring Sections, particularly since they no longer have the support of the Intergalactic Peace Project nor the Vitruvians, but some of these precautions seem less defense and more offense. It's making me a wee bit uncomfortable," Ivan confessed.

"What have you been asked to do?" Cepheus was curious. It was his understanding that Ivan and his team were to outfit some of the newer vessels with defensive armory against attack, along with non-lethal micro-bullets that shot out tiny signal disruptors, thereby throwing an assailant's spacecraft off course and cutting off communication with similar vessels. But that was all that he was aware of. Apparently, there was more.

"Well," Ivan let out a sigh, "it started off all normal-sounding to me, making sure our security team, the military and our local constables had upgraded uniforms to protect against most of the lethal weapons used in hand-to-hand combat. Things like that. But then it started to enter gray areas. My first day back at the lab, Renenet asked our team what it would involve to take a concoction created in the chemical lab and stuff it into a small handheld device. So that, when released into the atmosphere, it could specifically target certain species and make them ill."

Cepheus's sallow complexion grew even more yellow. This sounded like something the Royals would do and even what Earthlings would do, but certainly not peace-loving Erdelings.

Ivan pressed on. "Then, a few days ago, she asked for small, explosive-like devices that could be deployed from multiple-sized vessels at any moving or non-moving target."

"You mean, she asked you to create a bomb," Cepheus confirmed.

"Yeah, she tried very hard not to use that exact word but I knew whah she meant. I told her flat-out that I know nothing about explosives but she was quick to point out how I diffused a network of them months back when Jasper Set tried to kill us all. Hard to deny when hundreds of people were around to witness it."

"Where did you leave it?" Cepheus asked.

"I requested a meeting with Commander Royce and the PDL so they could tell me the *exact* purpose of said explosives and what *exact* specs it should have. She was none too happy but I figured it would stall them a bit. I can't create what they are reluctant to talk about."

"Let me know if you need my support or Tanager's," Cepheus answered. "I know we'd both be happy to offer our thoughts on these new…requests."

"Thanks, man. And ye know," Ivan continued, "it's not as if I'm not grateful for all ye have done for Fatima and me, getting us safety to Erde and securing my finances in the universal marketplace, but if these requests keep coming in, I'm tellin' ye right now—I'm out."

"I understand, my friend." Cepheus was saddened. "And I'm telling you, you won't be alone."

A loud murmur erupted down the hallway. Moments later, their conversation was interrupted by someone banging loudly on the office door. "Everyone out," the officer who had recently passed the hall flung the door open. "We're under attack. Achel needs to go on lockdown. Follow me to the basement."

They weren't alone. TARA was bustling that day. They met Tanager in the hall who paused to try and reach Lucene using his communication watch.

"Damn it," he swore out loud as a few more guards shuffled him onto a transporter where he was sandwiched in between Ivan and Cepheus, followed by at least a dozen other students and faculty members. "Lucene," he muttered to himself, "why don't you ever keep your damn watch on so I can reach you?"

"Hang on," the officer commanded, setting the transporter in motion with everyone struggling not to lose their footing. Fortunately, the sheer volume of people in the transporter meant they were packed in like sardines, so falling over was not really an issue.

Once on the underground level, the masses were shuffled into a newly developed safety shelter. There were cameras set up in the bunker, where outside, at least three diamond-shaped spacecrafts flew past the outside of the Makerspace and TARA and made a beeline for the Dragoste Healing Center a few blocks down.

"What the—" Ivan's face turned white. He recognized the markings on the side of one of the crafts—a bright orange stripe that contained a panel for sending an energy field around the craft enough to deflect sonic particles and assault from incoming fire power. It was one they recently developed in the transportation lab, with one major difference. This one wasn't surrounding itself with an energy field. Instead, the panel opened up and opened fire, directly at the medical center.

Ivan's watch began to receive an alert—Fatima.

"Hallo, my—"

"Where are you? Are you okay? I'm watching the news and freaking out!" Ivan could hear little Talula in the background beginning to cry as she picked up on her mom's stress.

"I'm okay. We're safe. What about you? What's happening there?"

Cepheus hung over Ivan's shoulder. He neglected to remember his watch that morning and had no way of checking on Moksha or Roman or anyone.

"I'm home. Moksha's here with us, too," Fatima answered. Cepheus let out a relieved sigh, overhearing Fatima through the small speaker. "There's nothing happening at the Crosses, at least not from what we've heard, but there were three vessels spotted entering the atmosphere about twenty minutes ago. Have you heard from

Lucene or Roman? Lucene left our training session over an hour ago, but I haven't been able to get in touch with her since—"

With that, all communication devices went silent and the cameras went blank.

"They've blocked the signal," Ivan yelled. "We need to get out of here and do something!" He ran to the doorway of the shelter. A rather small officer blocked him. Oddly, he was carrying a billy club. Ivan had never witnessed any of the security, nor the local constables for that matter, carrying a weapon before.

"Stand down, man!" the officer commanded. "I've heard from Commander Royce. The situation is being contained."

Ivan felt helpless. Were it not for the fact that he knew his family was safe, he wouldn't have left it alone. He would have fought his way out of the room, insisting that he had to do…something. Instead, he clenched his fists until they hurt. It was then that he noticed Tanager pacing back and forth, agitated.

"No Lucene?" he asked.

"No." Tanager ran his hand through his curly hair. He suspected Lucene may have gone to her usual meditation spot at the Eastern Cross but suspecting and knowing were two different things.

Ivan put a supportive hand on Tanager's shoulder but really didn't know what to say outside of that. An "I'm sure she's fine," didn't seem like a sensible response at that moment, as he had no idea if she really *was* fine.

From his high-home balcony, Roman watched as three vessels descended from the sky. At first, they flew directly toward the Makerspace at TARA. He held his breath but did not move. It was almost as if he were frozen in place and the world was slowing down and beginning to move at half speed. At the last moment, the three vessels shifted. They darted past his building at such close proximity that Roman could actually see that there were at least three people aboard one of the crafts. They all looked distinctly…human.

The crafts then formed a V-shape, the two blue ones in back following the leader. This one was white and had orange stripes. Roman didn't understand the distinction. Suddenly the one in front opened fire in front of the healing center. It let out three blasts at the front steps, demolishing the grand entranceway but leaving the hospital itself, intact. Then, as quickly as they arrived, they pointed their noses upward and shot out of the atmosphere.

Roman could see soldiers storming the healing center, ensuring everyone inside was safe and blocking off the scene. Most passersby ran for shelter as soon as they saw the vessels and heard the shots. But a few quickly began gathering around the now-demolished concrete steps of the building, in shock.

"Far was right," Roman muttered to himself. He looked down at his watch. *No one is calling to check on me,* he thought. In that moment of self-pity, it hadn't occurred to him to check on anyone else.

19

MALLORY'S RETURN (SORT OF)

TEN DAYS BEFORE THE END.

Mallory's Costume Shop remained closed until it could be determined what was to be done with it. Since he had no heirs, it would naturally go to the government to auction off. One of his clothiers, named Pelimar, offered to buy the shop, even drawing up a very precise business plan to apply for a bank loan. This, it would so happen, was the same man who designed Lucene's favorite French off-the-mannequin outfit that she found an excuse to wear at least once a week.

But Commander Royce had other plans, insisting that Pelimar's request would only be met if he agreed to use the shop to create military uniforms first. Only after those needs were met could he use the shop for his own clothing designs. While Pelimar was an artist first and businessman second, he had to admit that having the steady stream of commissioned uniforms would help get the business up and running quickly. So, with some reluctance, he agreed.

As Lucene passed the window, after a slight detour returning home from Moksha's training session at the Western Cross, she saw the sign *Re-opening Soon as Mallory and Pelimar's Costume Shop*. It would seem that Pelimar was sentimental, leaving Mallory's name on the door in respect to his mentor and former employer.

Lucene had no real reason to be there. And yet, every two weeks she found an excuse to visit the Eastern Cross, usually for specific herbs and pantry items that only the grocery store there stocked. This excuse would have been much more believable had it come from Fatima instead of Lucene.

In truth, there was a grocer not two blocks from the high-home that she now shared with Tanager but she had grown fond of the older couple who helped her in the Eastern Cross, and so she would make a special trip on the SpeedCircuit as often as she could. And each time she did, she would make it a point of stopping by the darkened doorsteps of Mallory's old shop which was just down the block from the food store.

She was saddened at the loss of one her first friends in this new world as she had entertained the idea that he would eventually become a confidant and person she could always count on, like Fatima, only jollier (if that was even possible).

Lucene strained to see through the darkened window, placing the edges of her palms against the glass to block out the streetlights and see more closely.

Suddenly, a ghostly face appeared in the window…Mallory's. Despite his gossamer form, his eyes still sparkled like multicolored prisms.

She sucked in her breath, blinked, and looked again.

Mallory was motioning her inside.

Lucene looked around but saw no one else on the street. She set her groceries on the ground before carefully reaching for the door handle. In true Erdeling form, it was unlocked. Lucene stepped inside, cautiously closing the door behind her.

"Mallory?" she asked quietly. "Tell me I'm not seeing things."

She heard a distant giggle. "Okay, you're not seeing things," the boisterous voice of Mallory called. He sounded far away as if he were speaking through a telephone.

"Where the heck are you?" Lucene was filled with both excitement and apprehension.

Nothing…there was only silence. She called out several more times but still she heard…nothing.

Lucene carefully wandered through the shop. While the racks of clothing remained, the walls were no longer covered with prom dresses and flashy costumes. Instead, they displayed military uniforms of varied ranks, along with non-military personnel support garb she had started seeing at TARA. Frankly, it was depressing. A sprawl of gray polyester-like pants with matching jackets was laying across the counter as if waiting to be sized and sorted.

Lucene crept into the sewing room in the back. *Odd,* she noticed, all of the sewing machines were upright and staggered across each side of the table, just as Mallory had wanted it so that seamstresses could talk to one another as they worked, without craning their necks. He thought this would be good for morale. But one sewing machine had been turned on its side. Lucene walked over to it and ran her hand across it.

She turned it upright and pressed the power button. It whirred loudly and vibrated as if agitated. But that was all. Lucene turned the power off and took a closer look. She didn't know a thing about sewing. Therefore, she couldn't have explained the problem she saw with the bobbin as she poked around, nor that the hook assembly was wonky, and that the thread uptake was locked. Yet, somehow, she knew how to fix this.

"Might want to unplug it first." Mallory appeared before her in gossamer form. "Just so you don't accidentally sew your fingers together or electrocute yourself. One of us dead is quite enough."

"Holy crap, Mallory. You scared the shit out of me!"

Mallory's ghost laughed heartily. "Oh my gosh, if you could see the look on your face, child."

"Wait, how?" Lucene pointed at him.

"Don't you know it's rude to point," he reprimanded. "I've been trying to connect with you for the past month, every time you walked back and forth in front of the shop window. I would have thought you were daft, but thus far, you are the only person who is able to see me!"

"What happened to you?" Lucene asked. "I mean, I sort of know. But where are you now?"

"Well, *A*…I was murdered. That part we all know. And *B*…some sort of limbo? I've always said that this shop is my life. Apparently, it's my death also!" He giggled some more. But then it turned into a sob as he put his hand over his face. Lucene tried to hug him but her hand merely felt cold air as it went through him.

"Cut that out," he complained. "It tickles."

"Sorry," Lucene apologized, pulling her hand back. Instead, she unplugged the machine.

"Why are you here, child?" Mallory asked.

Lucene's eyes grew red. "Well, I sort of missed you," she confessed.

"Aw," he pouted, "that's sweet. Now tell me the truth."

"That is the truth," she whined.

"And?" Mallory pressed her.

Lucene let out a sigh. "And, I have no discernible skills," Lucene explained as she—without thinking—took apart the hook assembly, used a cloth lying nearby to clean it—and then reassembled it. She also snapped the loose bobbin back in place, re-threaded the machine and adjusted the thread tension. "Unlike Amy," she wrinkled her nose, "I can't cook. I can't play the piano. I'm not an artist. I'm not a scholar. And, any special powers I had are now as uncontrollable as the weather, though they are, admittedly, getting a little better. Still, my ability to grow plants and magically re-energize broken car batteries are still in question." Lucene was in full-on self-pity mode. "But I thought maybe…"

"Yes?" Mallory was interested.

"Maybe I could learn to sew?" She looked up at Mallory who had his elbow resting on his forearm with a hand to his mouth as he tried not to laugh.

"Is that so funny?"

"No, my child. What's so funny is that you repaired the machine in five minutes that Pelimar has been fighting with for weeks.

"Are you sure?"

"See for yourself," Mallory challenged.

Lucene plugged it back in and picked up a piece of remnant fabric, looking up at Mallory, questioningly.

"Go ahead," he urged, "but keep your fingers on each side of the cloth and be mindful of the needle."

Lucene obeyed, turned it on and hesitantly placed the cloth under the feed dog. The machine appeared to have a clear display panel on the side of it where she tapped in instructions. It began to whir, and within moments, she had created a simple but effective straight stitch.

"Voila!" Mallory smiled.

Lucene smiled but then remembered the very important fact that Mallory was, in fact, dead. "Mallory, as happy as I am to see you, you can't stay here forever."

"Well, obviously," he chastised. "I was only planning on hanging around until I was sure this place was up and running again, and now I'm hanging around until these grotesque uniforms go away and this shop returns to its former glory."

"You may not have that kind of time," she explained. Even as she did so, his image began floating in and out.

"Whatever do you mean?"

"My friend, Isabella, accidentally created a leak of sorts, making it possible for lifeforms on different layers within this plane of existence to pass back and forth. That's probably why I can see you now."

"Well, what's so bad about that?"

"It's distorting reality and letting some beings out who are not as nice as you."

"Oh," Mallory thought for a minute. "That explains a few unsavory characters I've run into lately."

"The point is," Lucene continued, "once she seals the leak, I'm afraid you may be stuck in that realm with those entities, forever. I mean, I don't really know for sure—even Reverend Isabella isn't certain. But I worry…isn't there a different…better realm for you?"

"You mean like heaven?"

"I dunno, maybe?" Lucene wasn't sure herself. "Maybe it's that unfinished business idea. And when you're ready to let the shop go, you'll move on. Only, I'm afraid, you're short on time."

"My, my, aren't we morbid?" Mallory tsk-ed at her.

"What are you doing in my shop?" a male voice asked. Lucene jumped with a start, nearly sewing her fingers together in the process.

"I warned you," Mallory said.

Lucene quickly turned the power off and unplugged the machine.

"Uh," she looked down at the square of fabric. "I was, uh, fixing your machine?"

The young man standing in front of her had the brightest blood-red hair she had ever seen. It was molded to his head like one of those old troll dolls that they used to sell on the end of pencils, whose hair went wild when you spun the pencil between your palms. His face was narrow, oval shaped, and powder white. He was wearing black lipstick. In his hand was a metal hanger. He wielded it like a weapon.

"You broke into my shop to fix one of my damaged machines?" After he thought a moment, he realized the hanger wasn't going to be of much use to him, so he set it on the table and then crossed his arms, impatiently, waiting for an explanation.

"Just tell Pelimar the truth," Mallory encouraged.

"He won't believe me," she replied, looking at Mallory's hazy image as it floated behind the young man.

Pelimar looked over his shoulder, quizzically. "Who are you talking to?"

"Uh, listen, Pelimar—"

"How did you know my name?"

"Well, aside from it being on the shop sign," Lucene began, letting out a sigh, "Mallory told me."

"Oh, did he?" Pelimar laughed. "And when did you last talk to our old buddy Mallory?"

"Who are you calling old, red-headed Goth-i-mar!" Mallory retorted.

"About two seconds ago," she pointed.

Pelimar looked. He saw nothing. "You do know he's dead."

"I am aware of that, yes."

"So, you talk to dead people?"

"Apparently?" She wrinkled her nose. She was as confused about it as he was.

"Get out of my shop before I call the constable."

Lucene thought a moment, coming up with only one possible response. She pulled up a voice from her belly and answered jovially, "Who are you calling old, red-headed Goth-i-mar!" Lucene's impression was quite extraordinary.

"How did you know he used to call me that…as much as I asked him not to?" Pelimar furrowed his brow with a mix of suspicion and annoyance.

"Because he's still here."

"And I suppose he taught you how to fix my machine, is that it?"

"Don't be gauche, Goth-i-mar. I am an artiste. I don't fix machines. That's what I had *you* for." Mallory waved his hand for Lucene to relay the message.

"Don't be gauche, Goth-i-mar," Lucene imitated, "I am an artiste. I don't fix machines. That's what I had *you* for."

Pelimar let out a laugh. "You know, you've got him spot on. I just wish I believed in ghosts but I don't." Mallory stuck his tongue out at him. Lucene let out a laugh. "What's so funny?" Pelimar demanded.

"He just stuck his tongue out at you."

"Look, could you lose the whole 'Mallory is a ghost thing' and tell me what you want."

Mallory shot her a *well, go on* look.

"I want you to take me on as an apprentice and teach me how to sew." The words flowed with surprising ease because, up until that very moment, she wasn't entirely sure what, exactly, she wanted.

Mallory's eyes beat into Pelimar's brain. "Just agree, silly boy," he mumbled.

"Wouldn't there have been easier ways to ask for a job than to break into my shop?" Pelimar reasoned.

"I didn't break in," Lucene defended. "The door was open. And I came in because I thought I saw something…or…someone."

Pelimar waived a hand in the air. "I know, a ghost." It was clear from his expression that he had no intention of entertaining this idea.

"So?"

"So, what?"

"About my request?" Lucene scrunched up her face like a small child not entirely certain whether her parents were going to agree to her request or chastise her for even asking.

"Just agree, silly boy," Mallory tried again. "You could use the help, you know?" He looked toward Lucene to support her own cause. And so she did. *Just agree…agree.* Lucene focused her intentions as hard as she could.

"I can't believe I'm saying this," Pelimar poked a finger in his ear as if there were a fly buzzing around in it. "But I agree. I mean, what I'm saying is, okay, I will take you on as an apprentice. Uh, what's your name?"

"Lucene," she and Mallory answered in unison. Pelimar flicked at his ear again and looked in Mallory's direction, squinting in a confused manner.

"Okay, Lucene." He turned to face her. "I can't pay you much, but if a standard apprentice wage works for you, we can start there. If you prove useful, then we can negotiate a raise in three months. How does that sound?"

"That sounds perfect." Lucene put her hand out to shake Pelimar's, but he shook his head. Earth customs were clearly not his thing. He peered at her hand as if it carried with it a severe rash (it didn't). Lucene retracted her hand, awkwardly.

"When can you start?"

Lucene suddenly felt a chill and looked over Pelimar's shoulder. Mallory was gone.

Lucene returned home that evening to find Tanager pacing back and forth across the living room, muttering to himself.

"What's going on?" Lucene asked, surprised. She set her small bag of groceries on the table.

"Where have you been?" Tanager spat out before pulling her toward him in a bear hug.

"Okay, I'm confused. Getting really mixed messages here." Lucene returned the embrace with some hesitation.

"Fatima said you left the training with Moksha hours ago." He backed away, searching her face for an answer.

"I didn't know I had to check in with you as to my whereabouts," Lucene answered defensively. "If you must know, I made a side trip to the Eastern Cross to pick up red curry paste and dried ancho chili peppers…and a few other things."

"We have a store two blocks away."

"I like the store I used to go to," Lucene began raising her voice.

"Since when did you become picky about gourmet ingredients?" Tanager raised his voice to match hers.

Lucene angrily unpacked her tote bag, holding up the curry paste and chili peppers as evidence. "In case you thought I was lying to you."

"When have I ever accused you of lying to me?"

"I don't know. You seem awfully concerned about my whereabouts. I hadn't realized you were so suspicious."

"Suspicious?" Tanager was incredulous.

"Or controlling. Maybe both. I don't know." Lucene was flustered, her face becoming flushed.

"And now I'm controlling too?" Tanager ran a hand through his hair and then held his arm out as if he were about to give a speech. "Did it ever occur to you that I may have been worried about you?" His eyes widened as he searched her face for understanding. "That maybe a phone call to let me know you were running late might be a good idea so that I wouldn't pace the floor thinking something bad had happened to you? Oh, that's right," he continued, frustrated, "you never take your communication device with you."

Actually, it *hadn't* occurred to Lucene. This whole 'checking in with another person' concept was new to her. She felt a pang of guilt for her outburst. "I hadn't intended on staying that long, but then I stopped and talked to Mallory and time got away from me. And, why were you worried about me, anyway?"

"Just a moment," Tanager circled a finger in the air. "Back up… you talked to Mallory?"

Lucene let out a sigh. "Yes, but—"

"You know he's dead, right?"

"Clearly, I do, but—"

"Then, how exactly did you talk to him?"

"If you'd stop interrupting me, I'll tell you."

Lucene stopped to grab a pitcher from their refrigerator and a glass from the cupboard to pour herself a glass of iced turmeric tea.

She motioned the glass toward him in case he wanted one as well. He shook his head. They sat at the dining room table for the next ten minutes as Lucene recounted her interaction with Mallory's ghost and Pelimar, including the part about the apprenticeship. She finally concluded with, "I'm sorry I worried you. I'll call next time if I'm running late or at least have someone else call if I forget my watch."

But Tanager's mind was buzzing. He was already on to the next issue. "But you already have a job," he protested. "You are an agent of the PDL and you're my research assistant. I need you." Lucene placed a hand on his forearm. Before she could respond, he kept rambling on, "Assuming we can even return to TARA after today's attack…"

"Wait, what?" Lucene's grip on Tanager's arm grew stronger. "What attack?"

"Three fighter vessels entered the atmosphere as if targeting the Makerspace, but at the last moment, they veered off course and ended up destroying the steps of the healing center before vanishing."

"Holy crap. Was anyone hurt?"

"No, but now you know why I was so worried about you. Lucene, I thought something happened to you," his eyes were rimmed with red as he fought back tears.

With that, she wrapped her arms around his shoulders and hugged him fiercely.

20

CEPHEUS AND LUCENE
EIGHT DAYS BEFORE THE END.

For all the times that Commander Royce called the PDL agents together for one or her many meetings, she was surprisingly silent about the attack on the Dragoste Healing Center. When Ivan and Tanager requested a meeting with her to explain that the vessels the attackers were using had a striking resemblance to those Ivan and his team were building in the Makerspace (fitted with weapons to match) she dismissed them, citing that a top-secret investigation was underway and that she would reach out to them should she require their assistance.

This was a far different Commander Royce from the one who, just six months ago, gave them an open invitation to meet with her and speak freely about any concerning issues. In fact, this new version of Royce went so far as to tell them that given her current responsibilities, any requests for future face-to-face interactions should be made through Director Renenet.

Suspicious, Lucene decided to employ Kiki's sniffing skills to determine if Commander Royce, was in fact, Royce at all, instead of a shapeshifter posing as the commander. But the verdict came back with disappointing news. After Kiki had diligently tracked Royce at the PDL headquarters to her high-home in Achel, she determined that Royce was most likely an Erdeling. To be fair, Kiki hadn't actually smelled Royce prior, but she had the varied Vitruvian scents in her nasal directory, not to mention the sweet smell of Earthlings and the citrusy aroma of Erdelings. Royce was, decidedly, more citrusy. This left Lucene with more questions than answers, the main question being, was Commander Royce somehow involved with the latest attack? Or, at the very least, was she covering up for someone? Perhaps their suspicions were correct about her working with the Vitruvians…or someone else. The sourness in the pit of her stomach returned, a feeling that had been happening far too often lately.

Between the wolf onslaught, the attack on the healing center, the supernatural interactions spurred by the tear between the layers, her on again, off again empathic powers, not to mention her strained relationship with Tanager lately, Lucene's nerves were frayed. So she thought of the one person who might be able to help her gain clarity.

"Lucene, how nice to see you," Moksha greeted her at the door.

"Hi, Moksha. Sorry to bug you guys so close to dinner." Lucene was ushered inside Cepheus and Moksha's cottage. Lucene, who had taken to carrying a staff with her in case the wolves returned, set it by the front door. She had also come equipped with an ultrasonic wave handheld contraption that Ivan assured her was a high frequency that would irritate dogs, and would most certainly work on wolves. It was the best he could come up with on short notice, though he couldn't be sure if the irritation would make them more violent or send them running in pain. Therefore, the staff seemed like a good back-up plan. She unzipped her backpack and tucked away the contraption.

"He's expecting you," Moksha continued, "his study is just through there."

Of all the times Lucene had been to their cottage, she hadn't recalled ever seeing Cepheus's study. She expected it to be like his office at

TARA—cluttered with books, models of flying vessels, blueprints and all manner of gadgets thrown in disarray. But to her surprise, when she knocked lightly on the door, it opened to reveal a wall-to-wall bookshelf with a sturdy cherrywood desk in front of it. On the opposite wall were framed maps of Earth, Erde, and several neighboring planets in Section 1 of which she was still unaware. Unlike his office, this room was distinctly organized and minimalistic. Lucene suspected that Moksha had something to do with the present state of his study and his home.

"Lucene," Cepheus spoke softly, a warm glow crossing his face. "It's always nice to hear from you outside of work. Is this a social visit or is there something I can help you with?"

Lucene felt a pang of guilt, as aside from their monthly reunion dinner which now included Moksha but almost never included Roman, she'd been lax in her social visits. But to be fair, there seemed to have been one situation after another since her arrival on Erde.

"I wish it were merely social but I've come partially for advice and partially to ask a favor."

"Of course," he answered sincerely, "whatever you need. Please," he motioned to a club chair next to his desk, "make yourself comfortable. Would you care for a beverage? Moksha's just brewed a batch of reishi mushroom tea."

"No, I'm fine, thanks." Lucene fought to fit the words together in her mind.

"What's troubling you?" Cepheus asked calmly. "You know you can tell me anything."

"I know," Lucene sat down, hesitantly. "So, I've been thinking… you know how we stopped my meditation training on the vessel because I became a little…unstable…for a bit?" That was putting it mildly. She had to be put in hibernation for the remainder of the trip after becoming mentally unwell.

"Yes, of course," Cepheus confirmed.

"And then we started back up again at TARA with Tanager's class and then I sort of flaked out a second time?"

"I remember," Cepheus nodded calmly. Cepheus fought back the urge to defend her instability on the amount of stress she was under, the trauma she'd endured, genetic splicing, Jasper Set's influence and now, a confirmed virus. In fact, he thought she had recovered and adjusted remarkably well these past few months despite everything she'd been through. Instead, he paused and said nothing, giving her time to find the right words.

"Well, I've been afraid of resuming a meditation practice or developing any of my skills because I have been worried about short-circuiting again."

"What makes you think you would, as you say, 'short circuit' again?"

"Let's just say, my track record hasn't been all that great," Lucene admitted.

"But Lucene, you're a different person now than you were even a few months ago. And now you have the support of those of us who love you and understand what you're going through. Back on Earth, you knew you were in danger but didn't know why or from whom. Now, you've faced your demons—in some cases, quite literally, and look at the woman you've become."

Lucene wasn't sure who started tearing up first, but both were wiping their eyes. She knew Cepheus loved her and that he had become a part of her new family on Erde, but it was still nice to hear. "I wish I could see myself as you see me," she answered honestly, "because what I see in myself isn't all that great." Lucene sniffed as a few stray tears ran down her face.

"I wish you could, too," he answered in earnest, "because what I see is a pretty courageous woman." Lucene averted her gaze. After another awkward pause, Cepheus asked, "Do you *want* to continue your training?"

"I think so," Lucene replied quietly. "I mean, I think part of the problem before was that I became overwhelmed and lost my filtering system. All the sensory stuff came in at once and I lost the ability to let it in a little at a time."

"I know exactly what you mean." And he did, having spent a number of years *under watch* because of his own episodes, which fortunately, were now under control.

"But the thing is—"

"Yes?"

"Stuff is coming back, whether I like it or not—little things like manipulating energy for healing, telepathy, some telekinesis—"

"These are not little things, Lucene," Cepheus reasoned.

"Yeah, I guess not. And there's the ethical mind control, though, in recent use, it was more a matter of survival."

"The mind manipulation of the dessert gliders to overrun the dire wolves was quite impressive," Cepheus acknowledged.

"Thanks. And, you know, my memory is still a little fuzzy, but even that's getting better as I work through stuff. So, I guess if it's going to be there, like it as not, I should start training again. Otherwise, it's going to be erratic and unpredictable."

"That makes sense," Cepheus agreed.

"On the other hand," Lucene reasoned. "What *if* I go off balance again and become erratic and unpredictable?"

"I suppose that is always a risk."

"What should I do?"

"You know my immediate go-to is meditation, but since that's what we're talking about, perhaps begin by asking yourself four questions."

"What questions?"

"First, what do you have to lose by doing nothing?"

"Myself," Lucene answered without thinking.

Cepheus paused a moment at her revelation before continuing. "Second, what do you have to gain by doing nothing?"

"Nothing…it's just status quo."

"Third, what do you stand to lose by training your powers?"

"Myself."

There it was again. Cepheus persisted.

"And last, what do you stand to gain by training your powers?"

"The greatest potential of myself."

"So, what will you do?"

Lucene paused a moment, grinning. "That was five questions."

Cepheus let out a chuckle. "So it was. Still, what will you do?"

"If I decide to start meditating again—slowly, of course, just to see how it goes…will you work with me again?"

Cepheus tilted his head sideways forming a lopsided grin, his canine teeth sparkling. Anyone who didn't know Cepheus might have been frightened by it, but not Lucene.

Finally, he answered, "I thought you'd never ask."

Moksha insisted that Lucene stay for dinner and as the three of them sat, a strange howling began. At first, they thought it was the wind as a storm had begun brewing outside. But then they heard it—more wolves. Just then, an advisory notice began flashing on Lucene's watch. She hit play for those at the table to hear.

"Warning! Several packs of wolf and tiger-like creatures have been spotted in the Western Cross," the announcer said. "The PDL and all security units have issued a mandatory lockdown. Secure your outdoor farm animals as much as possible to prevent a possible feral attack and bring all pets inside. Furthermore, residents are required to stay inside until further notice."

Lucene was about to shut her watch off when a second alert came in. "Warning! A severe thunderstorm warning is in place across all the Crosses and the City of Achel. For your security, the PDL recommends that all residents take shelter until further notice."

Lucene turned off the alerts, looking at Moksha and Cepheus

whose hands seemed frozen in space, hovering over the noodle bowls Moksha had prepared.

"I sure picked a craptastic time to visit, huh? Want me to try and catch the next SpeedCircuit out before it's shut down? Otherwise, you'll be stuck with me for a while."

"Nonsense," Moksha answered. "The couch in the living room folds into a bed and we have extra blankets and pillows. You can sleep here tonight and catch the Circuit when it opens back up in the morning—providing the lockdown has been lifted by then, of course."

"I'm sorry," Lucene sighed. "I didn't mean to burden you."

Cepheus reached out a hand and took Lucene's supportively, giving it a father-like squeeze. "You are never a burden to us. Besides, we have work to do after dinner," he smiled.

Apparently, training was to resume sooner rather than later. Lucene squeezed his in return before remembering. "Oh, I almost forgot. Excuse me one second…"

To her host's surprise, Lucene dropped his hand and left the dinner table. She hit a button on her watch one more time.

"Lucene, where are you? Did you get the alerts about the storm and the ferals on the loose?" Tanager asked on the other end, fear clearly audible in his voice.

"I did," Lucene answered. "I just sat down to dinner with Moksha and Cepheus. I was planning on heading home right after but—"

Tanager let out a loud sigh. "You need to stay where you are, of course."

"I know. Sorry about that. But at least I remembered to call this time!"

"There's nothing to be sorry about. I'm just glad you are safe. All three of you, please be careful."

To emphasize his point, the howling resumed outside, closer this time. The storm became much stronger and rain began to beat down on the roof.

She could hear as Tanager sucked in his breath, having clearly heard the sounds from across the miles. Lucene watched as Moksha and Cepheus began triggering locks on the cottage that lowered see-through shields that barricaded the windows as if preparing for a hurricane.

"Don't worry, my friend," Cepheus called over Lucene's shoulder. "We won't let anything bad happen to her."

Lucene's stomach began to growl. After all, they hadn't had a chance to eat yet.

"Have you spoken to Fatima and Ivan yet?" Tanager asked.

"No, you're the first person I called. I suppose I should check on them."

"Go have dinner, Lucene. I'll give them a call. I promise to let you know if anything has happened."

"Okay, thanks. And, weather and circumstance permitting, I'll be home at first light."

"Take your time. Just be safe," Tanager spoke softly.

In the kitchen, Moksha and Cepheus had returned to the table, waiting politely for Lucene to join them again.

"I will be. Sleep well," Lucene's heart sank a little. It was then that she realized that she hadn't been away from Tanager for a single night since they'd moved in together. She hadn't expected the sudden hole she felt in the center of her heart. It wasn't so much that she couldn't bear a night apart. It was the fact that she had no choice in the matter. She was, for all intents and purposes, stuck.

"You, too, and Lucene…"

"Yes?"

"I love you."

She almost blurted out her usual, "I know" as the right words always got stuck in her throat. Perhaps it was the thunderstorm outside, the howling of the wolves and the realization that tomorrow was never really a given. So, instead she answered softly, "I love you, too."

21

THE WIND AND THE WOLVES

EIGHT DAYS BEFORE THE END.

Lucene and Cepheus sat on the floor of the study facing one another, several feet apart. Both were sitting cross-legged with eyes closed. Outside, the wind and the wolves were still howling.

Moksha assumed the role of security guard, telling the two to focus on their meditation; she would alert them if anything happened. So, with the windows and doors secure, Moksha sat in the living room, staff at the ready, just in case. At one point, she witnessed a tiger-like creature steaming up the window as it peered inside. But the hurricane-proof shutters worked against the strength of a supernatural wild animal as it pawed at the window in vain.

Instinctively, she touched her leg where the dire wolf had attacked her. Thanks to Lucene's energy healing and her own constitution, nothing was left but a scar where the wolves' teeth had broken the skin. This was not particularly interesting to Moksha who had a series of scars from her short time as a Royal assassin before escaping to Erde. In fact, most of the remaining scars she did retain were a result of her father beating her so that the Royals didn't learn that she had helped Cepheus escape. Oddly enough, she didn't look at these wounds as abuse—according to their dysfunctional culture, he was protecting her. Sadly, she didn't know what happened to him, or any of her family, for that matter.

Occasionally, Fatima would send a short message alert from their nearby home. Moksha smiled and sent an, "All is fine here. How about there?" message back. After her not-so-warm greeting from humans living on the preserves when she had first arrived, she was grateful for Fatima's friendship. Of course, those on the preserve had been there for quite some time and seem to have forgotten that they were once outsiders, too. But Fatima was new and hadn't forgotten. And, given her nature, Moksha was fairly certain that she never would.

"And Lucene?" Fatima asked.

"Meditating," Moksha messaged back.

"Oh, cool. But don't freak out if she starts screaming from sensory overload. She does that sometimes."

Moksha grinned, "Thanks for the warning."

Inside the study, Cepheus began with simple reviews, not unlike what they would practice when she was a young child and he was contacting her remotely from Erde. The same exercises that her own father would work with her on, as well. For example, he would think of a color, a shape or an object, and she would relay what it was. Then, she would send messages back. Then, they moved on to words and sentences. It seemed juvenile, at first, but it was almost as if they were re-calibrating her intuitive skills.

And as they did so, memories began flooding back. Lucene remembered calling out to Cepheus for help the night her parents died. But at the time, she thought of him more as an angel that could miraculously save her. As an adult, she now understood that while his skill level was much more advanced than the average human, he wasn't an angel or a deity. But he did try to help her. In fact, he had been looking after her for her entire life.

Finally, Lucene moved into the void, that is, a meditation that shifted from a place of breath awareness to that blissful space of nothingness. In there, it was quiet and peaceful. There, nothing unpleasant could get in.

"Did you miss-s-s- me, princes-s-s?"

"What the hell are you doing here?" Lucene spoke aloud, unnerved. This time, she wasn't even dreaming.

"What is it?" Cepheus opened his eyes, concerned. "Who's there?"

Lucene kept her eyes closed.

"Go ahead," Jasper encouraged. "Tell him."

"It's Jasper Set," Lucene whispered. She was becoming increasingly agitated.

"Lucene," Cepheus reminded her. "You control what experiences you let in. If you don't want to see him, block him out."

"You can do that…if you want," Jasper whispered back. "But then you won't be in on my little s-s-s-ecret."

"What secret?"

Jasper's image flew into view, more clearly than the last time, wearing an outdated three-piece tweed suit over his barrel-like body. His skinny legs were adorned with what could best be described as brown stockings. How his wings protruded from the suit she couldn't tell, but there he was, hovering in midair with a mixture of anger and absurdity.

"I've discovered a way out," he spat. "I couldn't seem to squeeze in and out between the layers like other beings, but then it occurred to me." He paused for dramatic effect. Lucene said nothing. She merely waited. "Go on! Ask me 'what?'!" he yelled, agitated.

Lucene felt a mixture of fear, anger, annoyance, and confusion all at once. She emotionally distanced herself as if the emotions floated all around her but could not attach themselves to her. Finally, in a moment of calm she asked, "What has occurred to you?"

"My energy is too big to fit through the tear unless the tear is bigger or the portal is opened altogether. My greatness-s-s was getting in my way!"

"Yeah," Lucene answered sarcastically, "that's always been the problem."

"Lucene," Cepheus whispered. "Talk to me. Are you okay?"

Jasper was confused for a moment. "Is that the guy I tossed into the field?"

Lucene ignored him. "I'll ask the same question I've asked you before. What do you want?"

"I want what I've always wanted…you, for starters. I still believe there's lots of dimension-hopping to be had, s-s-seeing what havoc I can wreak on other realms. See what my doppelgängers are doing. Your powers are returning, are they not?"

"How did you—"

"I know lots of things," he spat angrily. "I see everything from here. I jus-s-s-t can't always-s-s do anything about it…yet!"

"Couldn't we just try again?" Lucene reasoned. "Have Isabella send you into another dimension and you can see what the other Lucenes in their alternate lives are up to?"

"Rather irresponsible of you, isn't it?" Jasper offered. "To sic me on your other selves?"

Lucene had to admit that he had a point. Still, the *other* Lucenes —if parallel dimensions were actually a thing—hadn't exactly sent any new Jaspers to this realm, so perhaps they were better equipped to deal with him than she was.

"Besides," Jasper continued. "I've got issues with Rev…Rev…" he choked, "Is-s-abella. She trapped me like she trapped the kitty Hys-s-echia. The prieste-s-s-s seems to be making lots of enemies these days, don't you think?"

"So your grand plan is that I simply go with you to other dimensions, which we don't know how to get to and—"

"You're not a quick study, are you Lucene?" Jasper barked.

"Enlighten me," she answered flatly.

"The whole arms burning, ring of fire…*you* are the portal to other worlds. Is-s-s-abella may have had the coordinates off, but the concept is s-s-s-olid. You just need to figure out how to get us there."

"Where, exactly? You're not making any sense."

"Anywhere that isn't here!" he bellowed. Jasper's nerves were frazzled and he was even less coherent than usual.

"So, if I go with you, what's in it for me?"

"For you?" He thought a moment. "Not much, if I'm being honest. But in exchange, I will call my Null mamas and papas off. They're still looking for me, you know. You'd be saving your precious planet."

Lucene opened her eyes, momentarily. Cepheus was there at the ready. "What is it?" he asked, concerned.

"Jasper says if I go with him, he'll call the Null off from destroying Erde. Would your—" she stopped herself before saying 'father.' Instead, she reframed it. "Would Hamish have made a deal with Jasper without protecting Erde, given that you reside here?"

"Excuse me," Jasper flew into Cepheus's face, but Cepheus was unable to see him. "This is a private conversation." He turned to Lucene. "But I can answer that." He began bouncing up and down hysterically, like a small child. "I found a loopty-doopty-hole, as it were."

"A loophole?"

"That's what I just said! Stop repeating me." For a moment, he lost his train of thought. "That's right. I was permitted to do whatever I wanted on Erde, but not harm his precious Cepheus unless abs-s-solutly necess-s-sary. I suppose he assumed I would 'take the girl and run' so-to-speak. But then the plan changed."

"How did the plan change?"

Jasper knew he should have kept it to himself, he really did. But he was a braggart, and being stuck between the layers, he was left bragging to beings who didn't seem to adequately admire his capabilities. This annoyed him. "Hamish decided that Erde might be a better option for the Royals than Earth."

"Well, that makes sense," Lucene answered. "That's why Dallen and the Vitruvians were trying to work with Erde…to help protect it from the Royal invasion."

Jasper shook his head. "Oh, you poor, stupid girl." Lucene didn't react, she merely waited, knowing he couldn't help but tell her why. "The Vitruvians have no interest in helping Erde survive…quite the contrary. And I will keep my contract with Hamish and not harm his precious Cepheus…unless absolutely necessary."

"So, if I go with you—"

"Then I will redirect the Null."

"I don't understand."

"Of course, you don't. You're an idiot."

"Explain it to me," Lucene was not the least bit moved by the demon's insults.

"I will call the Null and redirect them to the space between the layers…Erde remains intact."

"But the other realms of reality? Won't they be in danger of being destroyed?"

"Who cares, so long as your friends are okay?"

"But that would be irresponsible, don't you think?"

"That's your deal, not mine." Jasper crossed his arms in front of him like a defiant teenager.

"One more question," Lucene thought a moment.

"What?"

"Why is it that you'd want to trap your surrogate family in an alternate reality?"

If it were possible for Jasper's face to become any more translucent, it would have. Instead, he merely looked dazed as if someone had slapped him hard across his jaw.

Lucene's empathic powers may still be under repair, but this one was obvious. "Oh," she answered, "I see. You're still afraid of them. In fact," she continued, "you're not calling them to rescue you. You're trying to bait them…so you can plan your permanent escape."

Jasper didn't answer. Instead, he began spinning like a cyclone, disappearing into a cloud of smoke.

22

MORPHINAE'S REALIZATION

SEVEN DAYS BEFORE THE END.

"You knew." Morphinae flew in as a falcon, transitioning into his male form once he reached the sands of Tranquil Beach, appearing to be anything but tranquil. In fact, he appeared angry—a rare emotion for Morphinae.

"You're back," Odessa's eyes lit up before she remembered that she was mad at him for disappearing on her after she'd made her declaration of love. Okay, she reasoned with herself. It was less of a declaration, and more of a simple, "I like you," but she hadn't expected him to run away like that and not contact her for months.

Morphinae ignored her. "How could you lie to me?" he demanded. "After I covered for you back on Earth?" He was referring to the time she stalled in returning to Vitruvia, claiming to be ill, giving herself time to escape to Erde and claim sanctuary.

"What are you talking about?" she squeaked out, nervously. His eyes seemed almost flame-like. He'd never gotten angry with her before.

"I'm talking about how Representative Dallen and other Vitruvian dignitaries made a side deal with Drake Cushing in exchange for

Lucene and for dibs on Earth, should it become uninhabitable by humans—"

"That's old news. They were trying to protect Lucene from the Royals. And, it was self-defense. If the Royals got her powers—"

"The Royals were never interested in Lucene's powers for themselves. They were just handing her off to Jasper Set in exchange for Earth. And later, protection from the Null."

"Again, old news—"

"Let me finish," Morphinae growled. Odessa fell silent.

"The Vitruvians *claim* non-interference, except in self-defense. Therefore, I thought it odd when they reached out to me, a member of the Balance-Keepers and asked for my help. Dallen said he feared for the safety of the Vitruvian people if the Royals took over Earth and spread to Erde. How long before they got to Vitruvia? And he *knew*!" Morphinae's voice grew louder before he remembered himself. "He knew that if he gained the extra support from the Balance-Keepers, that you would do anything to support the mission."

"What are you talking about?!" Odessa's eyes grew red. "Why would he assume that?" How could Dallen have known how Odessa felt about Morphinae, when she didn't even know it herself until recently? "As you can see, I abandoned my position. If I go back to Vitruvia now, they'll likely kill me."

"No, they wouldn't. This is exactly what Dallen wanted you to do."

"Oh, c'mon. You're not making any sense."

"The Vitruvians interfere and they interfere on a regular basis. They have every intention of occupying Earth and Erde and killing off the Royals—something which will become infinitely easier now that the Null has rolled over all Royal domains except for the training grounds. Sovereign Hamish was rather short-sighted in his planning when he made a deal with Jasper Set."

"Really? I had no idea—"

"Stop!" Morphine grit his teeth. "Stop lying to me. The only reason the Vitruvians wanted to make an alliance with Earth and Erde was when they thought they might have the protection of the IPP and surrounding Sections to guard against a Royal attack. Once that plan failed, they returned to the original plan, with one major difference."

Morphinae eyed Odessa, as if giving her the opportunity to confess. She opened her mouth to speak, but then shook her head.

"I can't," she whispered.

"How long have you been giving intel on Makerspace technology and the happenings on TARA and the preserves to Representative Dallen?"

Odessa thought about denying it, but she knew it was useless. And, she didn't want to lie to Morphinae. In a way, she was somewhat relieved. He turned away in disgust. All of his suspicions were true. "I never want to see you again, Odessa," he grumbled.

"They said they'd kill me," Odessa pleaded. Morphinae stopped, standing with his back to her. "I disobeyed orders by fleeing to Erde. Commander Royce was ready to send me home in a body bag until Representative Dallen thought I might be useful here after all."

"Commander Royce?" This surprised Morphinae. "Why would she do that?"

"Where do you think all the money came from to fund TARA and the Data Collector initiative to start with? This is a small and rather poor planet with lots of smart people but no funds to do anything. And yet, look at how advanced the Makerspace is. Who do you think privately funded all that?"

"Disappointing," Morphinae answered. "And here I thought the Erdelings were the only honest people among us…wrong again." With that, Morphinae transformed into a Peregrine Falcon and flew away.

Odessa stood there, numb. Of all the beings in the multiverse, she'd just lost the one she had expected to be by her side forever. And he had left her, not once, but twice. And this time, she feared, it was permanent.

She didn't have much time to wallow in self-pity. For there, in the distance, making their way toward her hut was none other than Lucene and Reverend Isabella. Lucene didn't wait to ask Odessa why she was crying, nor did she tap into the shapeshifter's emotion and realize that she was in the middle of heartbreak. She was on a mission and so was Isabella.

Instead, Lucene looked directly into Odessa's eyes and announced, "We need to talk."

23

OLLY

LAST OCTOBER, BEFORE THE NEW ASSEMBLY.

"Beggin' your pardon, my Liege, my Viceroy, my Marquess, my Baron, my Dauphin," the thick, elf-like being bowed, gesturing with his hands as his head nearly hit the floor.

"Who are you? How did you get in here?" Dallen asked, jumping from his high-backed chair that looked suspiciously like a throne…in a hotel room. He nearly knocked over the long-stem fluted glass he was holding, as he was sipping a fine Vitruvian port. "Guards!"

"Now, now," the elf answered. "Let's nah be hasty." He held his palms out as if to calm the ambassador down.

Dallen wasn't prone to yelling. In fact, when he wanted his guards, or a servant of any kind, he'd flick his fingers and they'd come running. If they weren't in the room, all he had to do was tap his lapel pin and a minimum of three attendants would appear. Realizing that his yelling hadn't worked, he began tapping the pin, fervently.

"Now, now," the elf tried again. "That won't not be necess'ry. I just wanna talk is all. I gave your serfs the night off just sos we can talk."

"You…what? How?" Dallen sniffed the air, distastefully. There was a strange aroma that wafted off the visitor, almost like olives… no, that wasn't it. Olive brine. He smelled like olive brine.

The elf-like creature stood there dressed in layers of dirty cloth and wore large boots that made a floppy sound as the sole of his left foot hung loose, while the toes of the right boot had a hole in it, revealing a hairy toe. The creature's face was large and round and seemed about two sizes too big for his torso and one size too small for his feet.

"I said, I gave 'em the night off sos we can talk. Mind if I sit down, my Liege, my Viceroy, my —"

"Ambassador or Representative Dallen is fine," Dallen interrupted. "Either of those titles are acceptable." Dallen really wasn't sure that he wanted the aromatic elf to sit down. He didn't even like having him in the otherwise immaculate room.

The elf plopped down on the carpet and crossed his legs under him, leaving Dallen to return to his chair-that-looked-like-a-throne and sit down. He looked down at the odd creature, expectantly. In his mind, he was cycling through all the neighboring Sections he knew. The elf certainly wasn't from Sections 0, 1 or 2, that was for certain. Unless the Royals were hiding a rare species, he couldn't be from Section 3. Could he be from one of the Trappist planets in Section 5?"

"I knows what you're thinking my Liege—" The elf caught himself. "Er, my Ambassador Dallen." He scratched an itch under his chin and flakes of skin floated to the carpet. Dallen's stomach turned, just a little. "But I'm not from any of those places."

"How did you—"

"Oh, I knows lots of things. But don't worry, I'm here to help you."

"Help me? Help me do what?"

"The way I sees it, is you want three things," the elf began ticking them off his thick hands. "You want the power. You want allegiance. And, you want the girl."

"What girl would that be?" Dallen began grinding his teeth.

"Why, Lucy," he answered.

"You mean, Lucene."

"Something like that," the elf waived his hands. "By the way, since you never bothered to ask, my name's Olly. Nice to meetcha, finally."

"Finally?"

"Are you always so…questioning?" Olly wanted to know. "Er, never mind. As I was saying, I was talking to this fine gent the other night. Goes by the name of Jasper. Ever heard of him?"

Dallen threw his hands in the air, frustrated. "No, of course I've never heard of him. And even if I did know a Jasper, it wouldn't likely be the same Jasper that you know, would it? The universe is a pretty big place, don't you think?"

"Now, now," Olly put his palms out to appease Dallen. "Don't get testy. I'm still getting caught up after being stuck in the Netherworld for so long."

"The Netherworld?"

Olly let out a snort. "There you go, questioning again." He laughed. "The Netherworld is the opposite of the Hitherworld, which is where we are now. In the Netherworld, a finely-dressed bloke by the name of Jasper Ssset—lots of esses in his last name, it would seem. He let on that you might be able to use someone of my skillset."

"So, you're looking for a job?"

"In a manner of speaking," Olly answered, lying on his side and leaning on a propped-up elbow. Dallen mimicked the movement by leaning his forearm on the arm of his high-backed, red not-a-throne. "You see, unlike my new friend, Jasper, I have only just recently discovered this kitschy new power whereby I can easily float between the Netherworld and the Hitherworld."

"And how does this help me?"

"I can bring you things."

"What sort of things?"

"For example," Olly held up Lucene's communication watch. "This here belongs to your lady friend. Only, she doesn't know it's missing yet, cuz it isn't. I snagged it at the dinner you haven't gone to yet."

"How did you know we were going to dinner?"

"I told you my Ambassador, my Representative Dallen, I knows a lot of things."

"You are very confusing."

"Thank you for not asking another question," Olly praised. "The thing of it is, the last time, I was a bit late and had to plant that watch in her home when she wasn't around."

"The last time? How many times, exactly, have you stolen her watch?"

"Er," Olly counted on his fingers again, only to realize he didn't have enough of them. "Two hundred and seventeen? Two hundred and nineteen times? Not really sure. You see, me and Jasper seem to be in a loop, of sorts. And, it's not just linear. It's sorta, five-dimensional and all."

"That doesn't make sense."

"Ah, but it does my—" Olly thought for a bit. "My Viceroy." He had gotten it wrong again. "The thing of it is, the loop we're stuck in is not just this timeline, but many parallel timelines. I've stolen that there watch hundreds of times, and it most always ends the same way."

"So, you fail every time. Then why would a high-ranking Vitruvian Ambassador, such as myself deign to hire you?"

"Well, my good sir, that's the funniest bit of all. See, I'm stuck. But you're not. Ergo, heretofore, I can bring things of consequence to you. For example, another gift…a trinket, if you like."

Olly handed over a tiny oblong silver box, not much bigger than a matchbox.

"What's this?" Dallen paused, not entirely certain whether or not accepting a gift from such a questionable source was a good idea.

"See for yourself…literally!" Olly's body quivered as he laughed to himself at a joke that only he got.

Dallen accepted it, hesitantly. Inside, lay two round, clear pieces of plastic. "You brought me Earth eyewear? I'm not even sure they use contact lenses anymore. And, my vision is perfect."

"Oh, these are quite different. Give 'em a try."

Dallen considered his options. His guards were not there to protect him. He had no reason to believe anything this little troll had to say and yet…curiosity got the better of him. He placed one of the lenses carefully in his non-dominant eye (making sure he'd at least have the good one if he needed it). Immediately, the vision in his eye began to adjust like a camera lens, in and out and finally focusing on Olly's right earlobe. There was a fly buzzing around it.

"That's not all," Olly smiled. "Blink and pause." He demonstrated.

Dallen blinked and paused for an additional second with his eyes closed. What flashed before him underneath his eyelid was a photo of Olly's ear, just for a moment before it disappeared.

"Now," Olly ordered, "check your fancy pin there."

Dallen didn't know how Olly was privy to that info, but he tapped his lapel pin in a distinct pattern, and images appeared and there it was—Olly's ear.

"You see, you don't need a camera or any special anything. You can snap photos of anything you'd like to remember—anything at all. It's a present for you, from me to you."

Dallen thought for a moment. "I do believe I would like to employ your services after all, Olly. But just answer for me one question, will you?"

"Certainly, my Liege."

"You said that in every parallel universe, 'It almost always ends the same way.'"

"That I did, my Vizier."

"So, thousands of them?"

"At least, my Lord."

"And in how many of them—"

"Yes?" Olly rubbed his hands together, eagerly.

"In how many of them," Dallen paused, "do I get the girl?"

Olly thought a moment, ticking away on his hand. "Only four, I'm afraid. At least, so far."

"That's okay," Dallen reasoned, smiling to himself. "I like a challenge."

24

MALLORY & PELIMAR'S COSTUME SHOP
SIX DAYS BEFORE THE END.

"Hey Lucene," Xeni called, enthusiastically, as she and Kiki burst through the doors of the newly renovated Mallory & Pelimar's Costume Shop. Pelimar looked up, at first with mild annoyance, but then he became transfixed, somehow.

Xeni smiled bashfully, as she tucked a strand of her hair behind her ear before realizing the cloche hat she was donning got in the way. She repositioned it to prevent it from falling to the carpet. "We were in the area on a class assignment and figured we'd stop in and see your new digs and bring you a sandwich. Here!" She thrust the bag over the counter at Lucene who was, at that moment, adding price tags to new inventory. Pelimar had been busy logging yesterday's sales receipts, yet he hadn't moved since the two women arrived.

"Thanks," Lucene answered. "That was thoughtful of you…and, I like your hat." For the first time, Xeni was actually wearing garb that was flattering, a simple scoop-neck off-white blouse and gray jeans. Oddly, her pink eyes looked blue today. *Contacts?* Lucene wondered.

"We weren't sure what you'd like, or who else was here," Xeni shot a hopeful glance in Pelimar's direction, "so we got one tuna sub and one tempeh avocado roll."

Lucene peeked into the bag. "Which one is which?" The two sandwiches were wrapped in identical paper.

"Let me see," Kiki offered, sniffing. "The one on the right is tuna." Kiki's attire was a little odder than Xeni's, with a high-collared blue button-down shirt that was camouflaged against her skin. The shirt was long, reaching almost to her knees. Underneath, she wore black leggings. This was quite different from what she wore on stage and not nearly as interesting.

"Cool place," Xeni scanned the small shop, approvingly. Once she noticed Lucene's pause, she added, "Oh, you go ahead. We already ate. We're on a mission to—"

Now, it was Kiki's turn to nudge Xeni. They were given explicit instructions not to share what they were doing in the Eastern Cross. It wasn't that they were doing anything particularly interesting, per say. It was more the school's way of teaching them to keep their eyes open and mouths shut.

"Snitches get stitches," Xeni would often say. It didn't make any sense in the context of the conversation. Lucene made a mental note to explain to Xeni one day just what that expression actually meant.

As it would so happen, Xeni opted to stay in the criminal justice training program at TARA. Since Commander Royce required all Data Collectors to resume their training, Xeni had to find a loophole by declaring a "double major." Kiki, who had become a fast friend, thought maybe it was time she went back to school. And, "detective-ing" seemed as good of a course study as any. After all, maybe she could put her nose to good use. Kiki was several years older than Xeni, and as much as she enjoyed singing, working as a coat-check receptionist at the Embassy Club was hardly fulfilling and certainly didn't do much to sustain her financially.

"Hey Pelimar," Lucene called over her shoulder. "Which one do you want?"

"Wha—" Pelimar was jolted from a daydream.

"Which one do you want?" Lucene repeated. "The tempeh or the tuna? Or, do you wanna go halfsies?"

"Which would you pick?" he asked while staring up at Kiki, batting his eyes and leaning one elbow on the counter and resting his chin on his upturned palm. *She was exquisite…her eyes, her voice, her blue skin…her aardvark-shaped nose…*

"Aw," Xeni blushed, sheepishly before it occurred to her that Pelimar wasn't talking to her. He was talking to Kiki. *What the heck am I doing wrong?* Xeni wondered.

"Oh." Kiki's gaze fell to the floor. She wasn't used to many people actually looking her straight in the eyes. Usually, they stared straight at her nose. Or worse, at the floor, to avoid looking at her nose. "I'm more of a tempeh gal, myself," she confessed.

"I'll have the tempeh, then," he smiled, never losing her gaze.

Lucene's eyes went from Pelimar, to Kiki, and back to Pelimar again before an exasperated glance at the ceiling. She shook her head, disbelieving. What is it with young people in love? They were so…obvious.

Xeni was crestfallen. She leaned on the counter and let out a sigh.

"Don't lose heart," Lucene whispered. "Your time will come. Hey, thanks for the sandwich."

Xeni's expression brightened a bit. "Ain't nothing but a chicken wing."

Lucene let out a sigh.

"C'mon Kiki," Xeni finally coaxed. "We have an investigation to finish."

"Call you later?" Pelimar asked Kiki.

"Mmm, hmm," Kiki nodded, shyly.

Wow. They didn't waste any time, Lucene thought.

Outside, Xeni and Kiki resumed their "class project" which was to essentially follow a pre-determined subject for half of the day, collect clues and document anything they could about the subject, all without making contact. It was a lesson in detective training not unlike Xeni's former Data Collecting training, save for two important factors. One, the Data Collectors were gathering as much information as possible on the entire species with the intention of helping the planet's survival as a whole. Whereas, in this case, they were following a mock trail in order to solve a pretend crime set up for training purposes. Second, they lacked their empathic, genetically engineered skills. In Xeni's case, it had been psychometry. And while her old powers floated in and out at random, they weren't reliable, forcing her to actually use the tools she was learning.

Xeni was envious of Kiki, not only for garnering Pelimar's attention, her amazing singing voice, but also for her uncanny tracking skills. There were a lot of reasons for Xeni to envy Kiki, but Kiki was unaware of this, and treated her new friendship as sacred.

"Okay, where did we leave off?" Xeni pulled her notepad out of her back pocket.

"Huh?" Kiki was smiling to herself.

"Snap out of it," Xeni chastised. "We're on assignment, remember?"

"Sorry," Kiki murmured.

Xeni immediately felt bad. After all, it wasn't her friend's fault that Pelimar liked her better. She also now had two very underwhelming dates behind her, all of which only made her even more convinced that Clusaladek was the one for her...he just didn't know it yet.

Xeni stopped at the SpeedCircuit platform and scanned her notes. "Our subject stopped here to meet someone."

"Allegedly," Kiki offered.

"Allegedly," Xeni acknowledged. "Except, that's what the class notes said, so I'm pretty sure that's the scenario we're going with." Xeni continued, "They left a clue behind, but what?" Xeni rested her hand on one of the guideposts designed to direct people toward the correct platform.

All of a sudden, a series of images flashed before her eyes. A drunk man…a monk…the smell of gin and cigarette smoke…war planes…an intense anger.

"What is it?" Kiki's eyes grew wide.

Xeni spotted Roman, dressed in a black coat with matching jeans and a flat cap. He was heading for the platform going to the Northern Cross. And given that the Northern Cross was an undeveloped wilderness, his attire was completely inappropriate.

"Change of plans. C'mon." Xeni took off, keeping a modest distance from Roman, leaving just enough time to catch the Circuit train before it left the station. "Two for the Northern Cross," Xeni declared to the attendant, flashing her watch. It registered two tickets, one for each of the young women.

"You sure about that?" the attendant asked, glancing at their attire.

"Don't worry, we just want to see it. We won't linger."

"Suit yourself." He waived at the train, indicating it should wait a few moments while they boarded.

On the circuit, Roman didn't bother to look up. Instead, he hugged himself, tucking his face low toward his chest. It was only then that they noticed that he had a small suitcase on the chair beside him, strapped in so that it didn't go flying about when the train took off at high speed.

"Last call. Take your seats and strap in," the attendant ordered.

The women obeyed, taking seats several rows behind Roman so they could keep an eye on him.

"What's this all about?" Kiki whispered.

"I'm not sure," Xeni confessed. "But I haven't had psychometric flashes like that since my powers fizzled out last year."

"Wow!" Kiki's eyes grew wide. And then she realized something. "Uh, what powers?"

"Shhh," Xeni hushed her. "Keep your voice down. I'll explain later."

Kiki was intrigued. She didn't know whether Xeni was onto something or should be on something…such as an antipsychotic medication. But truth be told, she was having fun. An adventure! She settled back into her seat while the SpeedCircuit took off.

They arrived at the Northern Cross an hour later. The weather there was unpredictable, cold and blustery one day, and hot and humid the next. Today, the clouds rested over the terrain, casting a continuous dark shadow over the rocky landscape. A few small tumbleweeds rushed past as the winds kicked up, causing the women to cough back dust. They had to stop several times to turn their backs to the wind as it whistled past their ears before taking cover behind a large bolder. There, they discovered, they could safely watch Roman at a distance. At that moment, he sat on his suitcase, facing the boulder where they hid not twenty feet away.

"What are we waiting for?" Kiki whispered, but Xeni couldn't hear her above the wind. She was about to yell louder when Xeni realized this and held a finger to her lips. Kiki fell silent.

Roman grew quickly impatient. He stood, arms outstretched as if on a crucifix. "Okay," he called. "I'm here. Where are you?!"

Xeni peeked around the corner just as a gust of wind blew her hat off, revealing a short mess of blue-black hair underneath. She let out a few expletives.

Kiki wasted no time, pitching her nose out and, literally, sucking the hat toward her like an elephant snatching its food. She grabbed it from her snout. "Got it," she mouthed. Xeni nodded, impressed. By the time she had the courage to look again, there was someone else standing with Roman—the monk from her vision. His back was toward her. The wind settled. She witnessed the monk outstretch his hand, but not before turning his head in her direction and grinning. She darted behind the bolder.

Xeni was afraid to look again, fearing she'd been spotted. Kiki gestured toward the top of the rock and before Xeni could stop her, she had scaled the side of it, peering carefully over the top.

"There's no one there!" she called to Xeni.

"What?" Xeni peered around the corner again. Kiki was right. Roman and the monk had vanished.

Xeni wasn't entirely sure what to do with the new information that she and Kiki had collected. Although, somehow, she understood that it was important. When her current professor dismissed her investigations as trivial, she went to the one teacher she respected most— Professor Tanager.

Unlike his colleague, Tanager was intrigued by the findings. When the young women were done telling their tale, Xeni asked, "But who was he and what does it all mean?"

Tanager cleared his throat, uncomfortably. "I can't tell you more at this time, Xeni." Xeni's face fell, disappointed. "But there's one thing I can tell you," he paused for dramatic effect, "the two of you are going to make fine detectives one day."

Kiki beamed proudly, even sticking her overabundant aardvark nose in the air triumphantly and letting out a strange toot. The two headed for the door in Tanager's office before a flash hit Xeni. The scene was suddenly vivid…not as memories are, but as if a person were reliving the exact moment. She turned to her teacher.

"Professor Tanager?" She asked.

"Yes, Xeni?" Tanager had been jotting down notes from their conversation to share with Lucene, Cepheus and their team.

"It didn't strike me until just this moment but…weren't the two men we saw today the same ones on the bridge with you the day you and Lucene almost got blown up?"

Tanager wasn't hardwired to lie, and he didn't have time to come up with a convenient diversion. Instead, he settled on the truth. "They were," he finally answered.

"Hmmm," Xeni attempted to replay the circumstances of that day in her mind, but there was some confusion. "Were those men the good guys or the bad guys?" Once again, her world was compartmentalized into the frame of the late-night detective movies on Earth, ones where the good guys and bad guys were clearly defined.

"Honestly, Xeni," Tanager answered, "I'm just not sure."

25

THE END FOR HAMISH
FIVE DAYS BEFORE THE END.

"Why are these doors open?" Hamish demanded of Far, who was at present, standing on the balcony overlooking the training grounds.

"Just breathing a little life into this place," Far explained. "Given how difficult it was getting them to budge, I venture a guess that they've never been opened before.

"No," Hamish stood beside Far, taking a deep breath. He wasn't sure why he hadn't thought of it before. But, he decided, he did enjoy the fresh air. "While I respect you as a prophet and spiritual advisor, Far, you are never to make decisions such as these without asking my permission. Is that clear?"

While Far didn't see why he would need to ask permission for as small a matter as opening a few glass doors, he nodded. "Yes, my Sovereign."

"Where is Fredo?" Hamish asked. "My guard is rarely out of range for any length of time."

"My apologies, Sovereign," Far answered. "I asked him to show Roman the training grounds. And, given that he is not of Royal descent, I was concerned how his presence would be received if he went unattended."

Hamish grew angry. "Once again, you overstep your bounds, Far!" He wasn't even looking at his prophet. Instead, he was staring over the balcony at nothing in particular, his eyes yellow with a sudden rage. "You don't open doors in my chamber without permission. You don't invite humans to this planet without getting it cleared through me. And, you certainly don't give orders to my Royal guard without asking me first! If Sovereign Sabrina were still alive, she would have had you hanged by now for insubordination!"

Far fumbled with something he held behind his back, tumbling its handle over and over as if weighing his options. Finally, he'd reached his decision.

"Yes…my Sovereign," Far answered forcefully, as he shoved a dagger into Hamish's back. Hamish was thicker than he anticipated, and during Hamish's moment of shock, Hamish took it upon himself to tug at the knife, both hands reaching behind his back in an effort to retrieve what was out of reach for his thick arms. Hamish fell face-first to the floor, and Far had to step on him to finally dig the blade out from between his shoulder blades. Far wasn't taking chances; he stabbed Hamish again, using both hands to thrust it in and twist the knife violently. After all, the Royals had fiercely strong regenerative skills. Far's plan had been tougher to execute than what he anticipated. In his mind, he would easily tip the sovereign over the balcony once he'd stabbed him. But that's not what happened, and now he had to figure a way to lift a large man up and toss him over the ledge.

"What are you doing?" Roman yelled in horror as he and Fredo burst into the room.

Another of Far's miscalculations. It's hard to pin Hamish's death on Roman—an angry Earthling who would do anything to protect his planet—when he was caught holding the weapon. Roman was supposed to be surveying the grounds, that part was true, but he wasn't accompanied by Fredo. Instead, Far arranged to have Fredo 'accidentally' locked in the underground prisons. Roman must have heard his screams and let him out.

Far had to think quickly. He dropped the knife and began shaking. "He…" Far stammered, drawing out tears with ease. "He attacked me," Far sobbed. "I had to defend myself."

Fredo's first concern was to his sovereign. He used his transmission watch to call for medics, before gently rolling Hamish onto his back to see if he was still alive.

Roman stood before Far. "He attacked *you*…" Roman put the pieces together. "And yet he was facing away from you. Why, pray tell, was he stabbed in the back?"

"What?" Far appeared helpless. "I don't understand! I was so frightened!" He moved toward Roman as if to hug him. Roman saw the blade, but it was too late as it made its way into Roman's side. Roman yet out a yelp as Far dove again. This time, Roman was prepared, sidestepping Far. With the ease of an ice-skater, Roman spun sideways, tossing Far's frail form over the ledge. He gasped for breath, watching in horror as his beloved hit the stone staircase on the mountain below and kept tumbling toward the ground. Several soldiers saw it, looking up at Far before rushing toward Hamish's chamber.

The medics arrived first. One moved toward Roman.

"Not him!" Fredo grumbled, motioning toward the fallen Hamish.

"That's right," Roman winced, bending over and holding his side as blood soaked his shirt. "Him first," he gestured with his free hand.

Three ran to Hamish. One took pity on Roman.

"Here, let's have a look at that," he said. He was wearing a black wetsuit-like uniform similar to Fredo's. He even had Fredo's red salamander shape but had a much smaller frame and a gentler voice. "I must admit, I'm not experienced at human emergency interventions, but so far, you appear to bleed the same way as we do. I'll see what I can do."

"Thanks," Roman winced again as the guard had him stand fully upright and roughly removed his bloody shirt and then attempted to tightly wrap a tourniquet around him. "I…appreciate…that!" Roman bit his lip in pain.

The solders burst in.

"Get this human to the hospital, immediately," the medic instructed the main soldier. "It can't wait." They paused for a moment, unsure why a non-Royal would be of any consequence to them, but since it came from one of Sovereign Hamish's chief medics, they followed instructions without question.

Hamish was not as lucky. The remaining medics shook their heads. It would only be a few moments now. While the Royals were hearty by nature and could even regrow limbs and were resistant to infection, there was little to be done if the heart had been punctured. Ironic, as it would seem that having a heart really *was* the key to their undoing.

The medics backed away to give Fredo room to speak to his Sovereign. He knelt beside him and for the first time in his life, he began sobbing.

"Why the tears?" Hamish whispered, coughing up a bit of blood. "I thought you hated me?"

"So did I," Fredo confessed. "But I have been sworn to protect you my entire life. Without you, my life has no purpose."

"It most certainly does," Hamish responded. "There is one more in line for the throne. You must continue to protect him with your life."

Fredo was taken aback. Surely his child, the illegitimate one born between he and Sabrina was not now to become the sovereign? Fredo's feeble mind wondered how a baby could rule anything. The most he could do is protect it and guard it until it grew older. But who would rule until that time? (It should be noted that never once did Fredo consider that he could assume a leadership role.)

"I will protect the baby with my life," he swore to Hamish.

Hamish realized he had misunderstood him but merely smiled. "Of course, you will," he answered. With that, his eyes rolled back in his head.

Hamish was gone.

26

HAMISH AND CEPHEUS

FOUR DAYS BEFORE THE END.

Hamish sat in Cepheus's living area, gazing back with interest at two gray foxes that were peering at him curiously through the glass doors to the back patio. "Ah," Hamish said to them. "So, you can see me, too?" One of the foxes perched his front two paws on the door at the sound of his voice. He was still wearing the robe he was murdered in, but somehow, the bloodstain where he had been stabbed was not visible. Hamish wondered if he had somehow manifested that effect to save Cepheus from seeing him that way. He wasn't sure.

Cepheus awoke from a fitful sleep in his bedroom. While it was getting easier, he still had better luck sleeping on the bench in his office at TARA. He was instantly on his feet, tip-toeing toward the living room at the noise. "Petrichor, is that you?" he asked.

"No, my son," Hamish answered. "It is not. And why would Petrichor be here?" He was curious. It never occurred to him that he shouldn't have even been able to be there, and yet, there he was.

Cepheus was taken aback, eyeing his father's gossamer-like visage with surprise. "Are you—?"

"Dead?" Hamish finished. "Yes, it would appear so."

"What happened?" Cepheus asked, suspiciously. One could not help but be suspicious around his parents, even ones that were dead.

"Far happened."

"Roman's beloved? He…killed you?

"Yes," he nodded solemnly. "Listen, I'd love to stay for a chat, but I seem to have an awareness of some portal closing soon…or, being opened and closed. I don't have the exact details, but your mother has resurfaced and has been clamoring at me nonstop since I arrived. And, I'd rather not be stuck here between the layers when the Null get here."

Cepheus thought a moment. He knew that since Lucene had visited him, that the Null were coming. He just didn't understand how it would affect his dead father.

"Then, why are you here?"

"I came to warn you."

"Warn me about what?"

"The baby."

"So, there is another heir." It was the one piece of the puzzle that Cepheus hadn't quite worked out yet.

"Yes, but with my untimely death, the Royals—what's left of them, that is—are under the rein of Far…unless, of course, Fredo actually gets the courage to overthrow him. But frankly, I don't see that happening, at least not until the boy gets older."

"The baby is a boy?"

"Yes," Hamish nodded sadly. "There was never any rite of passage. No ceremony. I'm not even entirely certain that any of the remaining Royal military brigade even knows of his existence. I suppose Far has a plan for that, too. I clearly underestimated that weak little scrap of a man."

If Far had been occupying the same realm, Hamish wasn't aware of it, just as he was unaware of Far's demise not long after his.

"What have you come to warn me about, exactly? A baby is not exactly intimidating."

"No, but if Far has his way, he will assume control as the boy's guardian…or worse. And, the way I left things…"

"Yes," Cepheus was growing impatient, but not with his father. He was frustrated about how long it was taking him to fit all the pieces of this puzzle together.

"The Royals were planning on taking over Erde first, then the surrounding planets under its jurisdiction, and then Earth—if Earth is still habitable at that time."

"Erde. Why? Earth is much larger than any of the worlds we occupy with much of the terrain and air qualities more easily adaptable by our people."

"True," Hamish agreed. "But with Erde no longer a part of the IPP, it no longer has the protection of surrounding Sections. All on its own, your little planet is an easy target. Frankly, I should have thought of it sooner, but I suppose I had a soft spot because you lived here."

"I didn't think you had any soft spots," Cepheus replied, roughly. But in truth, he didn't mean it. This was not the first time Hamish had attempted redemption for his past treatment of his son.

Hamish let out a sigh. "His name is Cefeus the Second…spelled with an 'f' instead of a 'ph'."

Cepheus ground his teeth anxiously, a bead of sweat forming on his brow as his pupils narrowed angrily. It wasn't just that it was a version of his name. It was more that one of his twins was to bear his name, but the Royals took his family away. His son never got to grow up, and now he's learning that his father dared name the second son after him.

"It was meant to be respectful," Hamish tried. "I realize I'm not good at doing the right thing, but…I missed you."

"You missed me?" Cepheus as aghast.

"Believe me, if I could do it all over again, things would have been different…better."

"You would have spared my family?"

"Yes, and I probably would have murdered your mother earlier on."

"I'm not sure that's better."

Hamish suddenly glanced up as if he heard a sound. "Shut up, my darling. I'm talking to our son." It would seem that his mother, Sabrina, was lurking between the layers as well.

Cepheus realized that he hadn't been visited by Petrichor in quite some time, not since she'd encouraged him to learn how to love again.

"Can you see Petrichor?" Cepheus asked. "It's been quite some time since she's come to see me."

"No," Hamish was confused. "I don't think so. This place is rather murky and quiet. If she's here, I certainly haven't seen her."

Hamish looked down at his arms. They were fading in and out. "We're running out of time, please let me finish."

"Okay," Cepheus finally sat in the chair across from his father. "Finish."

"There was an amendment to the new contract between myself and the demon called Jasper Set." Cepheus waited for Hamish to continue. "Cefeus the Second was next in line to assume control of the Royals should anything happen to me, which—as you can see—it did. Unless—"

"Unless what?"

"Unless Cepheus the Senior returns to reclaim the throne."

"What? Why would you do that?"

"The High Royals are no longer a threat. I made sure of that by having Jasper send the Null to roll over their domains, sending them into oblivion. You could turn the Royal military brigade around, use them to defend yourselves against the Vitruvians."

"The Vitruvians? But they are our allies."

"Are they?" Hamish began fading.

Cepheus thought for a moment. Mistakenly, the Data Collectors were trying to protect Earth from the Royals and potentially Vitruvia. He was furious with himself as everyone's true motives came to light. Somehow, throughout all of the wars and deception, now Earthlings, the Royal clan, and the Vitruvians were all seeking a new target—Erde.

"Just one more thing, Father," Cepheus called. Hamish came back into focus, his face breaking into a smile at his son acknowledging him as 'father.' It was the first time, in a long time, he'd remember him doing so.

"Yes, my son?"

"You didn't need to change the spelling of Cefeus the Second's name."

"Of course, I did. Look at how we destroyed your life."

"No, Father, you didn't. I have a very good life."

With that, Hamish reached out a hand as if to touch his son's face in an uncharacteristic show of affection. "When you find Jasper Set, remember to demand to see a copy of the contract. It was my last Royal act." And with that, Hamish was gone.

Cepheus wasted no time in telling Moksha about the visit, who listened solemnly but said nothing. She put on a brave face, but Cepheus knew what she was thinking. She thought he was going to abandon her on Erde, but that wasn't the case at all.

Instead, he had to put a few things in motion first. Namely, he had to let Tanager, Lucene and Isabella know about the interaction, so that when they opened the portal, and assuming that Hamish was right and Jasper would surface, he had to demand to see the new contract. Given Lucene's recent vision of Jasper, he was fairly certain that this was the case. He also needed to enlist the help of Ivan. After all, the borders were closed after the recent attack from what they came to learn were Earthlings possessing Erde technology. So, if he was going to escape, hopefully taking Moksha with him, a vessel had to be prepared in secret.

While all this weighed heavily on Cepheus's mind, not to mention all the work he'd have to do to change protocol and behaviors at the Training Grounds, somehow, he felt a warm glow at the center of his chest. Something about all of this was…right.

27

MAKERSPACE REUNION

THREE DAYS BEFORE THE END.

"You know I support any decision you make, but I still don't understand why you chose to work for a minimum apprentice wage at the costume shop," Tanager protested as he and Lucene walked hand-in-hand toward the Makerspace. In his other hand, he carried a small briefcase. As usual, Lucene preferred to carry her notepad and pen in the backpack currently strapped across her shoulders.

Tanager eyed their surroundings, nervously. Given the air attack a few days ago along with the emergence of dire wolves and storms, he had become increasingly protective of Lucene. She wouldn't have been at the Makerspace today were it not for her insistence.

"My serving part-time as an 'advisor' for Commander Royce isn't exactly fulfilling," Lucene complained. "And it certainly doesn't pay as well as she seems to think it does," She paused while the glass doors of the main entrance slid open for them. Tanager waited while Lucene entered first. They paused again while a guard summoned them through a pathway that scanned them for outside weaponry and to confirm that they were who they said they are and not shapeshifters…yet another of the new protocols put in place as the

Makerspace attempted to curtail outside threats. "And furthermore, you think I don't know that it's really so that Royce can keep an eye on me as my powers re-emerge? She's not being supportive. She's just using me."

"I don't think that's…exactly true," Tanager replied, walking through the pathway while the scanner confirmed that Tanager was, in fact, Tanager. Lucene's imagery always came through as a swirling circle of red energy, something the guard had been briefed on, since no one else's form looked like that. They simply looked like outlines of, well, people. "I think she values your contribution to our team."

"And what, exactly, do I contribute?"

Tanager let out a sigh once they had reached his office. "My darling…" Tanager set down his briefcase and scanned his communication watch in front of the door to unlock it, something that would not have happened just a few months prior. He paused, placing the palms of his hands on her upper arms, rubbing them affectionately. "You contribute your knowledge and experience. You help with research and lesson plans. You have excellent problem-solving skills. And—" his forehead wrinkled a little.

"What?"

"Nothing?"

"No," Lucene followed him inside his office. "Not nothing. You always wrinkle your forehead when something is bothering you. What is it?"

"It's just that," Tanager framed his words carefully, "do I not provide you with everything you need to be…happy? Is there something missing in our lifestyle that makes you feel the need to earn more money?"

"Honey," Lucene explained. "It has nothing to do with money, per say, but I would like to contribute more to the household and not have you take on the lion's share."

Tanager made a mental note to look up "lion's share" later. He hadn't heard this Earth expression before. He'd only just learned about "honey," a term of affection he decided that he rather liked.

"What I mean is," Lucene continued. "I need to find something I'm good at besides laundry and grocery shopping…and I'm not all that great at those to start with." She thought back to the now-pink shirt of Tanager's that used to be red. He told her that it looked better bleached a blotchy pastel but she knew that he was only being polite.

"But you are excellent at growing herbs and repairing light sockets," Tanager pointed out.

"I think that has more to do with my weird energy and are not necessarily skills," Lucene had to admit. "Why are you so opposed to my part-time job at Mallory's shop when Pelimar was nice enough to take me on as an apprentice, even though I have no experience whatsoever? He's training me and pays me an actual wage as I learn. And, I get to negotiate for a raise in three months. How about that?"

"So," Tanager tumbled the ideas over in his brain like clothes in a drying machine. "It's not that you're unhappy with me," he added carefully, "or us. It's that you want something purposeful so that you can be happy with…yourself."

"Yes," Lucene smiled. "That's it, exactly."

"Well then," Tanager smiled, kissing her forehead. "I support you, wholeheartedly."

Before Lucene could ask why he thought she may have been unhappy with him, there was a knock at the door. Amy peeked her head around the corner. "Oh," she seemed surprised to see Lucene. She was holding a plate of wrapped muffins. "Sorry to interrupt." Amy decided to ignore Lucene altogether, catching Tanager's gaze and holding it. "I was baking last night and I remembered how much you liked my poppyseed muffins. Thought I'd bring you a batch."

Not just poppyseed muffins, Lucene thought bitterly. *Her poppyseed muffins. Specifically. Of course, because Amy bakes.*

A long, awkward pause ensued before Tanager responded.

"Thank you, Amy. That was very thoughtful of you." He glanced over at Lucene. "We'll certainly enjoy them at lunch today."

Lucene smiled to herself. *At least he said 'we,'* letting Amy know that she and Tanager were, indeed, a "we."

"Perhaps you'll join us for lunch if you have the time? We can share these together," Tanager finished.

No! No! No! Lucene thought. *Why couldn't you have stopped after the 'we!'* She turned to Tanager. "Well, I'm off to the Crafting room," she explained. "I'll see you at lunch." She forced a smile-less grin, which was quite difficult to manage. She didn't wait for a reply before marching past Amy, wordless. Lucene didn't wait to hear what happened after she left, hopefully, nothing. She quickened her pace toward the Crafting room so she could flip through sewing designs and find something to bring to Pelimar to teach her when she showed up for her apprenticeship again in the morning. Instead of taking the Transporter, she decided to walk the winding Fibonacci ramp several floors as it finally spun her in front of her chosen location. It was surprisingly quiet. She was, as it turned out, the only person there at the moment.

The crafting room had a cozy feel about it, despite the size. The areas were sectioned off with translucent, noise-filtering drapes. Depending on the zone, one would find crochet and knitting materials, traditional watercolor and acrylic paints and easels, or, in the case of the sewing area, a few outdated industrial sewing machines and handmade wooden cabinets filled with cloth-cutting scissors, fabrics and an assortment of needles for hand-made projects. Suddenly, the sparsity of both materials and people made sense. If the Makerspace was now serving a military purpose, one would assume that traditional arts and crafts would slow progress down. And with places such as Mallory and Pelimar's Costume shop providing uniforms, duffel bags and other materials, there was little need for this space. Lucene didn't mind. She could use this as her personal play station, and learn, and mess up, quietly to herself until she'd developed some skills. By then, she reasoned, things might actually return to normal.

Lucene could have easily pulled up designs from the electronic library collection but there was something about the musty smell of old, worn-out books that she loved. Because, also in the cabinet was a collection of tall, faux-leather-bound design books. She found one on women's fashion from a place she had never heard of. She brought it carefully over to a work table and sat down on the end of a long bench and began carefully turning the heavy pages so as not to accidentally free any yellowed sheets from the binding.

One page featured a long, cream-colored chiffon skirt that was long in places and short in others with a lopsided blouse to match. *Maybe not for The Beacon,* she thought. *But this is definitely Bistro material. Eat your heart out, Brie.*

"Not something I would think to choose for you, but striking, nonetheless," a male voice announced over Lucene's shoulder. Lucene shuddered. She remembered that ego-filled accent…Dallen. The Vitruvian ambassador who she dated briefly last year before she realized that, for one thing, she didn't want to change everything about herself to be "worthy" of hanging on his arm. And, for another thing, she did not appreciate his talent for ghosting people. He and his representatives high-tailed it out of Erde when it became clear that an alliance between Erde and Vitruvia to rejoin the Intergalactic Peace Project would not be possible. And that was after he disappeared from her life without warning, only to resurface soon after and assume that their relationship would go on, business as usual.

"How did you get in here?" Lucene asked, candidly.

"Not exactly the greeting I was hoping for," he opened his arms, "no hug for your old friend?"

"We're not friends," Lucene reminded him.

"No," he agreed, "though I wish we were." Once he realized that a hug was not going to happen, he awkwardly lowered his arms, standing there in the exact same uniform with the exact same gold hair that was so bright it reflected light off of it.

"I'll ask again," Lucene was guarded, "how did you get in here without an escort? That was protocol even before the recent security changes."

"You simple girl," Dallen shook his head, "who do you think installed those measures in the first place?"

"So, it's true?" Lucene had been doubtful until this moment. "Commander Royce has been selling you information and technology in exchange for Vitruvians funding the Makerspace."

He leaned forward to run a finger down the side of her face. She grabbed it and bent it backward just as Moksha had taught her to do.

"Ouch!" he yelled, pulling his hand back. It was then that she noticed several men behind the noise-shielding drapes. "It's all right," he called to them. "Stand down." To Lucene, he asked, "What was that for? I thought you liked it when I was affectionate."

"Not anymore," she answered. "Keep your hands to yourself."

"My, we are feisty these days, aren't we?" He smiled, almost approvingly. "I think I like this more aggressive side of you."

Lucene felt a sudden bitterness in the pit of her stomach. She put her hand over her communication watch and twisted the ring around it once to the left and then tugged it upward to set off a silent alarm.

"I'm afraid that won't work," Dallen commented. "My system, remember? That was the first thing I had shut down. Helps that I also had access to your watch for necessary re-programming some time ago." He paused for the information to sink in. It was Dallen who was responsible for confiscating her watch at the Embassy Club that day, and Dallen who had it later returned to her cottage, leaving her to falsely believe that she had forgotten it, somehow. "Yes," he read her facial expressions. "I always know exactly where you are and when."

"And, *what exactly* do you want?" Lucene demanded, grabbing a pair of jagged cloth cutters from the cabinet. One of Dallen's guards immediately came up behind her and wrenched it from her right hand and attempted to wrap her neck in a chokehold. She stepped back, reflexively, scraping her heel against his shin as he let out a howl. She wrapped one arm around his waist and pivoted him across her hip, landing him with a loud thud onto the sewing table. Two more guards emerged but Dallen held his hand up, commanding them to be still.

"What I want," Dallen answered calmly, "is *you*. I thought that was obvious."

"I told you 'no' before and I'm unavailable now."

"Ah, yes," Dallen grinned, "Tanager." The guard on the table rolled over, steadying himself as he stood, shooting an angry glare in Lucene's direction. "While romance would be nice, that's not what I want you for."

"Then what? My powers are gone," she lied. "What use am I to you?"

"Well, you see…" Dallen took a step toward her before she shot him a warning glance. He held his hands up in surrender and took a step backward. "That's not exactly true, is it?"

"What are you talking about?" Lucene demanded.

"That shapeshifter you healed at the dance club…" he said. "What was that about?"

"How did you—" Lucene stopped herself. There were hundreds of people who could have reported it, but at that moment, there was only one who came to mind…Odessa. "Oh." Lucene fell silent.

"She proved to be useful after all," Dallen acknowledged. "I may know where you are but I can't always know what you're up to without informants." He watched her micro-expressions fluctuate between anger, horror and defeat and found it highly amusing. "I also learned about the little portal you opened up. So, you see, you may be the woman I *have* always dreamt about."

"A weapon," she stated flatly.

"A weapon, a healer, a tool—" he paused as her face crumbled.

"Oh, don't look so offended. That's all you really are here. Do you think Tanager would be half as interested in you if you weren't fascinatingly damaged with a hint of supernatural possibility? Intellectuals like that love a puzzle. And you, Lucene, are quite the puzzle."

"There are others who have this skill," Lucene caught herself before mentioning Morphinae's name, just in case Dallen didn't already know, or the Data Collectors in training such as Clusaladek, Xeni and Neroni. Though, she assumed that he did. "Why me?"

"Because I don't want them," Dallen stamped his foot like a small child. "I want you." He contorted his face. He thought emotions such as love were primitive and he didn't particularly like the way he felt about Lucene. Though, the emotions seemed less difficult when she was with him then when she was not. Therefore, he assumed that having her by his side was the simplest solution.

There were more guards that emerged from around the room, surrounding her. "Let's not make a scene. I simply want you to accompany me back to Vitruvia where you will become my dutiful companion. I promise you won't want for anything. And in exchange, you will help us in our efforts to occupy Erde."

"Wait…what?" Lucene was confused.

Dallen let out the most rambunctious laugh that she had ever heard. "Oh, you didn't know that part, did you?" He paused. She shook her head. He shook his head, mocking her. "That's the best part. All this time, your Data Collectors have been trying to protect Earth from invasion and environmental destruction, and yet, all this time, Vitruvia has been feeding Earth technology…Erde's technology. So, while you are doing the noble work of saving Earth, it's been trying to destroy you."

"No, that can't be true," Lucene protested. And yet, somewhere in the back of her mind, she feared it might be.

"Look around," Dallen challenged. "Vitruvia *did* want to align with Erde to defeat the Royals—a little matter that Sovereign Hamish and Jasper Set conveniently settled by having the Null destroy the major Royal clan. Vitruvia is a thriving planet. Erde has the same potential. Well, we couldn't very well offer Earthlings the opportunity to settle in our domain without a few rules in place, now, could we? Therefore, in exchange for jurisdiction and allegiance, we promised them—"

"Erde," Lucene finished, horrified.

"Perhaps you are not so simple after all. But you can be a good girl and accompany me to Vitruvia. If you do, I promise not to harm any of your Erde pals—not a single curly lock on your boyfriend Tanager's lovely little head."

"But there's only one thing I don't understand," Lucene questioned.

"Only one?" Dallen was skeptical. Lucene chose to ignore him.

"Inventors like Ivan were willing to help advance Earth and were shot down and pegged as terrorists before they could even get started. If they already had the technology in house…why?"

"I suppose it's all in the marketing," Dallen reasoned. "*Know your audience.* Isn't that what they say on Earth? *Read the room.* Your friend Ivan was empowering the masses. That's not what leaders want. They want to subdue the masses and empower the sovereigns. A simple truth that your very humanity-conscious friend, Ivan, never understood."

As if on cue, Ivan burst into the room with a Vitruvian guard strapped to his back and three more at his heels. "Lucene, are ye okay? I came as soon as I'd heard." He leaned over and flipped the guard on his back to the ground, seemingly with ease. Two others flanked him on each side.

"How?" Dallen asked, calmly. "I blocked the signal."

"Not from me, ye didn't," Ivan growled. "Workaround," he added in a huff, as it came to fisticuffs with the two men pursuing him. "Aww, c'mon then," he reasoned, "I left this kinda gang life years ago. Vowed never to go back. Don't make me embarrass ye in front of your sovereign, now…"

But Dallen's men were relentless and obviously less genteel with Ivan than with Lucene, as Dallen did nothing to keep them at bay. They pounded on Ivan mercilessly as his thick frame took a beating.

"Stop it!" Lucene wailed, coming to Ivan's aid. She landed a front kick to the side of one assailant's knees, causing a loud crunch as the man crumbled in pain. To the other, she dug an elbow into his spine, assisted by a press from her supporting hand. She followed this by reaching her arm around and digging her fingers under the man's chin, pulling his head back while pivoting her torso away from him and pressing her foot behind his knee. His knee buckled. She assisted his fall with her left hand as her right delivered a punch to his kidneys. He crumpled to the floor.

Moksha, you beautiful assassin, you, Lucene praised in her mind. *Thanks for the training.*

The persistent man rolled over and grabbed her ankle. Lucene was about to dig the heel of her opposite foot into the man's crotch, but by then, Dallen's men resorted to weaponry, now poising a laser gun at Ivan's head. Lucene stopped in her tracks, putting her foot down.

Somehow, Ivan could feel the heat of the laser. He put his hands up in surrender. But in an uncustomary surrender-like way he pleaded, "Look, man. I may have gotten into a wee mess of trouble as a young lad. But thah's not how I am today. I vowed never to kill another. Don't make me start today."

The man behind him found this funny, his finger on the trigger. But instead of aiming it at Ivan's head, he repositioned it to center a bright green beam on Lucene's forehead.

"No!" Ivan yelled, spinning around and knocking the guard's weapon free as it fired, grazing the top of Lucene's hairline. It burned her scalp lightly as it shot into the wall behind her. The man smacked the butt of the gun's handle into Ivan's temple, and it took only moments for the guard to reposition as a bloody Ivan clutched his head, trying to regain his wits enough to react.

"Not the girl," Dallen yelled, angrily at the guard. He didn't jump in front of Lucene to protect her, exactly. More like sidled up next to her and pushed her head down in an attempt to get her to duck. She fell on top of the man holding her ankle, knocking the wind out of him.

Not much of a hero, Lucene realized, rolling off of the guard. Not that she had ever expected that he would be.

Another shot rang out as Ivan tackled the guard that was attacking them. Dallen fell, a dribble of blood leaking from his neck.

"Ah no!" Ivan cried, head in hands. His worst nightmare come true. He ran over to Lucene first, now sitting up from her spill on the hard floor. "Ye okay?"

Lucene caught her breath and nodded.

Ivan turned his attention to Dallen, now lying in a heap on the floor. Ivan rolled him over as the ambassador's eyes rolled back in his head. Lucene crawled over and felt his pulse…light but steady. "He's alive," Lucene told Ivan, to his relief.

"Of course, he is," a female voice called, just as Commander Royce, Constable Melokuhle, and others rushed in, seizing Dallen's guards and subduing them. The voice belonged to none other than Amy.

It was then that Ivan and Lucene noticed something. There, in the neck of Dallen, was an ever-so-tiny hand-sculpted figurine of a soldier, with the tiniest of metal blades protruding from his head. It was one from the large model that Amy had been showing Lucene and Tanager earlier that month. "Don't worry," Amy reassured, "it's toxic enough to paralyze, but not to kill. He'll be fine in a few hours."

Ivan was relieved. Lucene…surprised. Had Amy not intervened, there was a good chance that she and Ivan would have been dead, or abducted. Either way, she was in the small-framed, red-haired woman's debt.

"Thank you," Lucene told Amy, quietly.

"Don't thank me," Amy answered, the rims of her eyes slightly red. "I didn't do it for you."

No, Lucene thought. *Of course, you didn't.*

Thirty Minutes Prior…in the Military Transportation Lab

Ivan was in the Military Transportation Lab during one of the only times he was confident that the Makerspace would be relatively quiet. Most of the work he did to prepare Cepheus's escape pod, he did in the middle of the night by disabling the tracker on his communication watch. And, on the off chance a security guard noticed his presence, he was able to convince them he was doing firmware updates that could only happen when computer devices were not being used by students or outside vendors renting the space.

He peeked under a black tarp that he used to cover the small vessel. At present, it was about the size of a compact car designed to unfold and enlarge into four times its size once out of Erde's atmosphere. Ivan laughed to himself. All he did was post an, "Out of Order" sign on the outside of the tarp, along with a second sign that read, "Dangerous voltage - Do not touch," and no one messed with his project.

Now, there was just one thing left to check. He had to be able to disable the security system so that no alarms would sound when Cepheus and, hopefully Moksha, made their escape.

He removed the cover of his communication watch using a simple 3-D printed eyeglass toolkit. (Yes, he invented that, too.) But when Ivan lifted the face off the frame of the watch, something was wrong.

"What the—" he took out a magnifying glass and looked closer. The little red beacon inside that was used as their "panic button" to set off the alarms had been disabled. It didn't flash blue periodically to show that it was working. Someone had already disabled it.

"Ivan!" A flushed Amy ran into the room. She was out of breath. "I…me…Transporter…Renenet…" She bent over and placed her hands on her knees to catch her breath. When she couldn't, she pointed. There, slumped over the door to the Transporter was Renenet. Her uniform was blood-soaked, forming a pool on the platform outside. Ivan ran over to her and felt for a pulse, but it was too late. Renenet's face and arms were bruised a deep purple from where she tried to fend off her attackers.

Ivan lost no time in returning to his abandoned watch. With a few split-second adjustments, it lit up and the entire Makerspace began wailing at the sound of the alarm. The Transporter that carried Renenet also sprang back to life.

"C'mon!" He grabbed Amy's hand and pulled her after him toward the vehicle. Amy braced herself, seeing her friend's mangled body.

"I can't!" she cried, pulling back as she fought off nausea.

It was then that the sound of voices and boots on the ground could be heard echoing through the winding halls that led to some of the internal, smaller rooms.

Ivan had no choice. "Sorry," he apologized to the dead Renenet as he dumped her body onto the platform and climbed inside. To Amy, he said, "Ye have to git in. I dunno who we're up against. But ye can't stay here alone!"

Amy sucked in a deep breath and nodded. She didn't even wait for Ivan to unlatch the door and slide it open for her; she put her hands on the door frame and vaulted herself over the wall. It was impressive. Even Ivan paused for a moment.

"Well?" She looked at the controls.

"Right."

They had intended to follow the shortest track to the safety of the outside world and wait for backup. Instead, what happened was an interception of the Transporter's signal, hauling them at great speed swirling down the circle, coming to a stop in front of the Crafting room where the Transporter stopped so abruptly that Amy and Ivan were thrown against the sides of it, and ended up landing on the metal floor in two heaps.

From the floor, Ivan's head spun dizzily. Then he heard people talking… *Lucene!* He realized, *she's in trouble.* As he fought with the door and spilled out onto the platform, two guards descended on him. He peered over his shoulder at the slight frame of Amy, still crumpled in the corner of the Transporter. She was so small; they didn't notice her. He took his foot and kicked at the Transporter's door, slamming it shut with Amy still inside.

The guards dragged him to his feet. It was then that Ivan the tinkerer, middle-aged man, father of Talula and husband of Fatima tapped into something he'd shut away a long time ago…his past. And for the first time since he was a teenager, he picked up fists and started punching.

28

ROYCE AND DALLEN FACE OFF
THREE DAYS BEFORE THE END.

"What the hell were you thinking?" Commander Royce screamed at Representative Dallen, slamming her fists on the table in the Planetary Defense League's Negotiation Room. He flinched slightly but was otherwise unaffected.

When Royce discovered Dallen in the Makerspace trying to abduct Lucene, she made a show of "arresting" him, though Ivan, Lucene and Amy couldn't help but notice that Constable Melokule and the security guards were awfully gentle with the dignitary. They hadn't even bothered to bind his hands behind his back, and yet he followed her, agreeably. The guards were rougher on Dallen's security team, particularly after they learned of Renenet's death.

"Come now, Commander Royce," Dallen flashed a smile. "Don't you think you're over-reacting?"

"You killed the PDL director who oversees TARA, a very trusted and loyal friend at that!" Royce, who hadn't previously exhibited obvious outbursts seemed about to throw a full-on fit.

"Unfortunately," Dallen replied, emotionless, "we didn't realize just how loyal. And, as a slight correction, I didn't kill her. One of my men did, in self-defense."

"Because they were where they shouldn't be, and she was following protocol to have them arrested!"

"I apologize for the aggressiveness of my men. However," he continued calmly, "they shouldn't have been apprehended. We have every right to be in the Makerspace. After all, Vitruvia pays for it."

"That wasn't part of our arrangement," Royce began grinding her teeth. "And I thought I told you that the girl was hand's off."

Dallen's face crumbled for the shortest of moments before recovering. "But—" he began defensively, before becoming silent.

"What?" Royce put her hands on the table, her gray-black hair spilling all over it. She leaned in ominously, which was no easy feat for a small woman with deep-set eyes and an abundance of wrinkles. And yet, Dallen was taken aback. "You're going to tell me that Vitruvia pays for her, too?"

Dallen slunk back in his chair. In the back of his mind, he wanted to answer, "her training, yes." But then he realized that even that was no longer true. In fact, when he had abandoned her last year, he also cut off funding to TARA's research, her training and the cottage where she lived. In a moment of something that resembles remorse, he had to admit that if Tanager and Cepheus hadn't stepped in to cover her expenses, unbeknownst to Lucene, and Royce hadn't taken pity on the girl making her an honorary "agent" of the PDL, Lucene could have actually become homeless on this planet. He thought for a moment that his actions may have been hasty, but then dismissed them. After all, he was a dignitary of the highest breed. They simply didn't make mistakes like that.

Dallen shrugged his shoulders as a stressed bird might ruffle its feathers. "I don't have time for this, Commander Royce. Just tell me how we can smooth over this little matter." He turned his head away. He wasn't even able to meet her gaze.

Royce took a deep breath, sighing it out heavily. "There is no *smoothing* over this little matter,'" she answered. "I want you and all Vitruvians—" she paused a moment, thinking of Odessa and other shapeshifters who'd sought sanctuary on Erde over the years. "All Vitruvians under your command, and not under the protection of Erde due to sanctuary laws, off of this planet immediately. We will no longer accept your financial support, nor will we turn over any new technological findings to Vitruvia. All new discoveries remain the intellectual property of Erde."

Dallen jumped from his seat. "But that's absurd? That research belongs to us! We paved the way for these discoveries!"

"Please let me finish," Commander Royce continued calmly. "In exchange for this agreement, we will not contact the Vitruvian government and seek to execute charges against you and your men for the death of my esteemed director, Officer Renenet. And we will overlook your attempt to abscond with our PDL agent, Lucene Jones, against her will."

"Agent…really, pshh—" he mocked.

"I assure you," Royce replied curtly, "she is a valued member of our team…and, a *human being*," Royce reminded him.

Dallen's gaze met Royce's. "Do you have any idea what you are doing? Earth already has much of your weaponry. Between Earth and Vitruvia, Erde doesn't stand a chance against us should we decide to occupy. And without our financial support, your economy would be in ruins."

For the first time in her long life, Commander Royce knew exactly what the Elders would have her do without waking them up. It was a gamble, and a leap of faith, but something worthy of the Peace-Keepers. "My offer stands," she answered. "Leave immediately, and we won't file charges against you. Just know that if any Vitruvian sets foot on this planet without express permission from the PDL, they will be arrested immediately."

Two guards who flanked Dallen on either side coughed uneasily. They didn't expect their leader to agree to this. They expected him to threaten immediate occupation of Erde and to hold Royce, herself, as hostage, to force Erde to bend to their will. But somehow… that isn't what happened. Whether this had anything to do with the blurred lines of reality or the sudden image Dallen had of Lucene burning in his brain, encouraging him to 'do the right thing,' he couldn't be sure. But, without any fanfare, he agreed to her terms.

Dallen, his guards, and fellow representatives moved out of Erde the next morning, leaving Erde to, as was always the case when Ambassador Dallen left the planet, pick up the pieces.

29

AT THE CROSSROADS
THE END. NOW.

If they hadn't realized where the Crossroads had been prior, it had become blatantly obvious now as storm clouds gathered directly over the Embassy Club, a swirling tornado-like funnel swarming slowly on the rooftop. The storms had been increasing each day as they got closer to the pink moon being full. With each swirl, more and more of the rooftop was jarred loose as the thunderous wind picked at pieces of the shingles that had been secured there. The ground shook, and it became challenging to remain upright.

"This way," Reverend Isabella summoned Lucene and Tanager to follow. Isabella had summoned Lucene the evening prior, letting her know that it was time. Tanager was not needed in the process as Isabella had informed him, more than once. But if Isabella's ceremony included using Lucene to close the portal, then he was going to be there…just in case. Just in case…what? He didn't know. But he refused to leave Lucene's side. Each of them carried a separate basket of supplies, the contents of which were unknown to everyone except for the priestess.

It was easy keeping the streets clear that day, as news reports of the strange weather encouraged everyone to stay indoors and take cover until it passed. A few reporters showed up at the Embassy Club with cameras and microphones but were quickly silenced by Commander Royce's team. Normally, she would not have been moved to do so as Erde had always permitted its people to speak freely. But given the gravity of this situation, coupled with the bull's eye she had now placed on her back, thanks to her sending Dallen and the Vitruvians packing, she wasn't taking chances nor risking sending Erdelings into a panic.

She had some knowledge of the 'other realms' from her meetings with the Elders over the years, much of which she shared with an untrusting Isabella, not that she blamed the priestess. Royce recognized that she had much to be regretful about. She understood what many did not, that if left unsealed, the leak could possibly grow and suck everyone into it…and let a few more beings out, including Jasper Set.

Reverend Isabella eyed the reporters as they were hastened away with disgust. It was half for them and their constant portrayal of her as a charlatan, and half directed toward herself. *How is it that, in spite of my best intentions, I manage to create a scene in lifetime after lifetime? How is it that I always mess up? Is this a testimony to me and my lineage?* She thought of Far and shook her head, sadly.

But enough of that. They had their 'team' in place, and it was show time.

Before entering the building, Isabella spotted Kiki "the nose" around the corner. She purposefully sniffed the air before vanishing, her way of letting them know that Hysechia was just around the bend. The three quickened their steps, making their way past the reception area and into the main dining hall of the Embassy Club. But this time, instead of a central stage for the band, there was a swirling pool of red that seemed to circle the orchestra pit like water circling a drain. If one were to peer over the edge, there was nothing by a turbulent mass of liquid and gas that bubbled up like lava. Tables and chairs surrounding the pit were either tossed on their sides or covered with shards of glass from broken vases and scattered rose petals from last night's dinner seating. Apparently, diners had to be evacuated quickly as this monstrosity of a wormhole opened up suddenly. The only positive note in all this is that the band had been delayed on account of Hysechia managing to tear up tracks on the SpeedCircuit, causing trains to have to divert and find alternate routes—yet another reason why Hysechia had to be stopped. She would have killed the band, and countless other people, if left to her own devices.

Isabella set to work, thrusting the basket toward Tanager. "You can make yourself useful by placing these stones around the vortex, about a foot apart and two feet away from the opening of the hole." He took the handle and dropped his arm slightly…heavy. He clasped it with both hands. Clearly, Reverend Isabella was as strong as an ox. "And don't fall in…lover-boy," she winked.

He let out a sigh. Tanager wasn't entirely sure that Isabella liked him very much. Or maybe she did but she didn't seem to respect him. *Lover-boy,* he thought to himself. *How demeaning.* Still, his first concern was Lucene. His second concern was everyone else, and… well, that about summed it up. Tanager followed instructions and started his trail of stones around the mouth of the opening. He peered curiously over the edge, sweat beginning to bead around his forehead. The pit was a swirling pool of red, and it kicked off the heat of a thousand suns (or maybe Tanager was exaggerating, but it was pretty damn hot). He could see no end to the abyss, and as the swirling continued, it slowly expanded. He worked more quickly.

"What can I do?" Lucene wanted to know.

"You can sit down and be quiet," Isabella answered. Lucine crinkled her lips and pursed them to one side. *Perhaps I am being a little harsh,* Isabella thought to herself. "You will have plenty to do soon enough. You need to conserve your energy," she softened. For whatever reason, Lucene bypassed actually setting one of the chairs upright and sitting on it, in favor of planting herself directly on the floor and crossing her legs underneath her. Somehow, this felt like the thing to do, although she wasn't sure why. Perhaps she just felt more grounded this way.

"So," Lucene spoke, "I'm confused. I thought we were re-opening the portal using yours truly. But it looks as if it's already open, all by itself," Lucene stated the obvious.

"Yes," Isabella answered, thoughtfully. "Ever have one of those loose flappers inside an old toilet?"

"Yes."

"At first, it stops sealing properly, and so the water never really fills the tank without someone pushing it back in place. Then, it opens up one day when triggered and refuses to close altogether."

"Not sure I follow," Lucene confessed.

"Too many beings able to wheedle their way in and out between the layers triggered a larger problem. I'm hoping you can help fix it."

"Am I the toilet flapper in this scenario?" Lucene wanted to know.

"I'm afraid so," Isabella confessed.

Outside, Hysechia crept cautiously up to the door with Marzipan's travel cage strapped to her back. Marzipan clung helplessly onto a few makeshift branches as the feline lumbered toward the Embassy entrance. Next to her, was another feline. He called himself Odin and he was very handsome. His fur was an odd blend of white mixed with light blue stripes—something that Hysechia had never witnessed before but quickly decided that she loved.

"Are you sure?" Hysechia asked her new partner. She had only met Odin recently, when she serendipitously ran into the fellow feline at a local park. Hysechia was there to feast on a new leash of foxes that had set up residence there. Odin, being rather clumsy, had alerted the foxes of his presence, sending them scattering in all directions. Hysechia would have normally been annoyed by this, given her current state of hunger. But Odin merely bared an innocent grin and flicked his tail with interest at the other feline predator in his midst. He enquired about the little half-boy and half-ladybug strapped to her back, and Hysechia was all too quick to fill him in. She had been between the layers for so long and it was certainly nice to have companionship.

"Most definitely," Odin nodded his thick head. "Given what you've told me about this…Isabella, is it? I'd say she has it coming."

Hysechia nodded. "She most certainly does. But—"

"But what?" Odin asked.

"What if I accidentally get trapped between the layers again? I may, once again, be reduced to a common house cat, unable to stalk and prey as I like."

"Would that be so terrible?" Odin asked. "To be cared for and fed regularly?"

"Of course, it would!" Hysechia hissed. "Would you want the life of a kept cat for yourself?"

"No," Odin had to admit, "I would not."

"Then, tell me why we're doing this again?" Hysechia challenged. She was beginning to doubt her knew partner.

"Because you want revenge on the person who reduced you to a common house cat," Odin reasoned. "Isn't that why you are so cross with Rev…" Odin caught himself. "This revolting human?"

Hysechia nodded. "Yes, it is true. But—"

"But what?" Odin persisted.

"I'm trying to weigh my options here and you're not helping!" Hysechia hissed.

"Forgive me, my lovely Hysechia. I did not mean to make someone as wondrous as yourself so angry."

Hysechia caught herself. Marzipan rolled his eyes and crossed his arms from his travel cage. He even kicked a fake pebble in annoyance. But that merely threw the cage off kilter and he was knocked sideways. Rubbing his hip, he stood.

"I'm not angry," Hysechia bared her teeth in a smile. "And," she relented, "I concur. The only solution is to go inside and toss the revolting Isabella into the vortex. Then, we seal her in it, just as she did to me."

"Purr-fect," Odin rolled his R's luxuriously. "Unless you want to scrap the whole 'revenge' thing and go hunting in the forest again. I support that, too."

"No," Hysechia lifted her upper lip defiantly. "She needs to be punished.

With that, Hysechia, Odin and Marzipan entered the Embassy Club as if they were dignitaries and had actually been invited.

The lobby was dark, but they made their way to the main hall, pausing at the archway, unseen. Tanager had finished putting the circle of stones around the hole and was now on to some strange saging ritual that Isabella had tasked him with. He had a vague notion of what to do after having watched Lucene perform this repeatedly in their high-home. For someone who was of no use, she seemed to be using him quite a lot, he thought. Every few moments, he glanced over at Lucene who was constantly peering around the room with a combination of bewilderment and fear. Occasionally, their eyes met and he would smile and then she would smile. For that micro-moment, everything in the world was okay.

As for the rest of the world, it was silent. Each detail was measured, thought out and protected. And so, Cepheus, Moksha, Ivan, Fatima and everyone else they knew were radio silent because anything might throw their plan off and cause it to fail.

"Mis-s-s—s me?" A familiar voice suddenly called. No one could see the infamous demon, Jasper Set, but his voice echoed the halls as vibrantly as an opera singer's final aria.

"Are you friggin' kidding me?" Lucene blurted out. They expected his arrival once the portal was officially re-opened, but not now.

"Nope, nope and…nope!" Jasper's voice sailed around her. "Not friggin' kidding you. Not even plain old kidding you! Just…here!"

"How?" Lucene asked as Tanager and Isabella held still. Even the two felines in the lobby with the poor little Marzipan in tow stopped, cautiously.

There was a loud rumbling sound outside, unlike anything they had ever heard before, almost as if thunderclouds were rolling in slow motion across the sky. This was followed by a cacophony of whistles and pops and an odd chattering that sounded like rattlesnakes.

"Uh oh," Jasper cupped his hand behind his ear, "sounds like the mamas and the papas are here."

"What?" Isabella was incredulous. "You brought the Null people…here? How…when you were trapped between the layers?" They knew his plan because he had not-so-discreetly shared it with Lucene during her meditation. What they couldn't figure out was how he was already out and about.

"Wrong, my dear Rev…Rev…" He still couldn't bring himself to say it. "Is-s-s-s-s-abella," he finished. "You trapped the future me between the layers. Remember, time is a wee bit behind here. In fact, I wonder if I might s-s-s-s-s-top you from s-s-s-s-s-ending me there in the fir-s-s-s-s-t place."

Isabella was at a loss. If she abandoned her efforts, then Jasper Set—the old one—would still be free and it would take only a matter of moments before the Null rolled over their planet and turned it into nothing but empty space.

While Isabella, Tanager and Lucene pondered on the gravity of the situation, Odin was busy unstrapping Marzipan from Hysechia's back.

"What are you doing?" Hysechia whispered.

"I am only getting the annoying little firefly prepared for—"

"I am not a firefly," Marzipan protested.

Odin leaned in closely, so close that when he inhaled, Marzipan almost got sucked into his left nostril. "Quiet, firefly," he warned. "You are hanging on by a wing and a prayer and only because you are useful."

There was a gleam in Odin's eyes, and suddenly, Marzipan saw it. He opened his mouth to speak. "Oh, you're—" but Marzipan caught himself, clasping his own hands over his mouth in case the words escaped, accidentally.

Hysechia became distracted, hunching low to the ground and wiggling her hind quarters like a cat about to pounce on her prey.

"It s-s-s-s-seems we have vis-s-s-itors," Jasper noted.

Isabella looked up in time to see Hysechia's feline form lunging toward her. She pounced…so did Odin. Just as Hysechia reached Isabella, Odin's giant paw stepped on the cat's tail. Hysechia let out a roar.

"You betray me!" Hysechia tugged at her tail with all her might. "Let me go!" Odin hung on tightly as Hysechia kept pulling.

"Very well," Odin answered finally, lifting his paw with the next tug. When he did, Hysechia catapulted past Isabella into the abyss. She reached a paw out and swatted at her nemesis before falling, and Isabella lost her balance. About to fall face-first after the feline who was now spiraling downward into the pit, Isabella felt an arm wrap around her waist and pull her backward. She landed on top of Lucene with a thud, accidentally jamming an elbow into Lucene's ribs.

"Ow!" Lucene whined. "How come all of our encounters end up with me falling on my ass with the wind knocked out of me?"

Lucene and Isabella rolled over and crawled to the edge of the pit in time to see Hysechia disappear moments later with nothing by the echo of a loud wail spiraling back upward. Odin peered over their shoulders. Isabella recoiled with a start. But not Lucene.

"Odessa," Lucene acknowledged, "you look good as a cat."

"Why thank you—" Odin's voice changed into its female counterpart but her cat form remained. "Hang on," Odessa was surprised, "how'd you know it was me?"

"Your smell," Lucene lied.

"Hmph," Odessa actually sat on her hind quarters and crossed her paws as if crossing her arms. "No, really." Lucene didn't answer. But somehow, she saw what little Marzipan had seen. There, deep in her pupils, was her soul. And it was the soul of one Vitruvian "not-a-mermaid."

"Are you all right?" Tanager gasped, having circumvented the pit and was now at Lucene's side, out of breath.

Lucene didn't have time to answer as the wind picked up with a thunderous roar, debris beginning to fall as the roof of the club was ripped off in its entirety. Overhead, the Null began to gather as if looking for someone…their lost son, Jasper.

"Hate to dis-s-s-sturb this s-s-s-s-weet little reunion. But I believe this is the end."

"But if you allow the Null to destroy us, won't you be killed too?" Lucene asked.

"Hmmm…hadn't really thought of that. What do you s-s-s-s-s-uggest?"

"I suggest you send your family into the portal and let us seal them inside," Lucene answered.

"How does this in anyway benefit me?" Jasper wanted to know. The angry sounds of hissing grew louder. His parents were upset with him and he knew it. Though, he wasn't sure if they were angry at the current version of him or the version stuck between the layers. Somehow, as a demon, he was aware of both of his "selves" simultaneously, across time, an awareness that left him with the nastiest of headaches.

Obviously, they were both the same demon, but still…was it that the Null assumed he ran away? That they learned how he diverted them from some planets and directed them toward others? Or had they caught on to his only fear…that they would realize that he wasn't a spawn of the Null nor a gift of the great Segue. He was just an ordinary demon, one that the Null would need to destroy just as they had done to all the others, along with their accompanying worlds.

He shrank his large torso as if a turtle trying to stuff his head back into his suit jacket. He wasn't having much success. "Okay, I s-s-s-s-ee your point," Jasper whispered, even though he was mostly sure the Null couldn't understand them. Perhaps his Null mamas and papas would, in fact, kill him, too. "I'm always up for a good bargain. I tell you what. Gather 'round children." He motioned for Isabella, Lucene, Tanager and Odessa to move closer. They did so with much reluctance, never taking their eyes off the demon. "There's a s-s-s-s-tory about a prophet leading the Null directly to the throne of the Mighty Segue. Perhaps-s-s-s one of you might," he motioned his eyes toward the pit, "take a tumble for the greater good? The Null will follow. I will make sure of that."

"Can't you lead them?" Tanager asked. "Surely, if you direct them, they will follow your direction and you can escape before we seal the portal."

"While I do appreciate your excellent plan," Jasper Set mocked, "pardon the pun, but it's hotter than hell down there…even for a demon! No thanks. I'll pas-s-s-s."

"I'll do it," Marzipan called from the travel cage. They had forgotten about the little firefly. "I can fly overtop and then buzz away really fast at the last minute. My wings are heat-resistant," he announced triumphantly.

Odessa pranced over to retrieve the cage, picking the handle up in her mouth and returning to the group. "I don't think so, little man," she mumbled, putting him down. "That heat will melt your wings in a heartbeat, despite your 'heat resistance.'" Given that his wings were already sticking to the side of his round body, he was forced to admit that she might be right. Still, it was brave of him to offer.

"No," everyone looked up to see Tanager was already perched on the edge of the pit. "I'll do it."

"No!" Lucene protested. "I can't let you do that!"

"Lucene, Isabella can't do it because she is the only one who knows how to seal the portal. You can't do it because she needs you to do it."

Just then, there were confused sounds emanating from the kitchen area. "How?" Lucene began to ask before remembering… time is different here. Commander Royce may have cleared the area of pedestrians in our time, but those at the back door were coming in for their night shift. They were from the past. This world was on a loop.

"Odessa, get them out of here!" Tanager commanded.

"Leave the bug," Isabella cautioned. "We need him." It was then that Lucene clued in to Marzipan's superpower. Why hadn't she realized it sooner? She had the sudden image of Marzipan gorging himself on too much sugary foods and…

Odessa nodded, taking off at tiger speed to chase the would-be workers out of the kitchen. The swift movement jarred Lucene away from her thoughts.

The Null began descending before anyone could argue with him. Lucene moved toward Tanager in an attempt to pull him away from the edge.

"I may not be very strong, or always say and do the right things," Tanager explained, his face dropping sadly, "but I can die for you."

Lucene's heart melted. She opened her mouth, but no sounds came out. It was not that she was at a loss for words. It was that Isabella had begun chanting and her throat was suddenly paralyzed. Within moments, Lucene's arms were glowing as the tree-like embers grew. As she transformed into a swirling pool of light, her energy somehow blended with that of the abyss.

"Will you keep your word, demon?" Tanager asked.

"I always do," Jasper Set giddily jumped up and down like a small child. Isabella's chanting grew louder.

"Then there's just one more thing…"

"And what's that?"

With that, Cepheus emerged from the shadows. He looked at his friend for a moment. "Are you sure? I could—" he motioned toward the abyss.

"Absolutely not," Tanager replied, "you have a planet to rule." He referred to their conversation soon after Hamish's ghost paid a visit to Cepheus. They need you. Erde needs you." Tanager shot a knowing look to Cepheus.

"What is-s-s-s he talking about?" Jasper looked between the two men, a visible mixture of confusion and impatience.

"I demand to see the final contract between you and my father, Sovereign Hamish of the High Royals."

"Oh, that," Jasper seemed almost disappointed. He was hoping it was something much grander. With a flick of his wrist and a snap of his fingers, a scroll appeared. "Here." He floated it over to Cepheus, the edges of it singed from the heat of the abyss. "Seems to have brought me nothing but grief and nothing to show for it to boot." He looked regretfully at Lucene, having failed to secure both her allegiance and the multi-dimensional plane-hopping support from Far. In fact, at this very moment, his world felt almost … hopeless.

And then something happened…

There was this inexplicable 'thing' that settled all at once in the center of Jasper's chest. What was it? He had watched a small firefly willing to risk his life for his friends. He watched as Tanager was going to unselfishly, and without hesitation, sacrifice his life for the woman he loved. Meanwhile his own Null family was ready to destroy this world and eat him for dinner for having betrayed them. He couldn't think of anyone who would make that kind of sacrifice for him. This thought bothered him.

"Hang on," he told Tanager. "I will give you the signal when it's time to jump." He spoke slowly, cleanly, without a single extra 's' in his words. With that, he winged his way up to meet his family. He waived his arms, hissed and popped, as if explaining something to them…probably that he hadn't betrayed them, that this was the will of the Mighty Segue. He was to deliver the prophet for them to follow, and he had done just that.

Jasper made one final survey of Tanager from the sky. "Oh well," he whispered to himself, "I always did wonder what would happen to a demon in the afterlife."

With that Jasper Set performed his one and only act of love.

He dove…headfirst into the pit with the entire Null following him as he did.

Tanager jumped back in shock, Cepheus grabbing his friend's arm to ensure he didn't accidentally fall into the abyss. After the final crustacean-like creature had flown into the dark portal, it began to close. As it did, the floor turned an ugly shade of gray with soot scattered everywhere. Lucene spun around several times before dropping to the ground in a heap. Tanager lunged to her aid. Isabella grabbed his arm. "Not yet, lover boy. Still charged up, remember?" He did remember from the last time, but instinct was instinct.

Lucene let out a cough. "Okay, Marzipan time to yack up lunch."

"Ew, that's gross," Marzipan protested. "That's not at all—"

"Eat, little bug," Isabella pulled a jar of actual marzipan from her basket. His eyes lit up.

"What is all this about?" Tanager enquired.

"I didn't realize it until now," Lucene explained. "But I got mental flashes from Marzipan's past." Tanager was visibly impressed by this as Lucene had never exhibited any psychic skills that would point to witnessing past events experienced by others. "Marzipan's old friend who rescued him from the desert gliders?" she continued. "He said that he manifested him because he was lonely. And maybe, in a way, he did. But what if—somehow—there was a leak between the layers back then and Marzi over there escaped. Not sure how he figured out he could seal the leak with firefly yack but—"

"I'm not a—" Marzipan's whining was interrupted by the regurgitation of what he had just ingested. And, there was a lot of it. Tanager coughed and turned away, his stomach beginning to cramp and heave. He had a terrible gag reflex.

"Come, help me," Isabella said to Lucene and Cepheus, ignoring Tanager. And for the next hour, the three spread firefly yack all over the blackened areas of the floor. Somehow, the expansion stopped at Isabella's stones, meaning Isabella was either exceptionally good at math or she was exceptionally good at protection spells. Either way, the stones were a guidepost for all the ground they needed to cover.

Meanwhile, Tanager dragged his cold, sweat-soaked body into the lobby and tried not to think about it, his stomach still queasy. "Some hero I turned out to be," he thought miserably. His one act of bravery was outshined by a weak stomach.

"It might take a few days for all of the anomalies to end," Isabella explained to Lucene and Cepheus, "but they will." Lucene thought for a moment about Not-Christopher and let out a somewhat disappointed sigh. Cepheus's mind went to Petrichor. Was she safe? He suspected so, since she hadn't revisited him in some time. Perhaps after her gentle nudge to move on, she was finally able to do so, herself.

And so, the leak between the layers was closed and the embers of Lucene's arms gently faded.

RECLAIMING THE THRONE

NOW...ONE DAY AFTER THE END.

"So, you are leaving?" Moksha watched, fighting back tears, when she arrived at Cepheus's office at TARA, only to find him packing an assortment of contraptions into a small suitcase. The room was still a mess, but somehow, he had no trouble rummaging through drawers and sifting through the piles of books and tools that littered the floor, finding the exact pieces he was searching for.

Cepheus paused, surprised at her presence. "How did you know where to find me?" he asked.

"Where else would you retreat to when you needed an escape… or tools for the journey?" Moksha leaned against the door frame. "Were you at least planning on saying 'good-bye'?" Her skin began to form a red hue as her face grew warm. She wasn't certain whether her feelings were anger or grief, most likely a combination of the two.

"Moksha, I—"

"I understand," she interrupted.

"No," he abandoned his packing to meet her at the door. "I don't think you do. Please, let me explain." He wrapped his arms around her, pulling her into his chest before Moksha's resistance gave out and she began sobbing, tears running down his shirt. "I have to go," Cepheus spoke gently. Moksha wrapped her arms around his waist and held onto Cepheus tightly. He continued, "If I don't, the Royals will continue their mission to take over Erde, and they won't stop there. But if I resume control, I can turn things around, and perhaps the Royals stand a chance at being the official military support of Erde and all of Section 1."

"You're wrong," she sobbed, sniffing between words. "I understand *why* you have to go. I just don't want you to."

Cepheus paused for what felt like an eternity.

"I want you to come with me," he finally said.

"What?" Moksha peered up at him in surprise. "You mean for military protection?" Cepheus paused for a moment before letting out a cat-like laugh. "What's so funny?" Moksha demanded.

"No, Moksha. I am not inviting you to be my personal guard. I'm asking you to become a sovereign—alongside me at the throne."

"Oh, come on," she backed away, socking him in the arm.

"Ow, what was that for?" Cepheus rubbed his arm.

"You shouldn't toy with my emotions like that. Look at me! I'm a former assassin. I know nothing of being…well…sovereignly!"

"Neither did my father when my mo—," he still couldn't get the word 'mother' out. "When Sabrina married my father. He too, was in the lower military caste."

"But I don't know the first thing about ruling."

Cepheus grinned. "Neither do I. But we can learn…together." He reached out and pulled her toward him a second time. "I confess, it won't be as glamorous as it sounds being a sovereign. The training grounds have become a waste-pit and the brigade are not going to be easy to decondition and re-train."

"Well, at least I can offer support in that area," Moksha smiled up at him. "I am a former assassin hell-bent on peace."

"Interesting choice of words," Cepheus's grin grew wider, displaying his saw-like teeth. "Is that your way of saying 'yes'?"

"Of course, it is, my love. Anywhere you are is where I want to be."

"I had another thought. But I must ask that you refrain from punching me in the arm again."

Moksha let out an uncharacteristic giggle. "Okay, I promise. What is it?"

"I was thinking of asking Isabella to accompany us as an advisor to replace Far."

Hamish had died before he got to see Far's death, and it would seem that the monk was not lurking in the other realm with Hamish and Sabrina. He was, presumably, someplace else.

"Are you sure that's wise?" Moksha looked up at him, surprised. "Some of her methods of persuasion have been…questionable," she finished, recounting in her mind the time Reverend Isabella put on a show for her followers, alongside Dallen, in order to garner support.

"While her actions have not always been ideal, her intentions are always with the highest good in mind. I believe we can work with her on, as you mentioned, her methods."

"If you think so, I trust your judgment," Moksha conceded before laughing. "And here I thought you were far too practical for crazy ideas."

"Oh, Moksha," Cepheus kissed the top of her head. "You are in for many more surprises. This, I can promise you."

31

___

THE NURSERY

NOW…ONE DAY AFTER THE END.

For as large of a salamander as Fredo was, he still gave the appearance of a small, lost child. He stood by the great window in his former sovereign's chamber, overlooking the training grounds. He even crossed his arms behind him as Hamish had done. And yet, it just wasn't right. Now that Hamish, Far and Sabrina were gone, there was no one left to rule. In this situation, the Royals would have likely sent one of their superiors to oversee the grounds, except that the Null had destroyed the entire race with the exception of those located on their small and dying planet in Section 3.

This meant that, technically, Fredo was now in charge. His subordinates expected it of him. There was just one small problem…while Fredo was built like a formidable beast, he was still dumb as a rock, a fact that he was becoming increasingly aware of as the sweat poured down his bright red salamander face. If he showed weakness, no doubt someone would challenge him, and he was terrified of what would become of their planet if that happened. He would be killed, and so would the baby.

"Excuse me…my Sovereign," a nurse cleared his throat as he peered his head around the large chamber door.

Fredo looked around for a moment, expecting to see Hamish. Then it occurred to him. The nurse was talking to him.

"What is it?" Fredo grumbled from deep in his throat.

"The baby is awake. Usually, our late sovereign would hold it each evening but since…" The nurse's voice trailed off.

Something in the center of Fredo's chest gave the littlest of pangs. *Would it be possible? Of course, it would. Why wouldn't it be?"* With a new flash of hope, his spirits brightened. "I'll be along in just a moment to…cradle it."

The nursery was not what one might expect. Instead of being filled with animal murals on the walls, pastel colors and a floating mobile above the baby's crib, this one was as stark as a sterile hospital room. No wonder the baby was fussy when Fredo arrived. Even a warrior such as himself thought the room could at least use a splash of color.

He approached the crib with caution. When Hamish had been alive, he wasn't allowed to touch the child, his child, born from a short-term affair with the former Sovereign Sabrina. He thought back on the encounter and fought back a tear. To her, he was just a plaything. Fredo, on the other hand, actually had feelings for his former sovereign that were possibly stronger than the man she'd actually chosen to rule with her had for her.

Fredo peered over the bars of the sleep station. The child had distinct lizard eyes and a tail. It likely wouldn't develop legs for several more months. Instead there were two round, leathery stumps where they would later form. Around its eyes and marking its face were peculiar red streaks. If it weren't apparent yet that the child was his, it soon would be.

"Would you like to hold the baby?" the nurse asked with uncustomary sympathy. Perhaps babies had a way of summoning compassion. Fredo nodded nervously. The nurse reached in and gently lifted the swaddled baby. A look of fear crossed the salamander's face. "Don't worry," the nurse reassured, "this one's made of tough stuff and isn't likely to break easily."

Fredo put out his thick arms to accept little Cefeus. It was then that emotion overtook him and he began sobbing for the second time in his still relatively young life. The nurse peered over his shoulder nervously at sounds from the next room. Several soldiers were in the examination room next door being treated from training injuries. They couldn't see this weakness in their new leader. The nurse quickly shut the door.

Fredo's mind began racing. *I know nothing about raising a child. I know even less about ruling an empire. But if I don't, someone else will and my child most definitely will not be allowed to live. He would be considered a threat. What am I to do?*

At that moment, he heard something through the walls. It was coming from the opposite side from where the soldiers were now blustering on about the range and depth of their injuries—of which they were enormously proud. It sounded like…humming. *Ah,* he thought to himself, *the human.* Even thinking about Roman next door left a bitter taste in his mouth. Humans were vermin, and he didn't like them. How could they have bothered to nurse this one back to health and…

A thought crossed his mind. Fredo didn't typically have many of them, and this one he savored for quite some time.

The baby wiggled a little in Fredo's arms, so he rocked it gently, making a little cooing sound that he'd heard Hamish doing around the baby and one that Sabrina had done on occasion when Cepheus had been born so many years ago. Young Cefeus let out a slurping sound and smiled. There it was again, that little pang in the center of Fredo's chest—one that was growing stronger all the time.

Fredo made his way toward the door, baby in arm. The nurse looked questioningly at him. "Stay here," he ordered, "we will return shortly."

The nurse nodded and offered. "Feeding time is in thirty minutes," he reminded Fredo. Fredo grunted that he understood.

Once in the hallway, he stood upright, puffing out his chest proudly as several soldiers passed. They each lowered their gaze deferentially as they did so. Once they were out of sight, he threw open the door that held the human. Roman looked up, surprised, and not without a hint of terror on his face. He opened his mouth to speak but had no idea what to say, so he closed it again.

Several days had passed and his wounds were healing nicely. It still hurt to sit up, and the carnivorous food they offered him did little to help his already sensitive digestive system. What Erde lacked in meat, the Royals made up for a hundred-fold. He was becoming so sickened from nothing but animal protein several times a day that he was certain that he was going to become a vegan as soon as he could get back to Erde. That is, he reasoned, if they let him return. He wasn't sure they would. The nurse had been kind—a rarity from the Royals. He tried to sneak him what he thought were vegetables but the greens he brought were varied palm fronds, grasses and inedible flowers.

Roman eyed the baby, curiously.

"It's a baby," Fredo grunted, as if Roman hadn't guessed.

"I can see that," Roman answered cautiously.

"I know nothing of raising a baby," Fredo spoke quietly to ensure no one else heard their conversation. He shut the door with his free arm. It made a loud thud, causing the baby to begin to wail out in frustration. Fredo tried cooing but it didn't work.

"May I?" Roman offered, putting his arms out.

Fredo eyed him distrustfully. "Don't hurt it," he cautioned.

"I won't," Roman answered, sitting as upright as possible in his bed.

Fredo handed him the bulky little baby. Roman began to purse his lips distastefully. Truth be told, it was the ugliest child he'd ever seen. He caught Fredo's dark expression and shifted into one of his well-practiced wide smiles. Roman started talking to the baby, reciting strange words that Fredo had never heard before, "For in and out, above and below, 'tis nothing but a magic shadow show, played in a box whose candle is the sun, round which we phantom figures come and go."

This all sounded like gibberish to the salamander. He could barely read, and even if he could, *The Rubayait of Omar Khayyam* would not likely have been his first choice. But the baby began cooing once again, soothed by Roman's calm voice. So the salamander let Roman continue with his gibberish.

When Roman had finished, Fredo spoke. "You know things," Fredo announced, gruffly.

"I like to think so," Roman refrained from his usual sarcasm. He valued his life too much.

"I was told you study people," Fredo was having trouble finding his words.

"Yes," Roman confirmed. "I taught anthropology for years on my planet and spent quite a bit of time studying your culture as well."

"Can you help me?" Fredo asked, realizing how weak and pathetic that sounded, and so he added sternly, "Help me understand how to rule the training grounds so there is no mutiny and I will let you live."

Something stirred inside Roman. His heart was still broken—once again—over Far, and with his death came a conclusion that he was somehow not ready for. He had felt abandoned by his friends on Erde, rejected from the school who fired him on Earth after his breakdown. He really couldn't remember the last time he actually felt…useful.

"I will gladly help you," Roman answered, sincerely. "With one small request."

"What's that?" Fredo asked, gruffly.

"Vegetables," he answered.

"Vegetables?" Fredo was confused.

"Beans…whole grains…fruit…seeds, even." Roman continued. "What's a guy got to do to get a meal that hasn't been slaughtered first?"

Fredo's mind circled around the request. Finally, he had an "aha" moment—possibly the first one in his life. Sovereign Sabrina brought back lots of exotic animals from varied planets, usually with no regard as to how they might react in their existing world. He remembered a menagerie of parakeets, conures and cockatoos that she brought from one of her Earth visits to her former Florida casino. They ate fruit and vegetables and seeds. He also remembered a pesky raccoon that kept unlocking chamber doors, and a salt marsh vole that had very poor hygiene and would leave his remains everywhere. Yet, he was pretty certain that they ate beans.

Funny, Fredo thought, *he's asking me to feed him like a Royal house pet.*

"Help me with the baby," Fredo finally answered, "and I will see to it that you have your requested…pet food."

32

THE SEAHORSE

NOW...ONE DAY AFTER THE END.

"Where are you off to?" Morphinae asked, flying in with wings outspread, still in his falcon form. He then transformed into his usual blue, life-sized crochet-doll frame—barechested, wearing tattered jeans. Odessa never did understand where he got the idea for this manifestation, and never really thought to ask. Instead, she turned to face him, grabbing the only weapon she could find—a conch shell she'd found on the beach. She wielded it, hesitantly. "What is that for?" Morphinae was surprised. He took a step toward Odessa, only to notice then that she backed away, her eyes wide. "Do you think that I would ever hurt you?" he asked.

"I dunno," Odessa confessed. "It's not as if you've never killed before. And you did say that you never wanted to see me again," her eyes began welling up with tears. She brushed them aside.

"I've killed a total of three times in my life, and it was only to restore balance," Morphinae explained. "You know as well as I do that the last one was necessary."

Odessa did know. He had mistakenly rescued a boy from drowning, who would grow into Drake Cushing, Lucene's former boss at the United Commonwealth on Earth. Doing so would later result in

Drake being involved in thousands of deaths, leaving Morphinae to feel partially responsible. In the end, he did the only thing an admirable Balance-Keeper could do—he drowned Drake in his adulthood, thereby restoring balance. Now, it seems that Drake's brother, Bryce, had taken the reins after his brother's death, and proved no better than his predecessor.

"And," Odessa asked cautiously…is this one of those times? A time where it's necessary?"

Morphinae surveyed the small shack that was Odessa's dream home. She had a bed made of bamboo strung together with reeds. The top of it was a pile of palm fronds where one would expect a mattress to be. On top of that sat a small, hand-woven suitcase that looked about as sturdy as the leaky thatched roof above their head. He eyed her with a mix of confusion as if he were seeing her for the first time.

"I have never and will never harm you," Morphinae told her. "I am surprised that I need to tell you such things." Morphinae wasn't one to get offended, and yet her words bothered him for some reason.

Odessa's face contorted as if it were about to crack as she broke down in tears, and cried between her sobbing, "I've failed my mission with the Vitruvians! I failed Isabella! I outed Lucene's powers and betrayed you! Even when I try to lead with good intentions, I seem to do a spectacular job of messing everything up." She covered her face with her palms, collapsing on the floor in front of the bed and pulling her knees into her chest.

"I don't feel betrayed," Morphinae answered softly.

Odessa looked up, cautiously, sniffling a little. "You don't?"

"No," Morphinae answered. "I'm used to leading with my head. I've always laughed at you for leading with your heart. But it has come to my attention that I could stand to be more…feeling."

"And what brought that to your attention?"

Morphinae put his hand out to help Odessa to her feet. "It was more a 'who.' You, of course."

"You don't hate me?" Odessa was surprised.

"Who could ever hate you?" Morphinae answered with a warmth that Odessa had never heard from him before. He was still holding her hand.

"Lots of people," she answered, wiping the tears from her eyes with the backs of her hands. "I was just packing to escape. But I have no idea where to go. Commander Royce has sealed the borders of Erde—no-one in and no-one out. If the Vitruvians discover my location, they will kill me. And this planet is so God-damned small that I would have to morph my way into an insect and spend the rest of my days as a bug in order to survive." Odessa may have been a bit melodramatic, but there was some truth to what she was saying.

"I have another idea," Morphinae shared.

"Really? What?"

"I don't know if it's possible," Morphinae explained. "But remember when you once asked the question about which of us would carry the baby if we were to have a child?"

"I remember," Odessa was shocked. "But I didn't think you had." Frankly, she thought, Morphinae all but laughed at the idea.

"Well, it got me thinking…about seahorses."

"Seahorses?" Odessa was confused, still bewildered that Morphinae had actually given thought to anything she said, particularly about suggestions about becoming a couple.

"Yes, seahorse males carry the baby to term."

"I'm afraid I'm not following."

"We know that we can shape-shift into male and female forms, and vary our outward appearance—"

"Obviously," Odessa answered, crossing her arms and waiving a hand in the air.

"But what if we could shape-shift and merge into one form?"

"I'm not sure that's possible." Odessa was skeptical.

"There are legends that we shape-shifting Vitruvians can go a step further then changing our personal forms. We can actually combine our energy to become a single new form."

"I've never heard that," Odessa challenged. "Is it true?"

"I'm willing to find out if you are," Morphinae answered, walking from the shadows of the shack and out into the sun while guiding Odessa by the hand.

"Where are we going?" Odessa followed, barefoot in the sand.

"To the sea, of course." They stopped at the water's edge, hand-in-hand and looking out at the setting sun over the water. "There's just one caveat," Morphinae added.

"What's that?"

"Unlike marriage and divorce and shifting from one form to another, I am not sure that, once merged, we could ever separate again."

Odessa paused carefully to think this through. "And," Odessa wanted to clarify, "you're willing to risk being stuck with me—a part of you—for the rest of our lives?" Odessa sucked in her breath.

"I have never been one to take on friends and yet you are my first friend—my best friend. I cannot ever see a time where I wouldn't want to be stuck with you," he answered practically.

"But—" Odessa started to speak.

"What?"

"Do you love me?" She winced, afraid of what the answer might be.

"I'm telling you that I want to spend the rest of my days co-mingled as a single entity." Morphinae grew impatient. "What do you think?"

"Is that a 'yes?'" Odessa grinned out of the corner of her mouth. "I'm gonna need a definitive 'yes'."

"Yes," Morphinae answered, uncomfortably, while averting his gaze. "I've already explained that I'm a thinker not a feeler. Why do you insist on making me say 'feely' things?"

Odessa smiled.

"So, what form are we taking?" she wanted to know, looking down at her female shape for what she assumed might be the last time. She had to admit to herself that a part of her would miss having breasts. There was something fun about them.

"I told you, a giant seahorse."

"No, you gave the seahorse as an example of—" Odessa caught herself. "You know what? Never mind. We are to become a giant seahorse, then?"

"Well, you do love the ocean and we could spend our days in this one," he gestured his long arm over the water as if Odessa couldn't see it.

"Is such a thing possible?" Odessa asked. "I mean, won't Erdelings find it odd?"

"The sea is pretty large. Who is to say that anyone will ever know?"

And with that, Morphinae and Odessa performed one final shape-shift, turning themselves into the most beautiful blue seahorse that any world has ever seen. They swam away together as one, never to be heard from again.

Years later, Fatima would tell her daughter Talula tales about the mythical seahorse. It was right up there with the Loch Ness Monster, Bigfoot and Santa Claus on Earth. And yet, somehow Talula sensed that there was some truth to this story, and often spent her younger years sitting on Tranquility Beach, gazing out over the sea, looking for the mythical seahorse. A few times, she was sure she spotted the united couple, Morphinae and Odessa, but it was always a quick flash out of the corner of her eye. So, she never could confirm it.

Still, without anyone really knowing who documented the story or why, the tale of Morphinae and Odessa became a legend in the Erde storybooks. The tale grew more and more incredible with each telling. It was cited as one of the most romantic stories of all time.

33

REDEMPTION

NOW...TWO DAYS AFTER THE END.

Commander Royce stood before the elders in a dark, circular dome located in a sectioned-off area of the PDL. They were larger than life as if they had morphed out of the red rocks of Sedona, towering over her in an equally intimidating and mystifying manner. The lead elder was soft-spoken with a long beard and tired eyes. He enjoyed his sleep and wasn't often awakened. And yet, this was the third time in a year. Only this time, Royce had not reached out to the elders. For the first time in her lifetime, they "requested" her presence. Royce was afraid. What vibrational shift had her actions caused that woke them up? Or, was it simply the recent shift as Reverend Isabella struggled to close the portal she'd accidentally left open?

"It seems we are faced with a dilemma," the eldest said. Except, when he spoke, it was as if the others were speaking in unison. They echoed him in hushed voices.

Royce suspected she knew exactly what the problem was (her), but she had to know for sure. "Of what problem do you speak?"

"Amina," he called her by her first name. No one else, except for the elders, actually knew it. She was Commander Royce for as long as anyone could remember. "You come from a long lineage of helpers. You, yourself, have spent a lifetime in service, and yet..." He paused, sadly. "What has happened?"

Amina's face dropped. Erde was a land of peace. But by living according to the morally "best" ways, instead of flourishing, it made them a target for intruders, unwelcome guests for those they wished to help (such as Earth), and financially bankrupt.

"I didn't think I had a choice," she cried softly. It was true. She hadn't intended to provide weaponry and technology to Vitruvia in exchange for financial support and protection. It happened slowly at first, and by the time she realized it, she was neck-high in deceit.

"Why didn't you come to us sooner?" The female elder next to the bearded one asked, softly.

"I thought I could handle it myself. And—" she paused. "I was embarrassed. I didn't want to seem...weak."

"We could have helped you...advised you. That's what we're here for," the old woman said.

"I'm sorry," was all that Royce could muster. After a long pause she asked, "What is my punishment? Is it death?" She assumed that her time had finally come. After all, she was old even by Erde standards, and in all likelihood she probably only had about forty years left of her life. She didn't want to die in disgrace, of course, but she had lived a full life. One hundred and ten years was a pretty good run, wasn't it?

"Death?" another elder, one of indeterminate gender, was surprised. "Do you mean to suggest that you think we'd murder you?" They seemed almost offended.

"Well, I don't know," Amina confessed, "I sold out my people by accepting money in exchange for weaponry and technology to the Vitruvians, knowing full well that they could use those resources against us..."

"And then their selling it to the earthlings?" the first elder questioned.

Amina let out a sigh. "I only learned of that recently."

"And tell us," the female elder asked softly, "what made you decide to make this arrangement with the Vitruvians?"

"I," Amina choked, "I thought it was for the best. As a small planet, less than the size of a country on Earth, without the IPP support, we had nothing. If TARA and the Makerspace shut down, there was little else to help keep the planet sustained and … relevant. Even if we could grow our own crops and keep ourselves fed and clothed, we had no protection against outside invaders, natural disasters…nothing."

"And, you believed the Vitruvians could provide that?"

"Yes."

There was a collective sigh among the elders. A murmur, as if they were in a back room somewhere discussing her fate, even though their faces were present. Finally, they returned.

"We have a proposal for you," they said in unison.

"A proposal?" Amina was confused.

"Yes, call it redemption, if you like. We have some specific suggestions for you to employ that will help Erdelings, all optional, of course, with the understanding that you will remain at your post for at least one more year."

Amina was surprised. She was due to retire last year and assumed after the mess she'd cause, they would want to be rid of her sooner, rather than later.

"Why are you not punishing me?" she asked.

"While misguided, you were acting according to what you believed was best. By our estimation, you went off track a year ago. Spend the next year correcting it, and all will be forgiven."

Amina thought a moment. "Like…karma?" she suggested.

"Call it as you like," the elders said as they began to fade. "We're very tired. Come back tomorrow, and we'll tell you all about our plan."

34

RESIGNATION
NOW…THREE DAYS AFTER THE END.

"Why are you here, Professor Tanager?" Commander Royce asked. It was the first time anyone had sought her out in her home. She invited Tanager into her high-home on the outskirts of Achel, which turned out to be walking distance from where he and Lucene currently resided. "And, how is it that you figured out where I lived? No one else has ever attempted to do this before."

"Forgive me, Commander Royce," Tanager apologized, removing the fedora that he wore for the occasion and holding it to his chest. "I didn't mean to intrude upon your personal space." He didn't answer the question about how he'd found her. That was thanks to Kiki's earlier efforts to ensure that Royce was not a shape-shifting imposter. It was the young girl who actually discovered Commander Royce's place of residence.

"Amina," she answered.

"I'm sorry, what?" Tanager was confused.

"Amina," she answered. "I'm not on duty. Therefore, you can call me by my first name.

Being on familiar terms made it more awkward for Tanager, but it did serve one purpose; it humanized Commander Royce, somehow.

"Amina," he repeated, circling the hat in his hands nervously. "Given everything that's happened lately, I thought you should be first to know before I give my official resignation in the morning."

Amina paused for a moment. "I see," she finally answered. "Please, sit down." Amina motioned for Tanager to have a seat on the wrap-around couch that took up most of her living room. "Reishi tea?" she offered, pouring herself a glass from the pitcher that sat on a glass table in front of the couch.

"Eh, no, thank you," he answered, sitting and resting his hat beside him.

Amina took her seat on the farthest corner of the couch, sipping her iced tea. After a moment of silence, Amina finally addressed Tanager's admission, "You are not giving your resignation in the morning."

Tanager was filled with a mixture of disbelief and indignation. Of course, he was. "Yes," he answered, "I am."

Amina let out a sigh. "Before you make your final decision, will you at least allow me to argue my case?"

What case? Tanager was very confused. Amina took his silence as permission to continue.

"I am aware that my decisions this past year have been unconscionable."

Tanager crossed one leg over the other and began tapping his fingers on his knee, uncomfortably.

Amina placed her glass on the table. *No coaster,* Tanager noticed. Lucene would have chastised him for that. He smiled to himself.

"Our entire planet was on the verge of bankruptcy, Professor Tanager," Amina spoke loudly to regain his attention. "I did what I thought I needed to do in order to save our economy and feed our planet."

"And for that, you were willing to sacrifice Lucene?" Tanager was angry. "One small price to pay for the good of the whole. Is that it?" He completely disregarded the fact that her actions also placed very large and lethal weapons into the wrong hands which impacted the entire planet. But at this moment, he had a very singular focus.

"No," Amina answered. "What I tried to do, and failed, was dance a fine line between giving them what they wanted and protecting our people."

"What is that supposed to mean?" Tanager challenged.

"I sold them weaponry—"

"To the Vitruvians—who you knew were going to give it to Earth. The very people we were trying to protect had plans all along to overthrow our planet."

"Yes, but there are pieces of which you are unaware."

"Such as?"

"Such as the fact that I did my best to have technicians at TARA alter some of the final blueprints before any weaponry or technology was given to the Vitruvians."

"Technicians?" Tanager immediately thought of Ivan. "Was my friend, Ivan, involved?"

"No," Amina answered. "I assure you that your friend was not privy to any of this. "And," she continued, "part of the agreement included a special clause."

"What kind of clause."

"Ambassador Dallen was not to lay a hand on Lucene. She was not part of the arrangement."

"You can see how that worked out."

"Yes," Amina sighed. "That was unfortunate."

"But this doesn't change the fact that I cannot support TARA and its current operations. Which is why I need to resign as lead professor of—"

"Stop," Amina said, elements of her 'work-self' creeping into her voice. "Give me three months."

"What?"

"Give me three months to turn TARA around. It won't be exactly what it used to be," Amina confessed. "But I promise you it will be closer to what it should be, and a place in which you can be proud to work."

"How, exactly, are you planning to do that?" Tanager was skeptical.

"Give me until tomorrow morning to make my proposal. I can meet you at TARA to discuss it. Let us just say, I have met with the Elders and I am seeking my redemption."

Tanager sat back on the couch for a moment, more confused than ever.

Amina leaned forward, resting her elbows on her knees for emphasis. For the first time in the years that he had known Commander Royce, she had tears in her eyes. "I can be better," she whispered regretfully.

The morning talk at TARA included Tanager, Lucene, Cepheus, Moksha, Isabella, Ivan, and for once, Fatima, with baby in tow. They sat around the table in the private Resource Room as Commander Royce established new guidelines for TARA.

She addressed Lucene first. "I know I haven't exactly given you a specific role as a PDL agent," she touched Lucene's arm in what was the only time Royce had shown any type of affection. "I'd like to change that."

"Okay," Lucene answered suspiciously. "What did you have in mind?" She was well aware of Tanager's move to resign yesterday and was still distrustful after Dallen almost succeeded in kidnapping her.

"Your healing ability has not gone unnoticed," Royce replied. "But I think we should officially pay you as a natural energy worker at the Dragoste Healing Center. We still need to see how your skills match up against traditional medicine, but I suspect we'll find that the cost of hiring you is a small investment compared with what they will save in long hospital visits, surgeries, and rehab which may or may not be necessary."

Moksha rubbed her knee, instinctively. She shuddered to think how she would have fared following the wolf attack were it not for Lucene's intervention.

"Is this one of those 'not really a request' requests?" Lucene challenged.

Royce smiled, knowingly. "No, this is an optional request. But I believe you can do a lot of good by accepting. It's only part time, of course, and as you grow into your skills, you can pass that on to students at TARA."

"Gimme a day or two to think on it?" Lucene finally answered.

"Of course," Royce replied.

Commander Royce then turned her attention to Tanager and Cepheus. "As for my esteemed professors, you will have the opportunity to continue running the Makerspace and TARA as you have done previously, leading the Data Collector training program and developing a self-defense weaponry program which, like it or not, we desperately need right now."

Tanager let out a sigh as if letting out hot air from a bicycle tire.

"Three months," she reminded him. "Give me three months to prove that I can help turn this planet around and make it worth you staying on at TARA." She didn't, however, have any idea how to address the fact that money was tight, and he was likely taking a pay cut.

Cepheus clung to Moksha's hand under the table, neither one letting Royce in on the fact that they had no intention of remaining on Erde for much longer. Still, he reasoned that any one of Tanager's lead students: Xeni, Clusaladek or Neroni would be able to support Tanager with the Data Collector training program.

"May I ask what it is we're training them to do, exactly," Tanager asked pointedly. "It's pointless to continue trying to collect environmental data on Earth—they clearly don't want us."

"I know," Royce explained. "But we still need those skills—not quite as militant as what we've seen in the past year in their training, but more of a…compromise."

"Compromise?" Tanager asked.

"Yes, we can still support neighboring planets in need, but we also need to prepare ourselves for the eventuality of war. And without the Vitruvians financial support and protections, we need to start training now, and training fast."

"Exactly how much 'financial support' are we talkin' about?" Ivan asked.

"I don't have the exact details in front of me but, why—"

"Er," Ivan rubbed his ear. "I might be able to provide modest support to your endeavors provided you're willing to grant me a wee request."

"What kind of request?" Royce wanted to know.

"It's just that, this border-closing thing… While I understand your reasons, there's got to be a way for certain parties to travel back and forth for specific reasons. Seems like planetary suicide to cut ourselves off from all outsiders."

Cepheus leaned forward as if to speak, but remained silent. Fatima reached out to give Ivan's knee a supportive squeeze. At that moment, Fatima and Cepheus exchanged knowing glances. Ivan was, once again, looking out for them.

35

TRANSITIONS – THREE

NOW…THREE WEEKS AFTER THE END.

"What's bothering you?" Lucene asked when Tanager met her on the steps of the newly refurbished Dragoste Healing Center. For the past week, Tanager had insisted on meeting Lucene for lunch on the days when she was working at the center or the costume shop. He would pace back and forth outside like an insistent cat until her break arrived. Sometimes, he'd bring lunch, like today. At other times, they would dart into a local cafe for a quick bite.

She didn't really need to ask. Even without using any of her telepathic skills, this one was pretty obvious.

"Here," Tanager handed her half of an almond butter and ginger seitan hoagie as she sat on one of the concrete steps. Tanager joined her. Oftentimes, other people on their lunch break sat nearby. But on this particular day, they were alone. He set down a satchel and produced a canteen of water. "Hope you don't mind sharing. I forgot to wash yours, so we'll have to drink out of just the one."

"Why would I mind?" Lucene took the canteen and gulped some of the water. She wiped her face haphazardly with the back of her hand before handing it back to Tanager.

"So," Tanager slid the sole of his foot across the new steps, absentmindedly, noticing how smooth they were. "How does it feel being the breadwinner of the household?" He forced a smile.

"Good one," Lucene acknowledged. She didn't recall having used that Earth expression around him. He must have figured it out all on his own. "But the better question is, why does it bother you so much?"

Tanager let out a sigh and thought a moment. "I don't mean to be old-fashioned. I really don't. But ever since I've known you, I've sort of had to…take care of you, in a way. Please don't take that the wrong way," he paused, awkwardly, waiting for the resentful remark that didn't come.

"I won't," Lucene answered calmly, taking a bite of the hoagie.

"Anyway, I didn't mind. Truth be told, I kinda of…liked it. It made me feel important, as if…you needed me."

"I do need you," Lucene interjected.

"No," Tanager shook his head. "You enjoy being with me. You've chosen to be with me. But you don't *need* me," he paused. "And, that's how it should be, I suppose. But now I feel...less than—"

"Less than what?"

"I think that's it…less than," Tanager finished.

"Is it so awful that I now have two very good careers that happen to support our home?"

Tanager took her hand. "I think it's wonderful. Some people spend their entire lives trying to find themselves and their purpose and you've found yours. It's just that, even with Ivan's generous investment, TARA has lost a great deal without Vitruvian backing. After a lifetime of service to the school, I'm now making about what I did as a teaching apprentice more than thirty years ago."

"But this is temporary—" Lucene objected.

"But what if it's not?" He looked her straight in the eyes. "What if this is the best I can ever do for us from here on out?"

"Do you love your work?" Lucene asked.

"Of course, I do," Tanager answered.

"And, do you love me?"

"More than anything. Why would you even ask that?"

"And between my contribution to the household, and your contribution, do you agree that we can continue to create a good life together?"

"That was never in question—"

Lucene leaned over and kissed him. "Then stop crunching the numbers and realize that this is a team effort that goes well beyond money or one person taking care of the other. We're in this for the long haul, right?"

Tanager's eyes began to well up, but he fought back tears. Instead, he hugged Lucene tightly to his chest and smiled. "I'm not entirely certain I understand what 'the long haul' is," he confessed. "But if it means that you and I are together for an eternity, then I'm all for it."

"There you go," Lucene smiled, hugging him back. "That's exactly what I mean."

At the Fortunata Household

"So, I've been meaning to talk to ya…about stuff you may have heard concerning the incident in the sewing room the other day." Ivan peered over Fatima's shoulder. She was giving Talula a bath in the kitchen sink. For some reason, kitchen sinks were the baby's favorite places—not the bathroom sink, the bathtub or even the deep utility sinks at TARA. No, Talula preferred kitchen sinks. They didn't know whether it was the scents from Fatima's cooking, or the shiny faucet, or the sound of the water running. Whatever it was, she gurgled with glee the entire time she was in there.

Ivan paused a moment to reach over Fatima's shoulder and tickle under Talula's chin, playfully. Talula grabbed his finger, her tiny hand not making it all of the way around it and held on tight.

"The grip of a tigress," he commented. Fatima suddenly got a chill, and shivered for a moment, but wasn't sure why. "So…about the other day."

"You mean where you saved Lucene from being kidnapped or killed and helped uncover Dallen's underhanded dealings with Commander Royce? Is that what you mean?" Fatima carefully rinsed the mild shampoo out of Talula's sparsely covered head.

"Er," Ivan tugged at his ear. "I s'pose you could look at it that way." He coughed.

Fatima grinned out of the corner of her mouth. "Or do you mean the part where you almost killed three of Dallen's guards in the process?"

"Er, yeah. That part."

"Here, hold this," Fatima handed him a large bath towel. "Baby, incoming." Fatima lifted Talula from the bathtub and handed her chubby little body over to Ivan who wrapped her securely in the towel, nice and warm. He felt a little perplexed. Fatima just acknowledged that he almost murdered three men and yet she felt comfortable handing their baby to him. Why?

Fatima went to the kitchen table where she had a cloth diaper and onesie at the ready. Ivan knew the routine and gently placed Talula on the table, still swaddled in the thick towel so that Fatima could put the baby's diaper on.

"You were defending my best friend. I'm glad you were there."

There was something odd about Fatima's voice. Perhaps that it was unusually calm as she proceeded to guide fat little baby arms through the sleeves of the onesie. She was typically more…boisterous.

"Fatima, it's more than what happened at TARA. There's something I have been meaning to discuss with you, fer the past year or so, if I'm being honest."

"Really?" Fatima lifted Talula up and the baby instinctively laid her head on her mother's chest as Fatima bounced her lightly up and down. Talula let out a loud yawn. Apparently, bath time was very tiring. "What is it? Should I be concerned?"

"There's a reason I've spent the better part of my adult life as a hermit, tinkering in my garage."

"You're an inventor. It's kind of your thing."

"But it's more than that," he rubbed the baby's back as Fatima continued to rock Talula gently. "I sort of had a rough time of it in my youth, got in with some not-so-great people. I wanted a different life for myself and I thought, if I could bring just one of my ideas to life, I could escape."

"And you did," Fatima touched the side of Ivan's face, lovingly. "Just look at what you've accomplished in the past few months alone when given access to new technology on this planet."

Ivan let out a sigh. "The reason I was targeted by the police, and the reason you are separated from your family now, is more than their fear of my inventions empowering the masses. They were looking for a reason to come after me." Ivan found himself fighting off becoming overly emotional.

"Hey now, what's this?"

"I haven't raised my fists in over twenty years and I vowed never to again. You should know…"

Fatima leaned over and kissed him lightly on the lips before he could finish his sentence. "Hush. That was a different lifetime."

"But, aren't you worried about me around the baby?"

"Unless our baby grows up and befriends a drug lord or opens a chop shop, I don't think we have anything to worry about."

"Wait," Ivan backed away. "You…knew?" How could she know all about his sordid past, his teenage years scraping by with no family to speak of, an orphan who took to the streets at thirteen, mixing with those he thought were his friends, but weren't.

"Of course, I did, silly," Fatima pulled him out of his daydream. "I may not be as tech savvy as you, but I do know how the Internet works."

Talula began to fuss, making a little sucking sound to indicate she was hungry…again.

"But about your family…" Ivan began.

"Yeah, I hope you don't mind, but they'll end up being in our neighborhood after Moksha and Cepheus abandon their house for a palace." The two were relocating to the Royal Training Grounds, a fact that was still unbelievable to everyone. "Aunt Keti and Tai are going to help me manage the vineyard for Moksha, possibly indefinitely."

"Wait, they're coming …here? To Erde?"

Fatima's eyes grew wide, followed by the largest smile Ivan had ever witnessed.

"Part of the trade negotiations to keep Earth and Erde borders open on a case-by-case basis. Many on the preserves are moving back to Earth, and thanks to your negotiations with Commander Royce, she sanctioned my parents, my brother, and my aunt and uncle to relocate here. I was going to tell you before you decided on this walk down memory lane." Fatima tilted her head back and leaned in closely, seductively (at least, as seductive as you can be while holding a baby). "So you see, my darling. You're not the only one with secrets."

The Animal Lab

"You're back!" Mati squealed, his long tail swishing from side to side. Now that the cat was no longer in quarantine, he could pick her up. Before the cat could protest, he scooped her into his arms and hugged her. "Tabby! Where have you been? Your parents will be so thrilled when I tell them you came back."

Where else was she going to go? Back in her house-cat form, her options were to scrounge for scraps on the street until an animal collector inevitably caught her or return to the animal lab where at least she would be reunited with her adoptive caretakers and be fed and sheltered for the remainder of her days…at least until the next lifetime.

"Put me down, you vermin," Hysechia tried to hiss at Mati. "You smell like a two-week-old sausage that's been left out in the sun!"

Unfortunately, the only thing that came out of her mouth was a pathetic, "Meow?"

36

GOODBYE, NOT CHRISTOPHER
NOW.

"Hello, Not Christopher," Lucene stood at the water's edge at Tranquil Beach as Not Christopher suddenly appeared beside her. This time, he was wearing a tan guayabera shirt with the same white linen pants. He was barefoot. Lucene wasn't sure why the change of wardrobe.

"Good to see you again, Lucene." He gazed over the horizon.

"I figured out who you are."

"Really?" Not Christopher turned to look at her. "How?"

"I thought you were going to ask, 'who?'"

"My question is far more interesting, don't you think?"

"Perhaps," Lucene smiled at him. "Please, sit a moment, if you don't mind getting sand on your clothes."

"You know I don't."

The two sat, Lucene crossing her legs in front of her and digging her fingers into the cool sand simply because she liked the way it felt.

Not Christopher sat beside her, stretching his legs out in front of him, one over the other and leaning back on his hands.

"The reason why I couldn't remember most of my crushes from

the past, except the one who tried to kill Reverend Isabella and hand me over to the Royals..." She waited.

As if reading her thoughts, Not Christopher nodded. "Trauma has a way of sticking," he acknowledged.

"Agreed."

"But the others?"

Lucene nodded her head, peering out over the water, seeking the right words. Of course, he already knew what those were.

"You were my ideal man, Not Christopher," Lucene answered simply. "I must have invented you around the age of twelve. And, once I did, who could live up to you? You were the perfect fantasy boy."

"What gave me away?"

"Aside from your obvious perfectness, I think it was the 'for me to know and you to find out' phrase that tipped me off. Not something most adults would say, is it?"

"I suppose not." Not Christopher blushed slightly at being described as 'perfect.' Of course, he would; Lucene imagined him that way. Humility was built in. "But I'm not so perfect anymore, am I?"

"No," Lucene admitted. "I mean, you are, but there's perfect and there's—"

"Perfect for you," Not Christopher finished.

"Exactly."

"On the one hand, I might never criticize you...never find another woman attractive...never become impatient or misunderstand you—"

"True," Lucene agreed.

"But on the other hand, I would never have imagined sacrificing myself to the Null people to save your life, or designing a high-home to remind you of the only home you'd known on Earth. And I certainly wouldn't have risked hell and high water to retrieve you from Earth, almost getting killed by the Royals in the process."

"No, who could have imagined that? But—"

"But, what?"

"Renenet said that Tanager called it off with Amy because he had this ideal vision of me, being of the same vibration and all."

"But he explained that to you. And, you didn't exactly turn out to be so perfect yourself, now did you?"

"Definitely, not."

"And yet, he didn't suddenly go running back to the arms of his ex-lover, now did he?"

"No," Lucene smiled, hugging herself. "He didn't."

"What did he do?"

Lucene paused. "He loved me even more."

"Flaws and all," Not Christopher agreed. "Though, I don't think Tanager views them as flaws. Frankly, I think he finds them charming. That's not something I would have ever done. Which brings us to the cold hard truth that—"

"I don't need you, anymore, Not Christopher. I'm sorry."

"You don't have to be sorry," he explained, "I'm a figment of your imagination. I could only be offended if you created me that way."

"One thing?"

"Yes?"

"Did I never think to give you a name?"

Not Christopher laughed. "No, I guess you did not. You created me with perfect hair, perfect teeth and skin. And I'm in pretty good shape, if I say so myself. I'm well-read and educated and like all the same things that you do. And yet…no name."

Lucene smiled, placing her hand on Not Christopher's arm. Surprisingly, she could feel it.

"The portal," he explained. "It messes up perceptions a bit. I seem to be flesh and blood, but I'm not. In fact," Not Christopher stood up, brushing sand from the back of his pants, "once the portal finishes closing, I won't be back anymore. Is there anything else you need to say to me before I go?"

"Just, thank you," Lucene's eyes began to turn red, just a little. "I believe I am going to miss you, Not Christopher."

"Goodbye, Lucene," Not Christopher said as his visage began to fade. Just then, his sandals washed in on an ocean wave. He stooped to pick them up. Before completely vanishing, he stood upright and said, "And not to worry. There's someone much better waiting for you at home."

The End ... For the Time Being.

ABOUT THE AUTHOR

Danielle Palli is a writer, business owner, multimedia specialist, mindfulness coach, and podcast producer and co-host. She lives in Southwest Florida with her husband and far too many pets. She also finds joy in nature, travel, theater and the arts, and is known for singing and dancing around the living room at any hour of the day or night. Also, you can convince her to attend almost any event if you promise her that she can wear a themed costume. Learn more at www.birdlandmediaworks.com.

www.ingramcontent.com/pod-product-compliance
Lightning Source LLC
Chambersburg PA
CBHW071424200726
48294CB00002B/507